EVERY FEAR

RICK MOFINA

MIRA

All the characters in this book have no existence outside the imagination of the author, and have no relation whatsoever to anyone bearing the same name or names. They are not even distantly inspired by any individual known or unknown to the author, and all the incidents are pure invention.

First published in Great Britain 2010.
MIRA Books, Eton House, 18-24 Paradise Road,
Richmond, Surrey, TW9 1SR

ISBN 978 0 7783 0367 1

58-0510

MIRA's policy is to use papers that are natural, renewable and recyclable products and made from wood grown in sustainable forests. The logging and manufacturing processes conform to the legal environmental regulations of the country of origin.

Printed in Great Britain
by Clays Ltd, St Ives plc

This book is for Stephen, Mary, Teresa and Amanda

And the king said, Divide the living child in two and give half to the one and half to the other.

Then spake the woman whose the living child was unto the king, for her bowels yearned upon her son, and she said, O my lord, give her the living child, and in no way slay it. But the other said, Let it be neither mine not thine, but divide it.

—Kings 1:3

DAY ONE

1

In the hour before sunrise, a blackbird slammed into Maria Colson's bedroom window, jolting her awake, its wings flapping in panic against the glass before it vanished.

She reached for Lee's side of the bed. He wasn't there. He'd gone out on a call around midnight. Something about a rig on I-5, up near Jackson Park. His whiskers had brushed her skin when he'd kissed her good-bye.

Maria considered the bird. It was crazy to worry. *Everything's fine,* she assured herself, nestling in the middle of the bed. By the light of the dying moon she saw Dylan's crib across the hall. Maybe she should check on him. A bird hitting the house was an omen her grandmother had always feared. But Maria was so exhausted. She had been up every hour with Dylan and all night last night. She was too tired to be superstitious. Unease prodded her until at last she heard him stir and sighed with relief.

Everything was fine, just a crazy bird and a silly old wives' tale.

Maria floated back to sleep but it was troubled. Her

dreams were haunted by the anguish she and Lee had endured over the last few years, grotesque flashes of the painful times and her irrational fears of something bad lurking out there.

Stop. Never again. Please.

Mercifully, her subconscious guided her to her sanctuary. A Caribbean beach, the warm azure water caressing her toes, palm fronds swaying in the breeze. The sound of a baby crying. *A baby?* Dylan was pulling her back to reality. She groaned awake.

"Oh honey. Just a few more minutes."

His crying intensified.

"All right, sweetie, I'm coming."

Stiff and tired, she dragged herself first to the bathroom, then downstairs to the kitchen, then back upstairs to Dylan's room. She took him into her arms. He was wet. She changed him, settled into her rocker, and fed him.

She kissed his fingers and his head.

Dylan was her miracle.

Because she'd injured her pelvis in her teens, the doctors had told her she would never be able to have children. But she had refused to believe them, refused to give up hope. She had begged God to let her have a baby, pleaded that if heaven allowed it, she would ask for nothing more.

And it happened.

After years of trying. Everyone was surprised.

Everyone but Maria.

She smiled at Dylan and rocked him gently, her heart aching with love for him, for Lee, for their life together.

It was not perfect. The dark times had strained their marriage. The hard times had strained their bank account. But things were better now.

Lee was earning a little more at the shop. It had been a struggle, but with his overtime and bonus they were adjusting to the reduced income while she stayed home with Dylan. Deep down Maria knew that as long as they had each other, everything would work out.

The sun had risen.

Dylan had fallen asleep. She put him back in his crib, showered, dressed in faded jeans, a Mariners T-shirt, and white sneakers. The kitchen was a mess in the wake of the last few hectic days with Dylan. Lee had done his best to clean up. She'd take care of it today, she thought, getting herself orange juice, a banana muffin, and the morning paper.

She unfolded the *Seattle Mirror* and gasped.

The large, front-page photo showed a fireball from a series of delayed explosions after a tanker had rolled on I-5 at the city's northern edge.

Lee's tow truck was in the chaos.

The phone rang and her heart skipped a beat.

Upstairs, Dylan began to cry. She stared at the news picture, then at the ringing phone. Lee's truck glowed. She couldn't see him.

Oh no.

Her mind raced and she forced herself to answer.

"Hey babe, it's me," her husband said over the chaos of compressors and steel striking steel.

"Lee! Thank God, you're okay!"

"Why wouldn't I be?"

"I just saw the picture in the *Mirror*."

"Oh, that. Wild, huh? I had just pulled up. The driver thought his pup trailer was empty, but there was some sort of vapor lock. Nobody got hurt."

"I'm so glad."

"Yeah, not a scratch on my truck. I went right to the shop after we finished up at the scene. How's it going at the homestead?"

"It's been a strange night. A bird hit our window."

"What? Did it break the glass?"

"No. It was just odd."

"How's Dylan?"

"Cranky. Cried all night and he's crying again. We're out of milk and bread. I'll take him over to the store."

"Listen, Lou told me this morning that he's serious about selling the towing business. I figure that when you go back full-time at the supermarket we might be able to swing a small loan. This could be our chance. What do you think?"

A few seconds of silence passed.

"Maria?"

"We should talk about it later. I've got to get Dylan."

"Sure, give him a kiss for me. I love you."

"Love you too. Be careful."

After dressing Dylan, Maria said, "Let's go, kid, we're taking this show on the road."

A few minutes later, Dylan was murmuring softly in his stroller.

The Colsons' small, two-story frame house was in Ballard, a sedate older neighborhood in northwest

Seattle. Located near Salmon Bay and the Ballard Locks, its history reached back to the late 1800s as a community of shipbuilders, most of whom had come from Scandinavia.

It was safe here.

Maria loved the tranquillity. Birdsong and breezes swept off Puget Sound through the maple, sycamore, and willow trees. Two doors down, the Stars and Stripes fluttered from the flagpole over the retired colonel's porch. He kept it so pretty, Maria thought, admiring the overflowing flower boxes.

Not much happened in this sleepy part of Ballard, except at the end of the street at the Lincoln place. The estate was renovating the big colonial house, and there was an influx of strangers. A lot of contractors' trucks coming and going. They were doing a beautiful job.

At the corner, while crossing the street, Maria thought how weird it was with the bird, Lee at the wreck, the picture in the *Mirror*. Lee would tease her about her *omen of doom*.

Then he'd want to talk about buying Lou out.

And what was she going to tell him? While he dreamed of owning his towing shop, she dreamed of staying home and trying to have another baby. They would have to talk it over. "Take stock of our situation," Lee would say. Maria looked at Dylan. The motion was making him drowsy.

Several blocks later, by the time they had arrived at Kim's Corner Store, Dylan was sound asleep. *Great,* Maria thought.

Kim's had a narrow, pioneer-style storefront with large windows and a small, two-stair, step-up entrance.

Shannon, the teenage clerk with the captive-bead ring in her pierced eyebrow, was out front sweeping the sidewalk. Music leaked from the headset of her CD player as she bent over to coo at Dylan.

"Ahh. He's such a little angel."

"He's been a little devil keeping me up these last few nights," Maria said as she began maneuvering the stroller through the doorway. Dylan started to cry. "All right. All right."

She stopped, parked the stroller on the sidewalk next to the store window, and picked him up. He cried harder, squirming in protest until she put him back down. Exhaustion rolled over her as she surrendered to the fact that Dylan wanted to sleep.

"You're killing me, kid."

Maria exhaled and Shannon slipped off her headset.

"You could leave him out here with me and let him sleep."

"That's so kind. Would you mind?"

"No problem."

"I just need to grab a few things, thanks so much."

Maria glanced up and down the street. Dylan would be fine outside with Shannon, just like the other times she'd left him with her. Maria was so tired, and he'd been so demanding these past few days. She would relish these few moments of peace.

The transom bells chimed.

Behind the counter Mrs. Kim smiled over her bifocals, her strong wrinkled fingers not losing a stitch of her needlepoint.

"Hello, Maria."

"Good morning, Mrs. Kim."

The worn wooden floorboards creaked as Maria headed to the back and the cooler. She heard a distant cell phone ringing. No other customers were in the store, it had to be Shannon's.

After selecting a carton of milk with the freshest date, Maria went to the bread shelf, glancing through the shoulder-high aisles to the front window. She could see the top of the stroller and Shannon talking outside on the phone. She looked upset.

Maria went to Mrs. Kim at the front counter to pay. She set the milk and bread down, snapped open her wallet, and checked the sidewalk.

"Baby's sleeping?" Mrs. Kim nodded pleasantly.

"Yes, he's been a fusspot for the last two days."

The transom bells jingled. Shannon strode to the rear of the store, phone pressed to her head, submerged in conversation. "That's *so not true* and I've got his letter in my bag. I'm getting it—"

Maria checked on Dylan's stroller, so close to her on the other side of the glass she could practically touch him. He was fine and she'd be finished in a few seconds.

As the register clicked, Maria noticed the revolving rack of the latest paperbacks near the counter, unaware of the large shadow that floated by out front. She needed a new book to read. A suspense thriller. Maybe she'd take Dylan to the park. The rack squeaked as she inventoried the titles. Catching something in her periphery, she looked up at Mrs. Kim, who was looking outside. The old woman's face was all wrong, contorting as her jaw worked but formed no words. Maria followed her attention to the street. Her heart slammed into her ribs.

Dylan's stroller had vanished.

In less than a second, part of Maria's brain screamed at her circuits to form the cognitive command to react. Her body spasmed and a deafening roar split her ears.

Adrenaline propelled her to the street. All of her senses were pushed to superhuman levels as she saw Dylan's stroller, rolling, toppling over the curb; saw the flash of his soft cotton blanket; heard the thud of a strange van's door, the growl of its engine; felt her hand on metal, felt her fingers grip a handle, a mirror, as the van began pulling away.

Maria threw herself onto the hood of the moving van and pounded on its windshield. She glimpsed fingers clenching Dylan's blanket, glimpsed his tiny arm, his hand, heard his screams blend with hers as she tried in vain to claw through the glass.

The van lurched, bucked, its motor snarling, brakes screeching until the world jerked to its side and the street flew up with a flash of brilliant light and pulled Maria to the ground. Through a galaxy of shooting stars she saw the van disappearing, Dylan's stroller on its side, its wheels spinning as warm blood webbed over her flickering eyes.

The last things Maria remembered were Dylan's sweet breath, Lee's whiskered kiss good-bye, and the blackbird that hit her window.

2

Jason Wade's stomach clenched as he walked to his desk in the empty newsroom.

Get ready for today's verdict.

He began each morning shift at the *Seattle Mirror* by adjusting the police scanners. The paper kept several going simultaneously, monitoring emergency frequencies 24-7 across metropolitan Seattle.

The job meant deciphering the constant chatter, determining what was insignificant and what was the first hint of a story that would stop the heart of the city, or break it. It was a skill Jason had mastered. He had to. On the crime beat, you lived and died by what came across the radios.

All quiet so far.

Now, the moment of truth: to see how the *Mirror* did against its competition. Scoops brought you short-lived praise. A tie was a win. But to get beat on a story—*to lose*—well, woe to the reporter who missed one.

Editors were unforgiving.

Tensing, he compared final editions of the *Times* and the *Post-Intelligencer* with the *Mirror*.

Everybody had the same stuff. The party girl who

fell to her death off the balcony near the university. Too much to drink. The drug bust with a few shots fired near Seola Beach. Nobody hurt. The stabbing in a bar fight in Burien. Victim will live. Even the late-breaker, the tanker fire on I-5 near Jackson Park. All stories matched. All nickel-and-dime stuff.

He relaxed a little, reached for his take-out coffee, hoping for a chance to work on his longer pieces.

There was an anniversary coming up for a shooting; he also had the sketchy terrorist thing out of Canada. Then the old cold case he'd found by chance while looking up something else in the archives. He'd wanted to follow up on them but never had the time.

Setting the papers aside, something caught his eye. Something about the tanker picture. The *Mirror*'s photo credit was "Special To The Mirror," indicating a free-lancer had taken it. Indicating a staff photographer was not there. Indicating that the night desk had likely missed it.

Not good.

Jason opened his e-mail for the overnight note just as he heard a female dispatcher relaying something about a traffic accident. Most wrecks were not news, but he picked up a trace of urgency, a tinge of emotion, in the dispatcher's voice.

"Caller was crying. Stand by. We've lost the line, we're trying to reconnect. Seventy-six?"

"Seventy-six. Ten-four."

"Stand by."

He blinked several times, locked two scanners onto the northwest channel, then looked outside. The *Mirror* was at Harrison and 4th, a few blocks north of downtown. The newsroom was on the seventh floor, its west wall was glass. Glimpsing the boats cutting across Elliott Bay, he suddenly felt old. He'd been on the beat for a year but was largely still considered a rookie. And it'd been a long time since he'd landed a good story. A long time since anything positive had happened in his life.

He glanced at the beaded bracelet on his wrist and thought of Valerie. She'd bought it for him at Pike Place Market. A long time ago. Then he turned to Karen Harding, staring from the tearsheets hanging from his lower wall. Jason wondered about both women.

Girls he used to know.

Things don't always work out, he thought before he resumed searching for the overnight note from the night cop reporter, Astrid Grant. Funny about her, how time hadn't softened her hard feelings toward him. That was her problem.

Astrid was hired on a contract after coming in second to Jason for a full-time spot in last year's internship competition. She was still bitter about it. She was the daughter of a Hollywood studio executive and accustomed to getting her way. After graduating from UCLA, Astrid had come to Seattle expecting to win a staff job. She was talented and beautiful, but had a reputation for attaching herself to other people's stories for a byline.

Jason was a loner who did his own work.

He grew up in a blue-collar neighborhood between the west bank of the Duwamish River and Highway

509. It was near Boeing Field and the shipyards, a place where all he'd wanted, since the day he started delivering the *Mirror*, was to be a newspaper reporter.

Pursuing that dream had not been easy for him.

His old man was a recovering alcoholic who'd worked in a brewery. Jason had driven a forklift there to put himself through community college. He also hung out with cops and sold crime features to Seattle's big dailies.

Impressed with his hustle, an editor at the *Mirror* offered him a last-minute spot on its intern program last year. It was his shot. He went up against five prima donnas, including Astrid, all of them from big J-schools with experience at big papers, all going full tilt for a single position. Jason won out. After he broke a major exclusive, the *Mirror* made him a full-time staff reporter.

But it almost didn't happen, thanks to his old man. To this day, his father refused to talk about the incident that forced him off the Seattle police force. It'd cost him his marriage and nearly took Jason down with him because the drinking strained their relationship to the breaking point.

The final embarrassment came last year when he showed up drunk in the newsroom looking for Jason. The shame of that night got his old man to admit he had a problem.

It got him to quit drinking and get help.

Almost a year sober now, and he was doing great. Hell, Jason was proud of him. He was a different man. He'd taken early retirement from the brewery, and a few courses to chase a dream of his own. Becoming a private investigator. And it was happening for him—an agency run by an old cop buddy had taken him on.

Jason's thoughts returned to the newsroom and the fact there was no overnight note from Astrid. Strange. While she'd never hidden the fact that she hated the night police beat and struggled on breaking news, she'd always left an overnight note. Except this time. Something wasn't right.

He went back to the scanners.

"All units on the Ballard situation, we've got a possible pedestrian injury accident. Stand by for confirmation."

"Seventy-six. Have you got paramedics rolling? Ten-four."

He flipped to a fresh page in his notebook, then jotted notes as he spotted Astrid's bag at her desk, which adjoined his.

Strange.

Her shift ended at 2:00 A.M.; she shouldn't be here. Maybe she'd forgotten it last night. He inventoried the large newsroom with its rows of half-walled cubicles, computer terminals, desks cluttered with towers of newspapers, reports, cafeteria plates, cutlery, and assorted crap.

Virtually empty. Nobody came in at this hour.

Nobody else in Metro, Business, Sports, Entertainment, or Lifestyles. A few copy editors worked alone on advance pages but they were far off from him, like sentries at distant posts. The editorial assistant was floating around and had left him a note from the assignment editor, who was going to be late because he'd blown a tire.

A door flew open.

He turned to his boss's glass-walled office to see Astrid Grant march to the cop desk. She opened her bag, then used both hands to thrust belongings from her drawers into it as if the building were on fire.

"Hey, what's going on?"

Her face and eyes were red.

"I've been fired."

"What? Why?"

"Ask dickhead." She nodded to the Metro editor's office. "Stupid damn tanker crash. I'm fed up with Rain Town. I'm going home to L.A."

Astrid grabbed her bag and hurried off, putting a hand to her face. He started after her but was stopped by the scanners.

"All units in the Ballard area. Update. Possible pedestrian injury now reported as a hit-and-run. Seventy-six, what's your ETA?"

"Seven maybe ten. Can we please confirm the address again?"

"Ten-four."

The dispatcher repeated the address over the air and Jason jotted it down. Hit-and-run? This could turn into something. Watching Astrid disappear toward the elevator he focused on the call, preparing to jump on it.

"Wade!" Spangler, the *Mirror*'s new Metro editor, summoned him.

Jason refused to leave the scanners. Not now. He waved off his boss.

Nobody waved off Fritz Spangler. He ran the *Mirror*'s largest editorial department. He controlled the professional lives of nearly one hundred people. Spangler was a son of Seattle who'd started with the *Post-Intelligencer* before moving to New York City and the *Daily News*. He'd worked his way up from One Police Plaza to assignment editor before being head-hunted by the *Mirror*.

He returned to Seattle with a mandate to reverse the paper's melting circulation by driving an agenda for hard news and exclusives.

The *Mirror* hadn't won a Pulitzer prize since the early 1990s. Even Jason's exclusive from last year had failed to earn a nomination. For Spangler, Jason's big story was old news and old news didn't cut it.

In fact, no story was ever good enough for Spangler. No reporter ever performed to his standards. Some four months ago, when Spangler arrived, thirty reporters worked in Metro. Word was, Spangler had orders to cut the number to twenty-two. His presence made staffers feel like swimmers who'd spotted a dorsal fin.

Spangler rarely spoke. He wore button-down shirts and never loosened his tie. His skin was wrapped tight around his head, accentuating his skull, making his eyes wide as if he were always pissed off. That was how he looked when he materialized at Jason's desk. Statue still and mute. Not a word about firing Astrid as he stood there listening to the scanner transmissions.

"All units, in Ballard. That report of a pedestrian hit-and-run is confirmed on scene. Mother with baby—"

Spangler shot Jason a look.

"Why are you still here?"

"Because it's breaking now."

"You should be out the door."

"I'm on it."

Collecting his notebook and his cell phone, Jason turned to Spangler, stood toe-to-toe with him, then nodded to the tearsheets displaying his old exclusive on Karen Harding.

"Just to remind you, I'm not Astrid. I know how to do my job."

Spangler eyeballed him.

"Go out and prove it then. This paper needs to kick some ass."

Jason held his fire long enough to let Spangler know he didn't fear him, he'd faced much worse and had the scars to prove it.

"Seventy-six, dispatch."

"Seventy-six."

Breathless officers were shouting over wailing sirens.

"Dispatch, from paramedics, the victim's injuries are life-threatening! It's real bad! She might not make it to hospital! Better alert Homicide!"

3

Sitting in an unmarked Chevrolet Malibu, Seattle Homicide Detective Grace Garner sipped raspberry tea from a commuter cup bearing the slogan, "Vengeance is mine, like this mug."

A present from her all-male squad.

It followed the real gift they'd given her the first day she'd joined the unit. The moment she'd stepped into the enclave of testosterone, she was escorted to a full-scale skeletal replica of a shooting victim.

"Detective Garner"—a grizzled bull exchanged conspiratorial glances with the rest of the squad—"tell us how we've determined its gender to be female." She studied the plastic bones amid sniggering, outwaiting the old cop until he provided the answer. "Because her head's got a hole in it," he said.

Grace smiled politely, ignoring the laughter. When it faded she said, "Pelvic opening's too narrow."

"Whaddya mean?"

"Your victim here's a male. *With a hole in his head.*"

The only person laughing now was the sergeant, Stan Boulder. He'd been watching from the back of the room.

Grinning at the memory, Grace looked at the parade of toddlers holding on to a rope near the daycare, next to the apartment where she was staking out a possible witness in a cold case.

The kids were adorable.

Would she ever have one? Not likely. And why not? Because she was alone, that's why. This was the life she'd made. Or, the one she'd let happen to her since *that day*.

Although she rarely admitted it, she traced her solitude to the day Roger Briscoe wore an eerie expression, a kind of know-it-all sneer, as he strode into Mr. Lorten's English class. Mr. Lorten had written two words on the blackboard—*Joseph Conrad*—looked at his students, and said, "Today, we'll start on *Heart of Darkness*, Conrad's master—"

A firecracker pop. Mr. Lorten's head snapped. He fell to the floor with Roger Briscoe standing over him, gripping the handgun he'd taken from the hiding spot in his mother's china cabinet—behind the gravy boat, next to the Jack Daniels.

"Not today, Lorten." Roger Briscoe then turned and pointed the gun at his classmates. "Today, you're going to learn about my pain. Pay attention, maggots. There will be a test."

There were screams.

Desks scraped and toppled in the stampede to the door. Someone pulled the fire alarm. Deafening ringing and a second shot. *"Nobody move!"* Roger Briscoe yelled, *"Today, I'm God!"*

Girls sobbed, boys cursed. Everyone cowered. But

not Grace Garner. Calm washed over her. She was not afraid as she inched toward him, looking directly into his eyes.

"Roger, please put the gun down."

"No."

"Please. Why are you doing this?"

"You know why, Grace."

"Roger, please. You don't want to hurt any more people."

"Yes, I do. I want to hurt everybody."

He pointed the gun at her.

"I want to hurt you."

Two members of the wrestling team, small, quick boys, got Roger Briscoe down, smashing the gun from him, pinning him until the sirens started in with the alarm, until it all became one prolonged scream. One she could never silence. She'd never forget Mr. Lorten's eyes staring wide at the ceiling.

They were closed in his casket.

The school, the city, and the Seattle Police Department gave her and the wrestlers awards for bravery. For preventing a tragedy from claiming more victims. That was when she'd decided to become a cop.

After college, where she'd achieved the highest grades, she'd considered applying to the FBI before deciding on the Seattle Police Department. She'd worked the street, was decorated for tackling a fleeing suspect who'd wounded a teller during a bank robbery; scored high in every course and had proven herself. A few months ago, despite grumbling by old-school detectives, she was handpicked to join Homicide.

This was her story so far.

A smart cop, isolated from the world with only her work and her ghosts for company. Well, she thought, sipping her tea, maybe she didn't want to be alone anymore. Maybe she could hear her clock ticking as she watched the little cutie-pies go by her window. Oh, enough of this poor me crap.

"Earth to Grace."

Detective Perelli stared at her from the passenger seat.

"Sorry, Dom. What'd you say?"

"I said, looks like our guy's a no-show. We'll give it another ten, fifteen, then go back downtown. Clear up some paperwork."

"Sure."

"By the way, I'm hearing that Jake in Robbery has got two tickets for Sunday's game. Expect a call."

"Quit trying to fix me up."

"Afraid I can't do that. Look at you, all googly-eyed watching those kids. You're giving off signals."

"Signals?"

"Like life's passing you by."

"What?"

He swallowed some cold black coffee.

"We've been partnered, what, ten months? And you know all about me. Eighteen years on the job, the last eight in Homicide. Wife, three kids, mortgage, and a bad back, makes me a part-time bastard."

"You got a point to make?"

"You never open up to me like you're supposed to."

"Like I'm supposed to?"

"Part of the code."

"What code?"

"Perelli's code."

"You're a nosy mother hen, Dominic."

"What're you, like twenty-eight, twenty-seven, right?"

"What does it matter?"

"Nobody makes Homicide that young. Not in my world. You're different. Know what the guys in Robbery told us about you just after you came to us?"

"I don't care."

"You're a sad young woman and we should find you a man to make you happy. Now take Jake in Internet Crimes, a bit of a computer geek, but so was Gates and look where—ouch."

Grace's elbow in Perelli's ribs ended his teasing just as her cell phone rang.

"Garner."

"It's Boulder. We got a woman in Ballard struck by a vehicle. Hit-and-run. Paramedics say she's not going to make it."

"Who's the primary?"

"You are, Grace. You and Dom haul it to the hospital now. Try for a declaration."

She reached into her blazer for her notebook, checked the time, and started logging.

"Where'd they take her?"

"Swedish. Ballard campus. Do what you can there, then hook up with Schaeffer and Berman at the scene. I'll get right back to you with her name and family details."

"All right."

Grace turned the ignition, then pointed to the dash cherry. Perelli fished it out.

"And Grace," Boulder said, "the FBI will be on this too."

"The FBI? Why?"

"Whoever ran her down abducted her baby boy."

A dying declaration is the last statement given by a crime victim. Grace knew it could make a case. She had taken one a few months back from an armored-car guard shot during a heist near the airport. Before he died, he described his shooter's belt buckle. It helped lead to the suspect and an arrest.

During the drive to Ballard, Perelli made calls for updates and more information on the victim. Some fifteen minutes after receiving Boulder's first call, Grace wheeled the Malibu off Barnes Avenue and into the ambulance entrance. Inside Emergency, the desk nurse pointed them to the room where they'd taken Maria Colson. Halfway there, Grace and Perelli came upon two nurses rolling her gurney into a large elevator. They stepped into the car with them.

"Sorry, no visitors," the older nurse said.

Grace flashed her badge.

"We need to talk to her as soon as possible."

"You've got to be kidding," the nurse said. "She's unconscious. She's suffered a head injury. We're taking her to OR."

The hospital sheet barely covered the woman who lay before them. Grace studied the young mother, dressed in the same clothes she'd slipped into to go to the corner store with her baby for milk and bread. Her white sneakers, her faded jeans, which were now torn and smeared with dirt. Her Mariners T-shirt, now ripped and soaked with blood. Fingers that earlier had caressed her son, Dylan, were now covered with lacerations. An IV tube ran from her arm, a clear oxygen mask cupped her face, which was darkened with a web of abrasions.

"How bad?" Perelli asked.

"It doesn't look good."

"How long will she be in surgery?"

"Hard to say, at least a few hours."

"She say anything at all about what happened?"

"Not to us, she's been out."

"What about on the way?" Grace asked.

"Try the paramedics. They're still here."

The elevator stopped. The nurses rolled Maria Colson out. Grace and Perelli caught up to the paramedics in the cafeteria.

"She was in rough shape when we got to her," one of them said. "Non-responsive. Sometimes they talk in the ER, but it's usually incomprehensible because they're in shock."

Grace and Perelli returned to Emergency and corralled some of the staff who'd first stabilized and prepped Maria Colson for surgery. None of them recalled her saying anything, except one trauma nurse.

"I heard her uttering something."

Grace's pen was poised over her notebook.

"She was out of it, but it was like, 'Why are they taking my baby?'"

"They," Grace repeated. "Are you certain she said 'they,' as in more than one?"

"Yes, 'they.'"

"Not 'he' or 'she'?—but 'they.'" Grace pressed. She needed the nurse to be absolutely sure.

"Yes."

"Anything else?"

A commotion coming from the hall interrupted them. The detectives stepped from the office to assess it. They went to the reception desk where two nurses were contending with a distraught man.

"Maria! Where's my wife? Maria!" he shouted.

"Mr. Colson," a nurse said. "Sir, we're taking care of her."

His navy work pants were stained with grease, his flannel shirt was untucked. Stubble covered the dark worry lines cutting deep into his weathered face. His eyes were rimmed red with intensity.

"Mr. Colson." Grace took his arm gently. "I'm Detective Garner, this is Detective Perelli. The doctors are helping Maria right now, they're doing everything they can."

"Let me see Dylan. Is he hurt bad? Where's my son?"

"No one told you?" Grace asked.

"Told me what?" Lee Colson's nostrils flared with his heavy breathing. "My dispatcher radioed my truck, she said Maria and Dylan were in an accident and they were taken here. Somebody tell me what the hell's going on!"

Grace traded glances with the others.

"You better come with us," she said.

4

Pulling out of the *Mirror* parking lot, Jason double-checked the address in his notebook, then charted the fastest way to the scene.

Elliott to 15th, north over the bridge to Shilshole and bang—you're there. Pushing his 1969 red Ford Falcon twenty miles over the posted limit, he couldn't leave the newsroom politics behind. Spangler had no sense of the depth of his staff. He regarded everyone in Metro as backwater bumpkins, compared to reporters in New York.

Jason rubbed the scar carved under his jawline, his prize for getting too close to a story. Confirmation of his investigative skills, but it meant squat to Spangler, who probably had him in his crosshairs. Just like Astrid.

To hell with it.

Crossing the Ballard Bridge over Salmon Bay, Jason thought it was too bad about Astrid. But the fact was, she constantly missed stuff on the scanners and at scenes, always charging in with demands, failing to find real news.

Observe, absorb, and squeeze gently for information, that's the way to operate, he reminded himself as he pulled up to the scene. Yellow tape cordoned off the street in front of Kim's Corner Store. Next to it there was a growing knot of bystanders, press, and police cars. Cross talk spilled from radios as emergency lights splashed the buildings with red.

Jason parked half a block back. Heading toward the reporters clustered near the tape, he came upon an unoccupied patrol car—and an opportunity. Like most major forces, Seattle police used the Computer-Aided Dispatch system to transmit information to cars equipped with Mobile Data Computers. No one was around to see him bend down, steal a glimpse of the MDC monitor to check it for any data.

Maria Jane Colson.
104 Shale St.

Lee William Colson.
104 Shale St.

There was more but he couldn't see it clearly. Memorizing the information, he moved off without anyone noticing. He stepped between two news vans then wrote everything down. Shale was close by. Before he could consider it further, a commanding baritone voice distracted him.

"There he is, a legend called Jason." White teeth flashed from the tanned, chiseled face of David Troy, WKKR's veteran crime reporter.

"What's shaking, Dave?"

"What I'm hearing is the mother and her baby were

run over by a truck that fled the scene. Mom's not going to make it."

"Yeah, I got that."

"We're waiting for a detective to talk to us. They're in the store."

"You got a name on the mother?"

"Not yet."

Jason took comfort in the hot lead he had in his notebook.

"What about witnesses?"

"Nobody so far."

"You're sure about that?"

"I'm sure you're not going to beat me, Skippy. By the time your rag reports this, it's yesterday's news." Troy watched the dish on WKKR's satellite news van position for transmission. "We're going live in minutes. Look at the images. Picture's worth a thousand damn words. Impact news." Troy pulled out a compact and began applying makeup for his stand-up.

Cameras were trained on the crime-scene people who were suiting up. Jason focused on the aftermath a few yards away, on the other side of the tape. The overturned baby stroller, the pool of blood near the curb, skid marks on the pavement. *Was that a windshield wiper?* He tried imagining how it had all happened. On the far side of the tape, he saw more TV and still news cameras, including Nate Hodge, a photog with the *Mirror*, who nodded.

As Jason studied the little he had, he got an idea. He slipped from the press pack and walked across the street to the vestibule of Arnie's Hardware. Out of earshot, he called the paper.

"*Mirror* library, Kelly Swan."

"Hey Kelly, Jason Wade. I'm at a hit-and-run in Ballard, which could turn out to be a homicide. I need your help."

"Sure, Jason."

Jason dictated the spellings for Maria Jane and Lee William Colson.

"Run the names through our archives see what comes up."

"Stay on the line." Kelly's keyboard clicked. "Nothing on Lee William Colson—wait, I got something on a Dylan Colson but he's, like, a baby."

"A baby? Call it up."

While Kelly clicked at her keyboard, he glanced inside the hardware store. His concentration switched tracks when he thought he could recognize a detective talking to an older man inside. *What's that about?* He made a mental note to follow it up later.

"Here we go," Kelly said. "It's not in the daily. It's in our community weekly. Zone Four. Oh, there's a citation for Maria Colson and Dylan Colson, together in one entry."

"What do you have?"

"No story. It's a cut line for a picture taken a few weeks ago at a Ballard community fund-raiser bake sale. A fluffy picture of Maria Colson and her son Dylan looking at baby toys at a rummage sale. What a little sweetheart."

"Can you send it to me?"

"Okay, you'll have it in a few minutes."

After hanging up, Jason looked at the Colsons' address. It wasn't far—three, maybe four blocks. He had a hunch and decided to gamble on it by leaving the scene. He called the *Mirror*'s photographer.

"Hodge."

"Nate, it's Jason. I've got to step away to check something out. Call me if the police make a statement."

"Sure, but listen." Hodge dropped his voice. "A cop friend of mine says it looks like they took the kid."

"What?"

"Whoever ran down the mom kidnapped her baby."

Kidnapped?

His pulse quickened. Man, this was more than a possible fatal hit-and-run, he thought, letting a few seconds of silence pass. "This could be a huge story. All right, call me if something pops."

A minute later, he received the picture on his phone. Maria Colson and her son, Dylan, smiled at him from the palm of his hand. Mother and child. Looking at them, he tried to get a handle on what had happened. He hadn't nailed anything yet. Was he even chasing the right angle? The right family?

As he walked around the corner, he got his answer. An SPD patrol car was parked in front of the Colsons' two-story house. Bingo. And no other press in sight. Sweet. He was a few doors away when he spotted a woman leaving the Colsons' driveway and coming his way.

"Excuse me." He stopped her and reached into his jacket for his ID and a business card. "Jason Wade, with the *Mirror*. Could I talk to you?"

She stared at his card but she was distracted with worry until he displayed the Colson picture on his phone and handed it to her.

"Do you know who this is?"

Tears came to her eyes and she nodded.

"That's Maria and her baby, Dylan."

"Colson?"

"That's right."

"Are you a relative or a friend?"

Passing back his phone, she indicated her house across the street. "Friend."

"Your name?"

She hesitated. Jason tried gentle persuasion.

"A story might help find who did this."

"Annette."

"Last name?"

"Tabor."

Jason pulled out his notebook, flipped to a clean page, and began making notes while she cupped her trembling hands to her face.

"I was looking for Lee but he's not there," she said.

"Lee?"

"Maria's husband. The officer thinks he's gone to the hospital where they took Maria. I wanted to find him, maybe get some things for her, but the police wouldn't let me in."

"Do you have any idea what really happened?"

"Only what Shannon told me."

"And Shannon is…?"

"My daughter. She works at the store. The detectives won't let me talk to her. She called me after—after it happened. But she didn't see—oh God—they took Dylan!"

"Who? Who took Dylan?"

"I don't know but they've got to find him! Did the police tell you anything about Maria? Is she hurt bad?"

"I don't know any details about her just yet."

"Anything about Dylan?"

"No, nothing. They're not saying much at this point."

"I've got a bad feeling." Annette Tabor looked back at the Colsons' house. "Dear Lord! Why Lee and Maria? They've been through so much! And now this!"

"What do you mean? What have they 'been through'?"

Annette Tabor shook her head. "Nothing. I shouldn't have said anything. I'm sorry. I have to go."

5

Angels looked down on Lee Colson from the stained-glass windows of the hospital's chapel.

A shaft of sun had pierced the clouds to find him. Grace Garner and Perelli seated him in one of the oak pews. A whispery air of reverence mingled with the smell of candle wax in the room's soft light. The flowing water of a hanging wall fountain failed to soothe him. His knuckles were scraped, his fingernails were worn, and his face carried the emotion of a man standing in the path of a freight train that was bearing down on him.

Dr. Raj Binder, a Harvard grad no older than Colson, joined them with a nurse, and spoke with the compassion of a lifelong friend.

"Lee, Maria is upstairs undergoing surgery at this time."

Colson looked to the others, then back to Binder.

"She's suffered a major concussion. Her brain was shaken by a blow to her head. It happened when her head struck the curb, shearing tiny nerve fibers. She's had an intracerebral hemorrhage. There's bleeding in her brain."

The train was getting closer.

"She was unconscious when she came to us, when we treated her. Our best neurological team is operating now. It could take hours. It's too soon for anyone to predict the outcome. Maria may make a complete recovery without memory loss, or she may have periodic amnesia. She may remain unconscious, or"— Binder touched Colson's shoulder—"she may never awaken. I'm very sorry."

"She could die?"

"Yes, I'm very sorry."

The train was upon him.

Colson's knuckles whitened as he clasped and unclasped his hands.

"How did this—I—I don't understand. I just can't— where's Dylan?"

The oak bench creaked sharply. Grace sat beside him.

"There's more," she said.

"More? What the hell's happened?"

"Lee." Grace knew time was hammering against them but waited until his eyes met hers. "Your son's been abducted."

"*Abducted?* What? Who—how?"

"From what we know, Maria left Dylan in front of Kim's Corner Store with an employee while she went inside to make a purchase. The employee, a teenage female, stepped into the store and during that time, a vehicle, we think a van, stopped. Someone got out, took Dylan, and fled in the van. Maria witnessed it from the store, rushed out, and when she tried to stop the van, she was struck by it. We're going to need your help now."

The train. Oh Christ. It's making the earth shake.

"Lee, do you have any idea who would want to do this?"

"No. NO!"

This was crazy. They're all nuts.

Colson's eyes searched Grace, Binder, Perelli, and Cindy, the nurse from psychiatric services, for a hint of deception, an error, the trace of a cruel joke that maybe the guys at the shop had set up because these people had to be joking, because you just don't tell a man that his wife is dying and his son's been stolen.

But staring into their sober faces; at Binder's scrubs, his white smock with the faded blue ink marks on his breast pocket; at Cindy's few strands of gray and small pearl earrings—*Maria loves pearls*—at the leather straps of Perelli's shoulder holster and the butt of his gun peeking from his jacket, Colson knew.

As columns of sunlight shifted through the stained glass and distant sirens rose over the gurgling fountain, he knew the godawful truth.

And when he surrendered to it, lightning flashed in the back of his skull, his skin began to prickle, his scalp tingled, and his intestines twisted as if the train had slammed through him, forcing bile to gush up his throat, causing a reflex gag, making him spasm forward before Grace and Binder steadied him.

Gasping, he studied the chapel like a trapped man.

In his job, Colson had helped people in distress, people stranded with a flat tire, a dead battery, or something. They were always so grateful because he'd rescued them, put them back on life's highway.

Then there were the times he was unable to help. Like with wrecks. When it was too late. When the bodies were still entwined in the metal. Firefighters covered them with tarps until they cut them out, leaving him to hoist their cars onto his truck; sometimes they dripped with blood and viscera the fire hoses had missed. But he was able to detach himself, even when he saw the beer cans, the brief-cases, cell phones, groceries, gifts, coats, shoes, baby seats, toys—the aftermath of lives terminated.

He kept a professional distance. He guarded his deepest hope—the hope of every paramedic, cop, and firefighter: that you never ever come upon your loved ones, that tragedies like this happened to other people.

Not to you. Never to you.

So this—this—bull that they're telling me is not real. See. It's just not real because I just spoke with Maria a few hours ago. She was fine. She was heading to the store with Dylan to get milk and bread. That's all. You don't pay with your life for goddamn milk and bread.

So this is a mistake.

It's not real because they haven't proved it. They've got to prove it's real.

"I want to see Maria!" Colson stood, shaking off Grace as he continued shouting. "I want to see my boy! My wife and son, now!"

"Take it easy, Lee."

Gently, Perelli and Binder got Colson back into the pew.

"It's not true, this can't be, because I was just talking

to her on the phone. I could hear Dylan crying. Last night I kissed them, this can't—we've got plans—it was just milk and bread and—"

There was a soft noise at the chapel door and a man in a dark suit entered and inventoried matters as he approached.

"Detective Garner?"

She caught FBI credentials for Special Agent Kirk Dupree.

"Can we speak privately?"

Outside the chapel, in the bright light of the hall, Grace noticed his neatly parted salt-and-pepper hair. His dark eyes, intense to the point of being hostile.

"That's Mr. Colson in there?" Dupree asked.

"Yes."

"I want a statement."

"We're getting to that. He's being notified about his wife and son."

"Anything from her?"

"She's unconscious and might not live."

"You're the primary then, is that correct?"

"Yes."

"We have jurisdiction over the abduction. I want Mr. Colson in his home immediately to set up for any contact from the kidnappers—phone, e-mail, courier. We've got our technical people rolling. Are you ready to put out an alert and set up a news conference with him?"

"We've blasted a forcewide description of the van."

"I'm talking about a public, statewide activation of the alert system: TV, radio stations, flashing traffic signs, do you understand?"

"We're gathering information for that as fast as we can."

"Not fast enough."

"Excuse me?"

"Detective Garner, are you aware that in most stranger child abductions, the victim is murdered within the first hours of being taken?"

"I'm fully aware."

"You've already lost an hour. Get my point? Colson can do nothing for his wife here. We need him to help save his child. Since you don't yet have a homicide, we'll take it from here."

"May I see your ID again?"

Dupree's brow creased as Grace studied it.

"I don't see it here."

"See what?"

"Where it says that you're an asshole with authority to supervise me."

His face tensed as she continued.

"We've had people working the scene since 911 took the call." Grace invaded Dupree's personal space, close enough to catch the mint on his breath. "We arrived here in time to see them wheel Maria Colson into surgery and for us to try talking to her and to her husband, who is barely coherent. Maybe it takes you longer to get down the elevator because in that time, you guys were invisible. *You've* lost an hour, Dupree, not us. *Get my point?"*

Grace's phone rang.

"Grace, Berman at the scene here. We may have something."

"What?"

"Security camera in the hardware store across the street may have recorded the whole thing."

6

"It should be here. Why isn't it here?"

Arnie Rockwell, seventy-four, replayed the tape from his surveillance camera yet again.

Fuzzy black-and-white images of his empty hardware store filled much of the small TV monitor on his counter. A sliver at the top of the screen offered a view of the street through his window. Stationary images of the store's interior were punctuated by jumpy stop-and-go frames of a car or person passing by. A patch of the street in front of Kim's Corner Store was visible.

Dylan Colson's abduction had not been captured.

"I don't get it."

Arnie's hand, speckled with age spots, scratched his head to coax a memory. His son had installed this cheap little security unit years ago after a pimple-faced teenager tried to steal a hunting knife. The system was ancient, but it still worked.

Kind of like Arnie, who'd kept his store going ever since he'd returned home from the Korean War with the need to hang on to something redemptive. He believed that hardware was the pillar of self-improvement. Your first stop to fix whatever ain't working in your life, he used to tell the boys down at Oscar's Bar.

That was long before his "forgetting" had worsened. Long before his wife, God bless her for keeping the shelves orderly, wanted him to retire. He refused. "Might as well lay me down and pat my face with a spade."

Arnie was at a loss.

"I don't understand. It should be here."

"Mr. Rockwell," Grace Garner said, battling time, "your tape has no date display. Are you certain your camera was operating today?"

"You bet. I save tapes and change them every week or so. I know I saved this one after what happened this morning."

"Where do you put the tapes you save?"

"In the back room."

"Show us."

Reeking of must, the room was a portrait of chaos that reflected Arnie's ailing memory. Boxes, supplies, and crates were stacked floor to ceiling. It was crammed with barrels and buckets of screws, bolts, and nails; the walls were covered with girlie calendars and license plates from the 1950s. A rolltop desk was cluttered with unopened mail, invoices, disorganized ledgers, outdated magazines, and a heap of videotapes.

Upward of fifty, Grace estimated. All unlabeled. She looked at Schaeffer and Berman.

"I thought we had it, Grace," Berman said.

"Go through these tapes with him and call me if you find it." She looked at her watch. "I'll be at Kim's."

* * *

They were losing time.

As much as Dupree was typical of the FBI's takeover style, Grace knew he was right. There was little hope they would find the baby alive. This case was going to draw a lot of heat. Crossing the cordoned-off street, reporters called to her from the other side of the tape.

"Detective! Can you give us a statement?"

Someone from downtown was supposed to be here to handle the press. Grace waved them off. She didn't need this now, not in what was shaping up to be a homicide-abduction.

The doctors had said it could be hours before Maria Colson *might* regain consciousness after surgery. They doubted she would live and had braced her husband for the worst. The FBI had taken him home in case Dylan's abductors made contact.

This one sucked, worse than most of them, Grace thought. Uncertain witnesses, unreliable security tape, no linchpin evidence, and no time. She glanced at the criminalists in their white jumpsuits scrutinizing the blood pool and the stroller, measuring distances. Anger twisted her stomach. No way was she giving up. All she needed was a break. Or something to point her to one.

Anything.

The transom bells rang when she entered Kim's.

Dominic Perelli was talking to a girl who looked to be in her teens. She had a bead ring in her brow. The open page of Perelli's notebook was filled with his neat script.

"This is Shannon Tabor, who works here." Perelli

turned toward the back of the store and a woman in her fifties, out of hearing range with two uniformed officers. "Down there is Betty Kim. She owns the store. Shannon, this is Detective Grace Garner."

Grace and Shannon nodded to each other.

Earlier, over the phone, Berman had briefed her and Perelli about what the women had seen. But Grace and Perelli needed to hear their accounts firsthand before taking them to the squad room later for formal statements, Grace explained, as she opened her notebook.

Shannon, who'd already been crying, rolled her eyes and sobbed.

"How many times do I have to tell you—it's not my fault! I just want to go home!"

"Nobody's pointing any fingers, just tell us what happened."

"I was sweeping the front. Maria asked me to watch Dylan while she came inside. I didn't see or hear anything. Then my friend calls me on my cell. I could see Maria was done and getting ready to come out to get Dylan. I thought she was coming out, so I went in the store, *okay*?"

"Who called you?"

Shannon sniffled and looked away.

"Shannon. *We don't have time.* Tell me, or I'll find out."

"Cody, my boyfriend. He's twenty-one and my mom would freak if she knew, *okay*?"

"Cody who?"

"Whitfield. He's working on the reno of the Lincoln house. He's a carpenter."

"I want his name, number, everything. I want to know why he called you at that time."

"It was just to talk."

"About what?"

"Going to a concert."

"Did you notice any strange vehicles, or anything out of the ordinary before it happened? Anything at all?"

Shannon covered her mouth and shook her head.

"I didn't see anything," she sobbed. "Is Maria going to be all right? We tried to help her. There was so much blood. She wouldn't stop bleeding, then her whole body started to, like, convulse, oh God! Is she going to be all right?"

"We don't know."

"You have to find Dylan!"

"We're doing all we can. It's important you tell us everything you think of now, anything you can remember."

Grace went to the back of the store to talk to Betty Kim. Her bifocals hung from a chain around her neck and she was touching a crumpled tissue to her eyes.

"Could you tell me what you saw?"

Betty Kim blinked several times.

"A van, a dark van stopped. I don't know what type. A person got out, could've been a man or a woman, they were wearing a hat. They picked up the baby and got back in the van. But it was fast. Like a dream—so fast I thought it wasn't even happening."

Grace looked around the store.

"Do you have a security camera?"

"No, my old one broke."

"Can you remember anything distinguishing about the van, or the suspect? Anything?"

Betty Kim buried her face in her hands and shook her head.

Grace's phone rang.

"It's Berman. They found the tape."

Grace and the other detectives huddled around Arnie Rockwell's monitor as Berman cued the tape, then played it in slow motion.

Again, because of the angle it was mounted on the wall, the camera only permitted a partial view of the street, in the top portion of the screen. Only Shannon Tabor's shoes and broom brush could be seen. Then the small wheels of Dylan's stroller and Maria Colson's shoes came into the frame.

There they are.

Maria vanished, leaving only Shannon and the stroller. A moment later, Shannon left the frame, leaving the stroller alone. Seconds ticked by until a shadow entered the frame. Only a partial view of the lower part of a van—its wheels, rocker panels—maybe a Dodge. It was red. It stopped and blocked the stroller from view. A shoe emerged from the van but the image flared, then disappeared from the frame.

Only the van was visible now.

Then nothing.

Then the van began pulling away, leaving the stroller rolling toward the curb where it was about to topple just as Maria Colson's shoes streaked into the frame— blurring, getting in front of the van before disappearing. As the van left the frame—

"Dammit!" Berman said.

Maria Colson's head smashed into the curb and bounced from it like a basketball bouncing from the rim. Betty Kim's shoes, followed by Shannon Tabor, then Arnie Rockwell hurried to the street. The three of them comforting Maria. Berman advanced the tape until paramedics arrived. Arnie trotted back to his store and the screen went blank.

"Hold it!" Grace said. "Back it up to when the van emerges."

"What is it?" Berman rewound the tape.

"There! There!" Grace tapped her pen to the monitor's lower corner. A person stepped into the frame. It was clear they were watching everything. "There's a witness in a position to have seen it all. Up close. Looks like a woman. Who is that?"

Arnie swallowed hard, nodding.

"One of my customers. She lives a block away on the other side of the park. She was in the store just before it happened. I think she's on the start of the tape."

Berman began rewinding.

7

Jason Wade walked back to the scene trying to make sense of what the Colsons' neighbor, Annette Tabor, had told him.

What did she mean by "they had already been through so much"?

He'd check that out later. Right now, he had to find Tabor's daughter Shannon and any other people who were at Kim's. He needed an account of what had happened. He needed to dig deeper into this story.

Walking through the neighborhood, Jason considered what he had so far: a mother who'd likely been killed when her baby was stolen from her in a sleepy northwest neighborhood. It was incredible. He needed more facts, more witnesses, and more color because this story was going to explode.

His phone rang.

"It's Spangler, what've you got?"

"Maybe a murder mystery. Looks like the mother, Maria Colson, late twenties, early thirties, isn't going to make it."

"TV's reported that already. What else do you have?"

What else? Give me a break, Fritz, I just got here.

"Anything else, Jason?"

Tell him, or hold back? All right, tell him before he finds out.

"They took her baby. Whoever ran her down took her son, Dylan."

The silence told Jason that he'd hit on something Spangler didn't know.

"Is the abduction all ours?"

"At the moment."

"Do you have the abduction confirmed by the FBI?"

"Not yet."

"Call me when you do. We'll get it up on our site. We need to be first to break news on this one. That's all you got?"

There was the bit the neighbor told him. But he'd better hold on to that. It was his angle, he'd check it out. Don't tell Spangler everything. Don't oversell.

"For now, yeah."

Spangler ended the call without another word. The prick. Jason rejected pondering him a second longer when his phone rang again. He checked his caller ID. Thankfully it was not Spangler again.

"Jason, it's Hodge. Where are you?"

"About two blocks from the scene. What's up?"

"Got a whole mess of detectives looking pretty serious in Arnie's Hardware Store. It's got to be important. Get your ass back here 'cause I'm telling you something's going on."

Hurrying through a small corner park, Jason saw an old woman sitting alone on a bench. Heavyset. White hair curling from her colorful babushka. She appeared forlorn, he thought, passing her until he was stopped by a detail.

The small plastic bag she was holding.

The writing on it said "Arnie's Hardware Store" and his gut linked it to the detective he'd spotted earlier inside the store, Nate Hodge's alert, and now this woman sitting before him, gazing off at nothing.

Maybe she knew something?

Might be worth a shot. He went to her, identified himself, then showed her Maria and Dylan's picture on his phone.

"Do you know who these people are, ma'am?"

Studying the photo, the woman's head tilted with the tender affection of a grandmother. A smile rose on her face then died. Her high red cheeks accentuated her Slavic features, pushing her bright eyes into tiny slits, as if to shut out the world—or her memories of it.

"Ma'am." Jason softened his voice. "Do you know what happened to these people? Did you see what happened?"

She looked at him for several moments before smiling.

"Tak."

Jason didn't understand, but, given her intonation, interpreted it as *yes* and opened his notebook.

But the old woman went away. Without moving a muscle, without leaving the bench, Lani Tychina resumed the journey she was on before Jason had interrupted her.

She was a retired professor at the University of Washington; a linguist fluent in five languages; a widow who lived alone in her house a few doors from the Colsons, the young couple with the beautiful baby.

Lani had gone to Arnie's first thing this morning to get a new hinge to repair her cat door so Buttons would no longer have to scratch the screen to get in and out. Walking home, she'd remembered she needed light-bulbs, turned around, and started back.

That was when she saw the van, the baby, Maria—*everything*.

It catapulted Lani back to Kiev, back through her life, before she married her American sweetheart—the handsome history student—and moved to Seattle. Back to when she was a little girl, back to Kiev's old castles in the hills, the silk-weaving mill, the market. Back to that day her Uncle Taras took her to the Podol and she was playing near the Dnieper River with her little cousin, Analise, back to when they heard the Soviet army trucks coming like sudden, angry thunder.

They came upon them so fast.

"Leave the ball, Analise! Take my hand! Analise!"

But her cousin's hand slipped from hers as the first truck launched Analise skyward. She fell to earth under the next truck, its big wheels firing her body like a rag doll to the gutter.

Lani rushed to Analise, took up her hand, refusing to let go, screaming. Then today, the horror she thought she'd buried in Kiev returned when she'd witnessed the horror in front of Kim's store.

Lani was paralyzed by it.

Too stunned to help or call, shocked with fear, she'd simply walked away, seeking comfort in the park that was like the banks of the Dnieper before the Soviet trucks; before death had brushed against her. And now this young man, Jason Wade from the newspaper, wanted Lani to tell him about it. She tried, but each time she replayed the details she was jolted.

It was too painful.

He kept speaking to her, this nice young man, repeating himself.

"Ma'am, please, can you tell me again? You said you saw the incident. What did you see? Can you tell me, please?"

Lani struggled. She wanted to help—had to help, but all she could see were the trucks and Analise until her thoughts shifted. Someone else was talking now. There was a woman with a pretty face also asking questions, like the police officers in Kiev.

"Lani Tychina?"

How does she know my name?

"Tak."

"I'm Detective Grace Garner." She showed her ID then abruptly turned to Jason. "Who are you?"

"Jason Wade, *Seattle Mirror,* and I was interviewing Lani Tie-Chee-Na," he said to Lani. "Is that correct, ma'am? Is that how you say your name?"

"Your interview's over," Grace said. "Leave."

"This is a public park, Detective."

"Don't make me tell you twice. This is police business."

Jason stood there, appraising her smooth skin, the way her hair was pulled back. She looked about his age, maybe a year or two older. Her face held something bright, strong. Behind her eyes, he perceived a hint of sadness. Maybe for the crime. Maybe for something personal.

"Did you hear me?"

Grace stepped closer, assessing him, the silver stud earring in his left lobe, then the few days' growth of whiskers that suggested a Vandyke. He was about six feet, strong build, with deep-set eyes that radiated an intelligent intensity bordering on dangerous.

"Police business, get lost."

"I got a right to ask questions."

"I've got the authority to arrest you for obstructing a police investigation."

Jason's jaw muscles pulsed, then he glanced at Lani, who had raised her hand, signaling that she had remembered.

"There was a man." Lani's voice still carried the thick accent of her childhood. "A man and a woman in the van."

"Describe them," Grace said. "Were they old? Young? White? Black?"

Narrow slits replaced Lani's eyes as she worked to remember.

"Lani, what about the van? Do you remember anything about the van? The model, color, license number?"

Her eyes opened.

"*Tak*, I maybe remember something about the van— on the back was a small picture of the sun and trees."

8

Two hours and forty minutes after Dylan Colson was stolen from his mother, images recorded by the hardware store's security camera filled the computer monitor at the desk of Seattle Detective Wes Delucca.

He worked flat-out to identify the red van.

The security tape only revealed the wheels to the lugs and the extreme lower portion of the vehicle. He studied the bottom door contours, lower front and rear quarters, and the beginnings of the bumper configurations. He enlarged, reduced, then checked the images against a list of other similar models. He compared the recovered wiper to manufacturer databases. The wiper pointed to a Chrysler but could've been a generic replacement part.

If anyone was going to identify this van, it was Delucca. He was a veteran of the Traffic Collision Investigation Squad, a court-certified expert on crimes involving vehicles. As his nine-year-old daughter smiled at him from the framed picture next to his phone, he clicked with the cadence of a heartbeat.

Let's go. Every second counts.

Delucca estimated tire size, wheelbase, and ground

clearance, again consulting a database of vehicle makes and models. Then, using a scaled template, he matched the attitude of the suspect vehicle and transposed images of existing makes and models over the security tape images. He clicked faster because he almost had it. Glancing at the time, he needed to be absolutely certain.

As his computer processed one more check, he consulted his notes. Lani Tychina, the confused eyewitness, was unable to provide any details on the plate. She didn't know if it was a Washington tag or an out-of-state plate. But she said the rear door had a small, customized mural showing the sun and trees. The computer beeped with confirmation. Delucca exhaled then sat up. *Here it is. The van in the security tape is a 2002 Chrysler Town & Country.*

Delucca reached for his phone.

Two hours and fifty-eight minutes after the abduction, Grace Garner, phone wedged between her ear and shoulder, took down Delucca's information.

"Good work, Wes, thanks."

Grace called the coordinator for the Washington State Patrol, who was poised to activate the alert system.

"We've got our lock on the vehicle from Records; the van is a 2002 Chrysler Town and Country." Grace paged through her notes from her preliminary interviews, quickly reviewing all she had from Lani Tychina, Betty Kim, and Arnie Rockwell.

"A 2002 Chrysler Town and Country," the coordinator repeated.

"Correct. You have everything now."

"Stay on the line, Detective."

The coordinator put Grace on speakerphone, connecting her with the analyst who was finalizing the text for the alert, double- and triple-checking details, facts, and circumstances with Grace.

The Seattle Police Department and Federal Bureau of Investigation were coinvestigating agencies on the hit-and-run abduction. The SPD had already preapproved a hotline for tips. FBI Special Agent Kirk Dupree was at the Colson home with Lee awaiting a potential ransom call or other contact from the suspects. Nothing had come at this stage. Dupree had been updated by e-mail and joined the call on his cell phone. The analyst read the script aloud to Grace and Dupree twice for accuracy.

"It's good. Move it," Dupree said.

"Good with me. Kick it now," Grace added.

Less than four minutes later, every TV and radio broadcast across Washington State was simultaneously interrupted with a burst tone alert followed by three shrill beeps, then the message:

This is an activation of the Alert System. The following is critical information on an abducted child in the Ballard area of Seattle in King County, Washington. The FBI and Seattle Police Department are seeking assistance locating Dylan James Colson, age seven months, abducted from the 3400 block of Calvington Avenue during a hit-and-run of his mother, Maria Jane Colson, age twenty-nine. Dylan James Colson is believed to be in danger. He has light hair and was last seen wearing a white T-shirt, blue jeans, and white sneakers. He may be in the company of a White female approximately 30 years of age and a White male, approximately 30 years of age. They may be traveling in a red 2002 Chrysler Town & Country minivan that is missing a windshield wiper. The rear door has a small customized mural showing the sun and trees. If you have any information on this matter contact the Seattle Police Department or the FBI immediately.

The alert was also flashed over electronic highway signs and was sent out by e-mails, faxes, and voice and text messages to websites, municipal, county, and state government transportation agencies, and to the fleets of private companies who participated in the alert system.

The alert did not stop within Washington's borders. It was also carried under agreement in the same manner in Oregon, California, Idaho, Montana, and British Columbia and Alberta, Canada.

"The alert is going to reach millions of people, Grace, it's going to boost our chances," Perelli said.

She didn't answer. She was watching the TV suspended from the ceiling in the hospital lounge, a few steps from the intensive care unit where Maria Colson had just come out of surgery.

The grim-faced surgeon had informed investigators that it would be several hours before there was any chance of her regaining consciousness.

Even if she did recover, could she tell me anything that would help—anything that would solve her own murder? Grace's fingertips touched the microcassette recorder in her pocket as she braced for a dying declaration.

Have we done everything? Are we missing anything? Grace wasn't one-hundred-percent certain. And there was that guy from the *Mirror*. She found his card. Jason Wade. He was right on the money, the way he'd found Lani Tychina. He was a good reporter. And she was a good detective.

So why was she doubting herself?

Maybe it was because she was worried the choices she'd made in her life were the wrong ones. Maybe she was tired of coming home to an empty apartment, tired of feeling that she was missing something.

The air in the room was oppressive with antiseptic smells. Maria's aunt and uncle talked softly in a far corner. As the clock over the nurses' station swept time forward, Grace took stock of the cheerless walls, the drab vinyl couches, the outdated copies of *Newsweek* and *People*, and a well-thumbed King James edition of the Bible.

This wasn't a waiting room, this was a terminal where hope confronted death; where frightened families pleaded with God and where a lonely Homicide detective and her partner awaited the outcome.

Perelli rubbed his tired eyes. For his part, he acknowledged he didn't know everything about Grace. Could you ever know all that a person carried in their heart? But what he knew of her, he knew well and her second-guessing was evident to him. He took her aside, speaking quietly. "We're doing all we can. We're doing it right. The alert will help us."

She looked at him and nodded.

In the corner, Maria Colson's sixty-two-year-old aunt, a retired secretary for Boeing, whispered prayers. They floated down the corridor, into the dimly lit room where her niece was fighting for her life. At that moment, the only other person with Maria was the intensive care nurse who was keeping vigil, watching the equipment monitoring Maria's heart rate, blood pressure, and breathing.

The room was bathed with the light of the muted television located in the high corner. The nurse had insisted it be left on for Maria, believing that if the young mother could subconsciously absorb the information on the massive search for her baby boy, it could help her.

Not long after the alert was broadcast, WKKR went to a live news report on the abduction. David Troy described the incident as the screen then showed the *Seattle Mirror*'s website with a story by Jason Wade accompanied by a large photo of Maria and Dylan together. A heartbreakingly beautiful picture, the nurse thought just as Maria's monitor ponged and her hand clenched.

Good Lord.

Maria remained unconscious. It was likely a coincidental muscle reflex. But the nurse believed, as she did with the many life-and-death cases she'd had on her floor, that Maria knew.

She must see her baby up there. Feel him up there, the nurse thought.

As the alert continued crawling across the bottom of the screen, the nurse turned to the window and the city beyond it.

Where was Dylan?

9

Several miles south of where Maria Colson lay in the hospital, Everett Sinclair was seething on the forty-fifth floor of the Bank of America building.

Three hours since the goddammed idiot in the van had sideswiped his Mercedes 450SL and his rage had not subsided.

No way.

The more he dwelled on it, the more it angered him. The scratches defacing his prized Benz sickened him. The deep gouges were wounds in the beautiful Jasper Blue finish.

And he couldn't bear to look at the stains on his suit. The new charcoal gray number he'd bought last month in San Francisco. Italian cut, woven wool, with pleated pants. Perfectly tailored. Nine hundred dollars.

Ruined.

Like his day.

This day of all days, when he was scheduled to make his presentation to the meeting. The entire board. It meant his shot at VP. If he got it, he'd be the youngest executive manager to sit in the chair.

"Your star's rising, Ev. This should be a slam dunk," Hadley assured him.

Dammit.

Set the fender bender aside, Sinclair told himself. But he couldn't. It was an affront and he couldn't stop replaying it.

As usual, that morning he'd rolled out of the cobblestone drive of his big colonial in Sunset Hills, with its view of Puget Sound and the Olympic Mountains. He'd left early enough to make his appointment with his accountant and leave plenty of time to get to the office and prepare. He had his briefcase open on the passenger seat and was glancing at his presentation at red lights, while he took hits of coffee.

He was in Ballard somewhere near Leary and 17th, reading, when the light had changed. A horn sounded behind him, he waved, signaling an apology for what? Being two seconds too slow in responding to the green. Then an engine growled, tires squcaled, something blurred and he felt a *scrape* as the idiot behind him suddenly cut ahead of him, grazing his Benz, forcing him to stand on his brakes.

His briefcase toppled; he fumbled his commuter mug and the lid came off, splashing scorching hot coffee on his lap, his papers, his car's leather interior. Dumbstruck, he glanced around. No one saw anything. If they did, they didn't care. He erupted with anger, smashing his foot on the accelerator.

His Mercedes roared with righteous wrath as he pursued the bastard. One block, two, three, four. Adrenaline coursed through his veins as he narrowed the distance to the bastard's rear bumper. He'd come within inches when he was suddenly staring into the horrified face of a cyclist. Brakes screeched as the acrid smell of burning rubber brought the Mercedes to a safe halt and Sinclair to his senses.

"Everett?"

Sinclair looked around the boardroom, at the massive mahogany table, the twenty-odd members in the high-backed chairs, the huge screen displaying his presentation, and the question in Hadley's face.

"The situation at our cross-border operation in Detroit, Everett?" Hadley repeated, "Your presentation touched onto our status there, which suggests a remedy."

"Yes." Sinclair lowered his head to feign serious consideration, doodling with his pen on the paper in his leather-bound briefing book. He noticed a coffee splotch from the incident. "I am confident we can address Detroit effectively by using our plant across the Detroit River in Windsor, as I outlined in the memo I sent out this week. If Detroit's on board with applying the El Paso scenario in Windsor, we can proceed."

Hadley's nod contained the right measure of approval. Then, while he took the Detroit issue around the table and across the country to the executives participating on the conference call, Sinclair resumed his private battle.

He'd abandoned chasing the jerk who'd hit his car. Kept his appointment with his accountant to hide away more assets in his numbered account in Aruba before he filed on his cheating whore wife. Parked his car, got to his office, changed into the wrinkled navy suit he'd kept in his closet, reproduced his presentation, and got on with business. During that short time, he'd set his fury aside, like a loaded gun, which he intended to use when he had a free moment.

There would be a reckoning. The son of a bitch would pay.

Sinclair studied his notes in his briefing book. *Knowledge is power,* he thought, as he circled the information he'd captured from the battlefield.

A red Chrysler minivan.

"Can you hear me, Everett?" the chief of operations at the Detroit plant said. "I acted on your memo immediately. We absolutely agree with your assessment."

"Wonderful, Jim. We're all on the same page."

A question hung in the air.

"Everett." The chief's long-distance voice filled the boardroom. "Are you in a position to do it? The sooner you get to Detroit-Windsor and approve the redesign the sooner we can start production. We've got three full shifts ready to go 24-7 once you green-light us. We can start ahead of schedule, thanks to your assessment."

An advanced startup impressed the board members. They murmured and nodded.

"I could be there the day after tomorrow," Sinclair said.

"How about today, after this meeting?" Hadley said.

"Today?"

"That's right."

"I still have the Tokyo project to send off."

"Langston will babysit Tokyo, Everett. Detroit's a

fifty-million-dollar contract. Early production positions us to triple the commitment over the next two years. We're talking two hundred million. I think we'd do well to maintain the momentum you've built."

"Understood."

Hadley pressed a button on his console. "Gloria?"

"Yes, sir."

"Get Ellen to make travel arrangements to get Everett Sinclair on the next flight to Detroit. I'm dispatching him immediately."

"Yes, sir."

"Okay," Hadley said to the group. "That's it for today. Thank you."

Sinclair exited the room through a flurry of back-slapping and attaboys. Hadley was dead-on. His star was rising.

While packing in his office, he glanced at his stained Italian suit and his anger bubbled. He went to the large window, looked down over Seattle, and thought for a moment before he went through his briefing book for his notes on Detroit. He stopped when he came to the page with the information he had on the asshole.

He powered up his laptop to download files for his trip, paused, then included the material from his camera phone. Pictures he'd taken. Evidence. The stains on his suit. The damage to his Mercedes 450SL.

The rear of the Chrysler and its license.

You will rue the day you fucked with Everett Sinclair.

Collecting his computer bag and the small toiletry kit from his office washroom, Sinclair headed down the hall to the office of Ellen Gorman, who handled executive travel arrangements.

"Hi, Ev, got everything right here," she said, putting papers into an envelope. "Your plane leaves in two hours for Chicago, where you connect to Detroit. The car's waiting for you downstairs."

"Thanks, Ellen."

Gorman's attention went back to the muted TV she had under her desk. Long ago Hadley insisted she have one on all the time to alert him to any breaking news that might impact the company. Sinclair knew she watched daytime talk shows.

"That's sad." Gorman did not take her eyes from the set.

"What's sad?" Sinclair asked. Not that he cared. He couldn't see or hear her TV. He was checking his travel envelope and the Detroit and Windsor reports he needed to read.

"It's one of those emergency alerts."

Sinclair grunted as Gorman watched the ribbon of information on Dylan Colson's abduction crawl across the bottom of her screen.

"A baby boy was abducted after his mother was run over this morning."

Sinclair wasn't listening. He was checking his reports, estimating if he'd have enough time to absorb them all, just as details and vehicle description flowed across Gorman's TV. None of the information reached Sinclair as he flipped through his travel arrangements. For a moment his thoughts shifted to how lucky he'd been not to have hit the cyclist. Moreover, Sinclair congratulated himself for nailing the info he needed to find the bastard who'd wronged him.

This is not over.

He tapped his bag.

"Thanks, Ellen, I'm off."

"We also booked you a room in Detroit and one on the Canadian side in Windsor. Good luck, Ev."

Gorman continued watching the reports on Dylan Colson, shaking her head.

10

"This will be difficult to watch."

FBI Special Agent Kirk Dupree slammed the hardware store security tape into the Colsons' big home system, which occupied one side of the living room. The sixty-inch screen gave the images such force Lee drew back.

The wheels of Dylan's stroller.

Maria's sneakers.

The van, as white shoes emerged from it. Someone scurried to Dylan's stroller, then scurried back to the van.

They had just stolen his son.

His breathing quickened. *This can't be.*

Only last night, he'd sat in this room in front of this TV holding Dylan in his arms. The little guy sucked happily on a warm bottle of formula. He'd felt so good in his cotton jumper; the one dotted with little elephants and giraffes. He'd smelled so sweet. And his eyes; his eyes were shining up at him like shooting stars.

Was that to be his last memory?.

He thought of Maria. How he'd kissed her in the darkness after getting out of bed at midnight to take the tanker call near Jackson Park.

Had he told her that he loved her?

The scenes flitted before him on the big screen.

Maria's sneakers as she rushed from the store to climb onto the van. The van lurched. The upper part of the screen blurred and Maria's head smashed to the street.

His insides twisted. The saliva in his mouth evaporated.

His wife was dying in the street and he was unable to do anything.

Dylan's stroller toppled, its wheels spun in a final chorus to the destruction of his world. The last images of his wife and son.

The FBI replayed the tape. Again and again, until Lee's thoughts became jumbled. Blood thundered in his ears as if he were underwater thrashing to the surface. He had nothing to grip but the arms of his chair. There was nothing to silence the typhoon of anguish as it began hurling blame.

What the hell was Maria thinking, leaving Dylan outside the store?

God, no. I take that back. I'm so sorry, Maria. Forgive me. Please.

A bolt of self-reproach hit Lee hard.

It was his fault.

He was supposed to protect his family. He'd gone out in the night to help strangers. Why wasn't he there to protect Maria and Dylan?

Why?

Lee drove his fingers into the chair's fabric until he seized a moment of clarity. He should be with his wife.

"I'm going back to the hospital now, I need to be with Maria."

"We know, Lee." Detective Grace Garner had arrived from the hospital moments earlier. "Maria's aunt and uncle are with her. Her condition's unchanged. We need your help here, then we'll take you to her."

"Have another look at the tape," Dupree said. "Do you know this van? It's a red Chrysler Town and Country. A witness told us that the rear has a custom-painted mural showing the sun and trees. You're a tow truck operator, you know vehicles. From what you see, do you recognize this van?"

"No. How many times do I have to tell you? How many times do I have to see this tape? Why are you certain I should know who did this?"

"I'm not. But there's always the chance that the person behind it has had contact with you, or your family, in some small way. Maybe a seemingly innocuous way. This happened too fast to be random."

"They were stalking us?"

"That's one scenario. We're looking at others."

Lee took stock of the living room and the adjoining dining room with the large oak table, a wedding gift from Maria's aunt. FBI agents had transformed it into a command desk with TVs to monitor news reports. They also had Global Positioning Satellite hardware, satellite phones, printers, laptop computers, and more phones with special lines in case Dylan's abductors called with demands.

Nothing so far.

Throughout the house, more somber-faced agents

wearing white latex gloves were searching everything, their voices low, creating a funereal air. The FBI was also screening calls from the press, friends, and well-wishers, while outside, uniformed Seattle police officers kept neighbors and reporters from approaching the door. Lee plunged his haggard face into his hands as Dupree glanced at his watch then resumed his questions.

"Does Dylan have any medical conditions, or require any special medication?"

"No, but I've given you his doctor's number."

"Do you know anyone who wanted children but can't have them, or anyone who recently lost a child?"

"No."

"Do you know anyone who paid unusual attention to Dylan? Anyone who made you and your wife uneasy?"

"No."

"Any recent altercations with anyone? Anyone who threatened you or Maria in any way?"

"No."

"Any strange visitors at your door that she may have mentioned?"

Lee shook his head.

"Anyone lost looking for directions, hang-up calls, anything?"

"Nothing like that."

"You use a babysitter?"

"No. Only family."

"Did Maria take prenatal classes?"

"Yes."

"We'd like a contact name."

"It's in her address book, in her purse." Lee indicated the dining room.

"Do you know anyone with a grudge against you, your family, the company you work for?" Dupree asked.

"No."

"Do you or your wife use drugs, or gamble? Do you have any outstanding debts to anyone for drugs, gambling, anything like that? Anything illegal?"

"What are you suggesting?"

"We need to know everything, Lee," Grace said.

"We will find out, Lee," Dupree added. "If you're truthful with us now, it'll save time that may help us find Dylan faster."

"The answer is no."

"Any vindictive girlfriends from your past?"

"No."

"Ever have an affair?"

"God, no."

"Or keep anything secret from your wife that may be a factor in this?"

Lee shook his head.

"Any criminal history in this family?"

"Haven't you checked already, Dupree?"

"Please, we're asking you to cooperate."

"We haven't broken any laws." Lee glared at Dupree. "I don't get you people. Someone tried to kill my wife while stealing our baby and you treat me like I'm involved."

"It's been known to happen," Dupree said. "Four

months ago, you doubled your wife's life insurance policy to two hundred thousand dollars."

Lee looked at Dupree, then Grace. "We updated our policies when we got one for Dylan."

"A policy for fifty thousand?"

"That's right."

"We understand you recently talked to the bank about a six-figure loan."

"I made enquiries about qualifying and terms. I'd like to buy the towing business. I discussed it with Maria."

"When?"

"This morning. What? You think I'd kill my wife and ransom my son to own a towing business?"

"Mr. Colson, we want to eliminate you as a potential suspect as soon as possible and to do that we need your fullest cooperation."

Lee's left jaw muscle twitched.

"My fullest cooperation?" He'd already volunteered everything. His fingerprints for a comparison set, should they find evidence. Phone, bank, credit, and online records. The FBI was going through their mail and personal papers. Two agents were doing things to their home computer he'd never seen done before, tracking all of their e-mails and Internet activity. Out back, forensic experts were searching his truck, their cars, going through the garbage; while upstairs more agents were sifting through all of their belongings, probably going through his socks and underwear.

Why aren't they scouring Seattle for his son?

"I am cooperating, Dupree. What're you doing?

Besides sitting here and asking me if I'm a crook, a liar, or if I've cheated on my wife? What the hell are you doing to find my boy? Why aren't you looking for him?" Lee pointed at the frame showing the partial view of the van frozen on the big TV. "That's who ran down my wife and took my son. *Find them!*"

Dupree let a beat pass.

"Mr. Colson, my sworn duty is to effect the safe return of your son and see to the arrest and prosecution of the people who took him and hurt your wife." Dupree scanned the room. "The alert's been broadcast to millions of people in the Pacific Northwest and in Canada. It will be replayed continuously all day long. We've entered the case data in the National Crime Information Center, to alert police across the country and compare it to similar crimes. Our Evidence Response Team is working with Seattle PD, and a Rapid Response Team has been deployed to help coordinate leads. Now, I could continue detailing every other single thing that we're doing but that would cost us time. What I will tell you is that we will open every door and follow every lead, without fear and without favor, in order to return Dylan to his home. *Every door. Every lead.*"

Lee didn't respond. His anger at Dupree had ebbed. He had nothing to hide and resigned himself to do whatever Dupree wanted just as the phone rang again. The source came up on one of the FBI's computers. "Another press call, the *Seattle Mirror*," an agent said.

"Take it, Foley," Dupree said.

Foley answered, then put his hand over the mouthpiece.

"They want a statement from Lee Colson."

"Tell them there will be a news conference in forty-five minutes," Dupree said. "At the front of the house here in Ballard. Give them the address. Then tell our press office to put out a notice." Dupree looked at Lee. "We expect Dylan's abductors will be watching. We'd like you to consider making a plea to them. Use the news conference to talk directly to them, to get a public appeal out."

"I'll do whatever it takes."

Lee nodded. "Another thing we'll need is Dylan's footprint."

"His footprint?"

"Babies are too small for fingerprints. We use the footprint the hospital takes as a method of identification."

"Like with a dead person?"

"We're watching the airports, bus and train stations, car rentals. If we stop someone with a baby whom we suspect might be Dylan, the footprint will determine identity. We can copy it here and shoot it out instantly. We need it now."

Lee nodded.

"Maria has it in Dylan's baby book upstairs. I'll get it."

"I'll go with you," Grace said.

The Colsons' renovated master bedroom had oak flooring, soft green walls, and a handmade quilt over the queen-size bed. This was Maria's sanctuary and today it offered a reprieve from the intense activity in the rest of the house.

A female FBI agent was standing near Maria's closet, flipping through photo albums and old high-school yearbooks. It sickened Lee the way the tragedy had engulfed them with white-gloved strangers pawing through every intimate corner of their lives.

"Could you give us a minute alone here," Grace said, waiting until the agent closed the door before telling Lee, "Believe me, I know Dupree might come off as a jerk but he's just doing his job."

"What's this? Good cop, bad cop?"

"He's led a lot of kidnapping investigations for the bureau. Some have had parental involvement. Lee, he's got to push every angle as quickly and as far as possible. It's standard police work."

"So is remembering who the victims are."

She let him have that. He was entitled. "After the news conference we'll take you to the hospital."

He didn't say anything; he was looking at his wife's clothes, the Seahawks shirt she wore to bed, her hairbrush on her dresser. The lotion she used. He breathed in Maria's scent, as if she were still here.

It took him back to Lincoln High.

That Friday night dance and Maria all alone against the wall. A slow song had started. He wasn't much of a dancer, never even went to school dances. He was more comfortable working on cars and trucks, pretending they were more important than girls. But sometimes the loneliness ate at him, until he couldn't take any more and suddenly found himself standing in the school gym in front of a teenage girl named Maria.

She was wearing a blue dress and a tiny pearl necklace, and seemed a little nervous herself.

His pulse had upshifted and even though he'd showered and shaved without nicking his chin, he knew there was still a bit of grease on his knuckles, enough to make him painfully self-conscious as he faced the moment of truth.

"Want to dance?"

"Sure."

He took her into his arms and something happened.

Holding her so close, she felt so right as "Ruby Tuesday" echoed and a thousand points of light rained on them from the mirror ball. When the song ended they knew that the rest of their lives together had just begun.

Noises pulled Lee from the gym to the bedroom.

Shouting, then a hydraulic whir. Through the window he saw the TV trucks positioning their satellite dishes. The street was lined with a growing number of police vehicles, news crews, reporters, neighbors, kids on skateboards, bikes.

God.

"Is this it?" Grace pointed to a pastel-shaded book labeled "Baby's First Year." The kind you can get at most department stores.

Lee opened it to the first few pages, coming to the one with the inky black swirls and whorls, impressions of his son's tiny feet taken by a nurse shortly after he was born.

He turned to Maria's entry for Dylan's birth. *"Today God granted me a miracle,"* she'd written in her neat script. *"I'm bursting with love for him, my answered prayer."*

As he traced the letters, the words began to blur. He rubbed his eyes, then saw the snapshot of the three of them taken at the hospital. Dylan, barely an hour old, his little face scrunched. Maria, radiant as she held him. And there was Lee: the proud father, so happy he wasn't sure his feet were touching the earth.

Why was this happening? Hadn't they been through enough?

He turned to read more of Maria's words, her love letter to their son: *"To Mommy's Angel, No one believed we would have you, except me. I always believed you would come to me."*

11

Jason Wade paced outside the Better Price Supermart.

He was outside because the bow-tied assistant manager, "Mitch Decoli," according to his nameplate, had busted him talking to a clerk at the customer service counter.

"No interviews with my staff inside the store."

"Why not?"

"Company policy. I'm sorry, you'll have to leave."

After considering his options, Jason put his notebook away. As he walked by the checkouts, a husky-voiced cashier—"Pam," according to her tag—pulled him aside. "Candy and I are taking our break outside in five minutes. Hang around, we'll talk to you."

"Sure."

That was fifteen minutes ago.

Jason continued pacing near the shopping cart corral. While waiting he'd managed to get a call answered at the Colsons' home. But the FBI wouldn't put Lee Colson on the line, saying there'd be a news conference in forty-five minutes, hinting that Lee would be there. Jason checked his watch. How much more time could he afford to wait here?

Ten more minutes, then he'd bail.

Tapping his notebook against his leg, he ran through his thoughts. After his encounter with Grace Garner, he got nothing more from bewildered eyewitness Lani Tychina, other than her address and phone number. Then he'd returned to the pack at the scene where little was happening, until he noticed something the others had missed.

Movement behind Kim's Corner Store.

A teenage girl leaving with Annette Tabor, the Colsons' neighbor. It had to be Shannon, Annette's daughter. He followed his hunch to the Tabor house and rang the bell. To his surprise, Annette and Shannon came to the door, their faces taut with worry.

"My daughter's not granting any interviews."

"No, Mom. I need to tell him." Shannon kept him on the doorstep. He wrote quickly as she gave him a terse account of what had happened, ending it by stating: "You've got to write that this was not my fault. *It was not my fault!*" Shannon's hand flew to her mouth as her mother pulled her away and tried to close the door.

"Wait." He flipped through his pages. "Mrs. Tabor, you told me earlier that the Colsons had already 'been through so much! And now this!' Please, what does that mean?"

"This is just too upsetting," she said and began shutting the door.

"But Mrs. Tabor, I'm just looking for people who might know—"

"Try the cashiers at the Supermart where Maria worked," Shannon shouted to him before her mother closed the door.

As he drove to the local Better Price Supermart, he looked anxiously into his rearview mirror at the satellite news trucks gathering in front of the Colsons' home.

It was eight minutes away.

He stood a good chance of learning more about Maria with the cashiers. From stories he'd done on supermarket robberies, he knew how hard they worked. Standing on their feet all day. Some got varicose veins or backaches. They contended with scanners that malfunctioned, dealt with bitchy customers and management that plotted to claw back hard-won wages and benefits. It helped color the unfolding picture of Maria Colson's life.

"Who're you with?"

He turned to face Pam the cashier as she blew a stream of cigarette smoke skyward.

"*Seattle Mirror.*" Jason produced business cards for Pam and Candice, the younger cashier with her who was snapping her gum and looking around as if she were guilty of something.

"Mitch's going to freak out," she said.

"Screw him. It's our time." Pam studied his card. "We saw some of what happened on the TV in the lunchroom. The produce manager told us about the alert. It's horrible. Is Maria still alive?"

"As far as I know," Jason said.

"Did they find Dylan yet?" Pam asked.

"Not yet."

"Where's Lee?" Candice asked.

"Either at the hospital, or at home with the police, in case there's a ransom call or something. That's what I've heard."

"Is it true? Did it happen like we're hearing? Someone just snatched Dylan from her then ran her down?" Pam asked.

"The details are still sketchy," he said.

Candice touched the corners of her eyes. "It's just so awful. How could anyone do this? Do the police have any idea who did it?"

"I'm not sure. There's going to be a news conference." Jason opened his notebook. "Maria worked here, as a cashier?"

Both women nodded.

"She was on mat leave," Pam said. "Used some parental leave and banked vacation time to stretch it out. She has the seniority because she's been working at BPS—cripes, since she graduated from high school."

"She worked, like, right up until her time," Candice added. "I used to tease her about reaching the till."

"Quickly"—Jason checked his watch as he wrote—"what can you tell me about Maria and Lee?"

"High-school sweethearts. They both went to Lincoln," Pam said. "He's a good-looking, hardworking man devoted to her. She's so cute. They're in love. The real deal. He'd do anything for her."

"For the longest time, Maria wanted to marry Lee, have babies, have the white-picket dream," Candice said. "Having babies was all she ever talked about."

Pam nodded, dragging on her cigarette. "Yeah, Maria was desperate to have kids. Really. Seems that's all she lived for. She was baby crazy."

"Baby crazy?"

Candice rummaged through her bag and produced a

snapshot. Candice, Pam, and several other smiling women were bunched around Maria Colson, whose face glowed in the light shining from the candles of the cake in front of her.

"We threw a shower for her. Look how happy she is."

"Can I borrow this to use this in the *Mirror*?"

Candice looked at Pam.

"It's your photo, your property, right?" Jason said. "The more attention on the story, the better the chances of it helping."

Candice nodded. "Take it."

"I'll talk to Chip in the deli," Pam said, "about taking up a collection with the chain and he can call Lee's guys at the towing shop to join in, for a reward. There's talk about a community search team to help pass out fliers and look for stuff. And we'll go see Maria as soon as we get off."

Before they returned to work, Jason got their full names, contact numbers, and their promise to call him with any new information.

"Hold it," he said, glancing at his watch before they left. "One thing, a neighbor I talked to said something odd. Hold on."

Jason looked through his notes.

"Like that what happened today sort of followed another bad thing that happened to the Colsons. Here's what she said: 'Why Lee and Maria? They've been through so much. And now this.'" Jason looked up from his notebook. "Do you know what that might mean?"

Pam and Candice looked at each, then shrugged.

"Not really," Pam said.

"Well, was there some kind of other tragedy in their lives, maybe?"

Candice shook her head, then nodded to Mitch Decoli, who was watching them from the other side of the supermarket's front window and tapping his watch. Pam sneered and took a final pull from her cigarette before crushing the butt under her foot.

"I know she had a hell of a time getting pregnant and that used to get her down. I think one time a doctor told her that she couldn't have kids, or would have a hard time, or something like that."

"Really?" Jason jotted some notes. "But she had Dylan?"

The women nodded.

"I mean"—Jason flipped over the baby shower picture—"it's pretty obvious she's pregnant here."

"Pam, we have to go," Candice said.

12

Four hours after Maria Colson left her home pushing Dylan's stroller to Kim's Corner Store, FBI agents were setting up a video monitor beside a table and folding chairs in her driveway.

Preparations for the news conference.

For Lee Colson to plead for his son's life.

"Have your IDs ready," Special Agent Ron Foley said as he approached the yellow tape keeping reporters and neighbors on the street. "Only accredited press will be let onto the property to set up for the news briefing. For you people going live, that's nineteen minutes from now. Let's go."

Some sixty news types jostled to claim a piece of the Colsons' pavement. Metal clanked as TV crews erected tripods and called for cables, switches, and batteries to be ferried from satellite trucks. Harried cell phone calls were made to editors, patched through to booths and networks. Data about birds, dishes, coordinates, feeds, airtime, and sound tests were exchanged. Overgroomed TV reporters checked their hair, teeth, earpieces, and mikes and helped with white balances by holding notebooks before cameras.

"We're going live through New York!" a red-haired TV reporter, hand cupped to one ear, repeated into her camera.

A mountain of portable recorders and microphones with station flags rose at the center of the table as reporters settled into spots while taking calls from their desks.

Jason nodded to Nate Hodge to check out the agent testing the video monitor. The agent was cueing up a tape that appeared to be footage from a surveillance camera. Hodge raised his Nikon, squinted through the viewfinder to line up a shot.

Another agent began distributing sheets of paper. Jason studied it. A summary of facts and descriptions. Nothing he didn't already know. A spread of color photos. One of Maria Colson. One of Dylan. One of a red Chrysler minivan over a note that read, "Seeking information related to a vehicle similar to this model." *And what's this one?* It looked like a frame taken from a security tape. His phone rang.

"It's Spangler, are you at the news conference?"

"Yes, with Hodge."

"Update me."

He looked around, then dropped his voice to guard his information. "Got a fairly good inside account of what happened. I talked to the corner store clerk who was there and supposedly watching over the baby."

"Fine, they got a suspect yet?"

"No one so far. At least no one they're talking about. But the way they're setting up for us here, looks like they may have caught something on a security camera."

"What do you know about the Colsons? Sinners, saints, what kind of people are they?"

"Blue-collar high-school sweethearts. Maria's a supermarket cashier on maternity leave. Lee's a tow truck driver."

"Sounds like a Springsteen song. Anything else? Police getting any solid leads or tips from the alert? What're they saying?"

"Nothing yet."

"That's it? Come on, Wade. We need to break news on this story."

"I'm doing the best I can. We were first to report the abduction, got it up on our site, and scooped everybody. The FOX affiliate and the Associated Press credited us, and that went national."

"It's history now, Wade. *MetroPulse News* is reporting that Maria Colson is in a coma, brain-dead."

"I haven't heard anything like that." Jason's attention went to the suits emerging from the house. FBI agents, Seattle police detectives, including Grace Garner. They formed a protective ring around a distressed man wearing jeans and a white T-shirt. That had to be Lee Colson. "Looks like it's going to start."

Colson took the center chair before the microphones. To his left he was flanked by Special Agent Kirk Dupree; to his right, another agent. Grace drifted off to the side as TV lights and strobe flashes showered the people at the table. After making introductions Dupree read a brief summary of the case verbatim from the handout.

"Now," he said after he'd finished, "I'd also like to

clear up some erroneous reporting regarding Maria Colson's condition. She is *not* brain-dead and on life support, as some outlets have suggested. The FBI confirms that Maria Colson is alive, in critical condition; and we are not prepared to elaborate. At this time, Mr. Colson will make a statement."

Cameras tightened on him and the anguish carved into his haggard face. He looked toward the group, or through it, as if he were gazing at a distant dreadful land.

"I just want to ask anyone…" He paused. "I'm asking anyone who knows who might have my son, Dylan, to ask them to return him safely. Please."

As Colson spoke, one of the all-news networks broadcasting live framed him with large still photos of Maria and Dylan over the graphic: FATHER PLEADS FOR ABDUCTED INFANT—FBI SAYS MOTHER'S CONDITION CRITICAL. "Dylan is our only child. Don't harm him. I'm sure that whoever has Dylan is taking care of him. Dylan's a good baby. We love him. He's our world. We need him so we can be a whole family again. Please, if you know who has Dylan, tell them not to be afraid. Tell them they can make everything better by just taking him to someone's door, anyone's door, ring the bell or knock. Please, Dylan's our only son. He's our miracle. Please take care of him and return him. Please."

Lee Colson covered his eyes with his hand as an agent took his shoulder to comfort him and Dupree took over.

"As you know, we're looking for a red 2002 Chrysler Town and Country minivan that may be related to this case. According to witness reports, the rear bears a small customized painting of the sun and trees. We're now going to run a few seconds of security tape taken by a camera in a store across the street from the abduction. We'll make copies available, as well as still frames. We believe what you're seeing is a very limited view of Maria Colson and a person and vehicle that are of interest to us. We're asking that if anything in this sequence looks familiar to any member of the public, that they immediately call the hotline at the FBI or Seattle Police."

Murmurs rippled through the group as the tape played on the monitor, then Dupree asked reporters to identify themselves as he took questions.

"Agent Dupree, David Troy, WKKR. With this tape you must have a prime suspect?"

"We won't rule out anything but our focus now is on Dylan's safe return."

"Cathy Cain, Pacific Post Syndicate. Has there been any contact, directly or indirectly, with Dylan Colson's abductors? Any demands?"

"That's an area we're not prepared to discuss."

"Is that a confirmation, sir?"

"It's a subject we're not prepared to discuss. Our goal at this stage is to make sure Dylan is reunited with his family. Next question, over there."

"Jason Wade, *Seattle Mirror*. I have a question for Mr. Colson."

Grace sharpened her attention to assess Jason, impressed by how he'd found Lani Tychina so fast. She didn't know much about him other than having read his stories in the *Mirror*. He seemed to be a cut above the other reporters. *Let's see what you've got here, Jason,* she thought.

"Sir, I know that this is a difficult time, but I understand there may have been other difficult times for you and Maria?"

"I don't know what you're asking."

"You called Dylan your miracle, can you explain what you mean by that?"

Colson thought, then said, "He means everything to us."

After watching their exchange, Grace stayed on Jason's question. It was cryptic. *Does he know something?* she wondered as Dupree brought things to an end. "Last question," he said.

"Amy Quan, *Action News*. Mr. Colson, tell us when you last saw your son?"

Colson blinked several times. "Last night, when I held him, I—" His chin crumpled and he shook his head, unable to continue. Dupree wrapped things up.

"We're asking anyone who knows anything about this case, who has any concerns, no matter how seemingly insignificant, any unease about something, or someone they know, to please contact us. Thank you."

Dupree and the other agent helped Colson back into the house as reporters lobbed parting questions.

"Is there a reward?"

"When's the next briefing?"

"We'll let you know," Dupree said.

Jason shouldered through the crowd toward the table and his recorder, testing it to ensure it had picked up everything. It had.

His cell phone rang. He figured it had to be Spangler.

"Jason Wade, *Seattle Mirror*."

"Grace Garner."

He looked around until he saw her standing alone at the side of the house, looking directly at him.

"What were you getting at with your question?"

"What do you mean?"

"Your question was odd. What do you know, or think you know?"

Now, she'd hit a nerve with him. She'd crossed a line, expecting him to cough up information for her.

"You confuse me. First you prevent me from doing my job when I was interviewing Lani Tychina in a public park, now you want information from me. I've got a question for you, Detective Garner, just—" *Just who the hell do you think you are?* But he stopped before finishing, realizing this call was something he could use to his advantage.

"Go ahead."

"Forget it," he said.

"I was curious that you seemed to be headed somewhere with your strange question."

"Hold it. Look—maybe we could talk?"

"Talk?"

"Like the movies, a little quid pro quo."

"This isn't a movie."

"Poor choice of words. You know what I mean. Besides, you called me."

She continued looking at him a few seconds more.

"Let me think about it—I've got to go."

13

In the Seattle community of Lake City, at Duke Piston's gas station, the attendant, Ritchie Sneed, read the oil dipstick of the van he was filling at the pumps.

Down a quart. Excellent chance for a small-parts commission, Ritchie thought as he tapped the driver's window. It lowered about two inches, giving him a sliver view of the man at the wheel and the woman in the passenger seat who was contending with a crying baby.

"What's the problem?" the man asked.

"You're down a quart, sir. Want me to put one in?"

"No, we don't have time. I'll catch it next time."

"It'll only take a minute."

"Just the gas, and hurry it up here."

Three crumpled tens appeared at the window. After taking the money, Ritchie took control of the gas nozzle to finish the fill. The baby's crying was muffled but there was a lot of movement inside. He ended the flow at exactly thirty dollars, capped the tank, then tried to close the van's small gas door.

It was stuck and wouldn't shut.

Suddenly the van's motor started, forcing him to

step back quickly as the van moved toward the station's exit, where it stopped to wait for a break in the traffic.

Definitely some sort of family crap going on there.

At the counter, as Ritchie rang up the sale, he resumed staring at the battered TV atop the steel file cabinet next to the pyramid display of oil bottles and the shelves with batteries, fuses, and lightbulbs.

Another breaking news bulletin about that thing in Ballard. They'd been running a lot of them. He'd been too busy to pay much attention until he noticed something he'd missed earlier. A fax had come in from the alert network. Ritchie scanned the data about Dylan Colson's abduction while glancing up at the TV.

What the hell?

He absorbed the key details: police were looking for a man and woman who stole a baby and drove off in a red 2002 Chrysler Town & Country minivan with small custom art on the rear showing the sun and trees. His head snapped to the lot.

Just like the one pulling out of the station right now!

Ritchie bolted from the counter to grab the van's license plate but he was too late. It vanished into northbound traffic. With the baby's crying still fresh in his ears, he ran back to the office, picked up the phone, and began jabbing the hotline number.

In Ballard, at the towing and salvage shop where Lee Colson worked, Gina Shepherd twisted the cuff of her faded denim shirt.

"Lee worships Dylan and Maria. There's nothing he

wouldn't do for his family. What kind of person steals a baby?"

Gina was sitting in the cab of her tow truck with the door open. Other workers at the shop had gathered to talk to Jason Wade about Lee Colson. All of them had seen the news conference. Some had been to the house. They were organizing volunteer search groups with other tow companies and taking up a collection for a possible reward.

"What kind of person would just steal their child?" Gina said.

"They must be deranged," said a bearded man in a stained ball cap. "None of this makes one damned bit of sense to us. You reporters always know something. What do you figure?"

"I don't know," Jason said, "it appears—excuse me."

A Chevy Blazer screeched to a halt in the lot. It was Nate Hodge, gesturing urgently for Jason to approach him.

"They've got a good tip on the van!"

"Where?"

"Lake City. It's breaking right now on the scanners, get in!"

Hodge gunned his engine; the Blazer's tires squealed, creating a cloud of blue smoke and leaving two strips of burning rubber.

Upstairs at the Colsons' home, Detective Grace Garner was helping Lee Colson gather some personal items for Maria as they prepared to leave for the hospital.

Downstairs, the hum of FBI agents and detectives at the makeshift command post in the dining room turned into a commotion when the special phone lines began ringing at virtually the same time as cell phones.

Perelli entered the bedroom to alert Grace just as her phone went off.

"Grace, it's Boulder. We've caught a good lead on a van from a gas station. Right color, custom art on the back, crying baby inside. All happening now in Lake City! Get rolling, I'll call with more."

"We're on our way."

Grace and Perelli hurried down the stairs, where FBI Agents Kirk Dupree and Ron Foley were collecting files before rushing to their car. As investigators scrambled from his house, Lee wanted Grace to tell him what was happening.

"We've got a van fitting the description with a baby inside."

"Where?"

"Lake City. We're heading there now."

"I'm going with you."

"Lee, it's better that you wait."

"He's my son. I'm going with you."

Grace looked at Perelli, both of them knowing that one way or another, Colson would get to the scene.

"All right, Lee. Let's go."

Seattle Police Officer Kip Henley was northbound two blocks from Duke Piston's station when the dispatch went out on the van suspected in Dylan Colson's abduction.

Henley, a traffic cop, kept his siren and emergency lights off. He carefully navigated his unmarked Crown Victoria through traffic until *bingo*, he spotted the red Chrysler Town & Country with its telltale open gas door and a painting that showed mountain forests in the sunset.

Henley edged up unnoticed behind it, locked on to the license plate, then called it in, making an urgent query for all data to be cross-checked with a number of police databases holding local, state, and federal crime information. His response came back in less than a minute.

"Registered owner is a Charles Robert Burkeyne. White male, approximately thirty-five years, of the 3300 block of 123rd Street, Seattle. One outstanding warrant for firearms violation. BATF shows failure to update registration of a nine millimeter, semiautomatic handgun and a hunting rifle. So heads up."

"Ten-four," Henley said.

Keying off of Henley's position, Seattle PD updated police agencies across the region, including the FBI, Washington State Patrol, and the King County Sheriff's Office, which put up its "Guardian One" helicopter over Lake City.

A stalled city bus slowed traffic, buying police time to gather resources. As Henley maintained visual surveillance of the van, calling in its location every few seconds, FBI and Seattle police commanders reviewed their options and made several immediate decisions.

Seattle's SWAT team was activated to begin rolling

to the area, but the situation was mobile, and things could unfold before they arrived. The baby's safety was the paramount concern. Not a second would be wasted to rescue the child.

Best option: a lightning takedown at the right moment.

The Seattle police marshaled every available unmarked unit in the zone while others headed into the area. All of them kept their lights and sirens off. Marked police cars took up ever-changing choke points in inner and outer perimeters, as the operation flowed with the suspect's direction.

The van led police through a neighborhood dotted with porn shops, rough-looking restaurants, used-car lots, barred-up liquor stores, strip clubs, and strip malls. It pulled off the main street, and slowed into a parking lot at a large office plaza.

"Okay, this is it. They're stopping." Henley pinpointed the address over the radio. In less than thirty seconds, half a dozen unmarked police cars glided into the lot, taking strategic positions around the van, poised to seal off any attempt to escape.

The police helicopter thudded high above them.

The woman stepped from the van, holding a crying baby, and began walking quickly through the lot toward an office storefront.

Police sirens yelped as two unmarked sedans lurched toward her, boxing her in. Car doors swung open, guns were pointed at her, a voice over a loudspeaker barked orders.

"Police! Sit on the ground now!"

"What? Why?"

She shot a look to her van. The man had been ordered out. His hands were above his head. Three police cars, their lights now flashing, had encircled him. Using their doors as shields, officers aimed rifles and pistols at him.

"Charlie!" the woman cried, tightening her grip on the baby.

"Mandy!"

Afraid and confused, the woman lowered herself to the pavement. An officer rushed to her and snatched the crying baby from her arms while another handcuffed her.

"No! What're you doing? Give me my baby! Charlie!"

At the far end of the lot, Jason Wade and Nate Hodge watched with the other news crews who were first on the scene. TV and still cameras recorded the drama as the officer hurried with the baby to another unmarked car a safe distance away. Jason recognized Detective Garner and Lee Colson inside.

"Lee?" Grace Garner turned to Colson.

After watching the takedown from the backseat, he stepped from Grace's car to stare at the baby. Slowly, he began to shake his head, then he covered his face with his hands as news cameras captured his reaction.

"It's not Dylan. That's not my son."

But no one heard Colson over the screams of the woman who was handcuffed and hysterical on the ground, staring at guns pointed at her face. Or the cursing of the man being patted down for weapons before he was handcuffed and put into the back of Dupree's car.

It took senior officers nearly an hour to sort out and confirm the facts.

Charlie and Mandy Burkeyne were taking Crystal, their baby girl, to a doctor's appointment to treat an ear infection. The doctor's office confirmed through medical records that the Burkeynes were the baby's parents.

Photos of the van's windshield were e-mailed to the crime scene investigators. The van was not missing a wiper, like the one Maria Colson had ripped from the vehicle.

Charlie Burkeyne was a welder "between jobs." Money was tight and he was a procrastinator, had never fixed the gas door or updated his gun registration.

Police regretted any inconvenience the Burkeynes had experienced after being arrested, but they refused to apologize for making the stop, asserting that under the circumstances, they had made the right call.

"If Crystal were taken from you," Sergeant Stan Boulder said softly to Charlie and Mandy Burkeyne, "wouldn't you want us to do everything and look everywhere to find her?"

Mandy Burkeyne kissed her daughter's head tenderly, then nodded.

So went the search for Dylan Colson.

In the wake of the alert and news conference, the FBI and Seattle Police hotline received a steady flow of tips, reflecting the concern of people making a heartfelt attempt to help. Unfortunately, most of the information was useless, with calls like: "I saw a van, not sure where, when or what color"; or, "My neighbor's weird because his dog barks a lot." Calls with something a little substantive usually dead-ended.

All were saved and stored.

In the hours after Dylan Colson was stolen and his mother left to die on the street, police were no closer to the truth.

14

The deadline for the *Seattle Mirror*'s first edition was less than two hours away.

It ticked in the back of Jason Wade's mind as the elevator doors opened to the newsroom. His stomach was growling. On the way to his desk he stopped at the coffee room to grab something to eat.

As his coins bonged through the vending machines he mulled over everything; the abduction, the possible homicide, the news conference, the dramatic takedown, that bit from Lee Colson about Dylan being a "miracle baby." As he considered what he would eat, one strange aspect of the day niggled at him—Grace Garner's call at the news conference.

What was behind it?

It was unusual for a Homicide detective to press him for information the way she did. Maybe he should call her later, push her a bit, he thought, collecting his soda, cupcakes, and potato chips, for the lunch and supper he'd missed.

Leanne Belmont watched him over her cup of herbal tea. The silver-haired copy editor had been a crime reporter with the *Mirror* long before she left to raise four children at home.

"That junk will kill you, Jason."

"It'll be a sweet death."

"Quite a story you've got. That takedown looked scary. Anything to it?"

"Nope, just people who fit the description."

"Is Maria Colson still alive?"

"She was last time I checked with the hospital."

"What an ordeal. It's horrible." Belmont stepped closer and touched his shoulder. "Forgive me for changing the subject, but anything to the rumor that Spangler fired Astrid?"

"It's true." Jason kept an eye on the time as they walked to the newsroom. "It happened this morning. She missed one too many stories."

"Spangler's scary. Astrid should talk to the union."

"She should've done her job." He glanced at the nearest clock. It was in the sports department, above a life-size blowup of a Seahawks touchdown. "Where's Fritz? I gotta talk to him."

Belmont nodded across the Metro section to the boardroom, where the day's final story meeting was breaking up. Spangler emerged gripping a clipboard. Tie loosened, sleeves rolled up, he pointed directly at Jason, then to his office.

"Watch your back," Belmont whispered.

One wall of Spangler's office was a shrine to himself. Front pages of his biggest Seattle and New York stories. Framed and signed photographs of Spangler meeting presidents, governors, the Rolling Stones, Madonna, Springsteen. Glory days.

"It's late. Where the hell you been, Wade?"

"On the story."

"You didn't answer when I called after the conference."

"I was on other calls, or interviewing someone."

"Answer your damn phone when I call, got that?" Spangler glanced at his clipboard notes and remained standing. "You'll have the lead on this story until I say otherwise, got it?"

"Got it."

"You're writing our main story, which will go page one and jump."

Jason set his snacks on the edge of Spangler's desk, then pulled out his notebook. "How long do I go with it?"

Spangler stared at the food, offended that Jason hadn't sought permission to use his desk. "Go as long as you need to, it'll turn to an inside double truck. We've got strong art." Spangler's large monitor showed Nate Hodge's crisp, vivid photos of Lee Colson's heartbroken face, forensic experts in white moon suits working the scene, insets of Maria and Dylan, a powerful shot of Dylan's overturned carriage next to a dark, red puddle—*his mother's blood*.

"What else is coming?"

"Munroe Wicker's doing a column. Sleepy community victimized. I've sent Phil Tucker to Ballard for more info. He'll feed his quotes and color to you, give them a files credit."

After jotting notes, Jason met Spangler's cold stare.

"Shut the door," the Metro chief ordered.

He closed it. Spangler remained standing.

"You listen to what I'm going to tell you, Wade, and you listen good. A radio station's reporting a reward for the kid; Channel 99 says there are neighborhood patrols, and CNN is talking to former FBI agents on investigations. We've heard that the *Seattle Post-Intelligencer* has nailed an interview with parents in Ohio or Florida whose baby was abducted and murdered ten years ago—the woman who did it committed suicide in prison.

"All of Seattle is feasting on this 'baby-snatched-mother-in-coma' story. It's national news. Our circulation is melting. We need to be out front on this one. We need to break exclusives. It's our shot at a Pulitzer. Anything less is unacceptable. I'm warning you now, if you miss a single angle, or allow us to get beat by anyone on anything, *it's your ass*. Do I make myself clear?"

A rush of anger churned in the pit of Jason's stomach as his memory streaked through the nightmares he'd faced in his life.

"I think you're forgetting something," he said.

"Excuse me?"

"Before you got here, I was already breaking exclusive stories. While you were in Manhattan contemplating a career move, I was bleeding for this paper. I live and breathe my beat; don't tell me how to work it and don't threaten me."

Spangler's face hardened.

"You listen to me, slick. House-trained pups have long since crapped on your 'exclusives.' Your old stories don't do a damned thing for us now. And that big chip you've got on your shoulder is sitting there perilously. So unless you want your employment to end here and now, get your ass in your chair and get to work, because your deadline is looming."

Jason collected his cupcakes, potato chips, and soda.

"And one more thing: talk to me like that again and you're gone."

Jason shot a parting glare at Spangler, then left, adrenaline pumping as he settled in at his desk, fired up his computer, and adjusted the scanners. Forget about it. Concentrate, he told himself.

He glanced at Astrid's empty chair. It was always empty around this time. *But this time*—man. He looked at her desk, at the things she'd left behind, her open notebook, uncapped pen, half-finished granola bar, card pulled from her organizer, dates circled on her calendar. It held the eerie air of a crime scene, the aftermath of execution-style management.

His computer beeped amid the scanner chatter, pushing Spangler from his head. He worked the fight out of his system by going through his notes page by page, rapidly typing all the information he'd gathered that day into a story file.

He crafted a rough lead, a couple of nut grafs, then mapped out the story. He went to his e-mail, collected the files from the other reporters. They weren't bad, he thought as he went through them.

He read the data the news librarian had researched for him. "Jason—These are weighty but good. I've highlighted relevant parts for you," said the note she'd attached to several academic articles and published studies on baby abductions. He'd written about child abductions before but she'd found updated stats, he thought, eating his cupcakes and potato chips as he read.

It was clear the FBI had gone by the book and had cautioned Lee Colson before the news conference so he wouldn't publicly antagonize whoever stole Dylan. He didn't threaten them, get angry, or call them names. Kidnappers usually followed news reports.

The studies suggested that some 5,000 children were abducted each year by strangers. Baby abductions were rare. They averaged a dozen each year. Babies that were recovered were usually found within hours or weeks and within 75 miles of their home.

The babies that were killed died within three to six hours of their abduction.

Man.

He looked to the window, where the fading afternoon sun and early evening shadows had yielded to the night. Lights twinkled from the traffic moving along the edge of Elliott Bay. Time was ticking against him.

His keyboard clicked as he wove in facts, statistics, opinions, quotes, and color from the other sources. He worked on transitions, keeping a smooth flow as time galloped by. The story ran long, some fifty inches. He sent it electronically to Vic Beale, the *Mirror*'s night editor.

Twenty minutes under deadline.

Jason rubbed the tension at the back of his neck and paced the newsroom. Still hungry, he thought of the vending machines, then rejected the idea of more junk food. He'd pick up something after work, he thought, after Beale cleared him for departure.

"It's good. Get the hell outta here."

Except for the editors and deskers who were busy putting the paper together, most of the day staff had gone home. Slipping on his jacket, Jason decided to take a detour out of the building.

He went to a door at the far corner of the editorial floor. It led to a narrow corridor. Its walls displayed mounted front pages of the *Mirror*'s coverage of major events, going back to the late 1800s and the first paper. He stopped at the large window with its panoramic view of the giant German-made presses below.

Pressmen in dirty blue overalls moved along the line preparing for the first edition. Massive rolls of white newsprint were loaded. The smells of ink and hydraulic fluid filled the air as the deadline neared. As he waited, he grew anxious about his story because he hadn't reported everything he had on the Colsons.

Like what the neighbor had said. *They've been through so much. And now this.* And the cashier at the supermarket. *She had a hell of a time getting pregnant and that used to get her down... the doctor told her she'd never conceive.* And the way Grace had reacted to his news conference question. *What do you know, or think you know?*

Had he hit on something? Was there more beneath the surface? He didn't have anything concrete, just bits and pieces. He hadn't told Spangler about Grace, or the other fragments.

Was that a mistake?

It was a risk. But he just didn't have enough to use the information. It would've been dangerous to put undeveloped threads out there, it would've been inaccurate, unfair to readers. The only thing it would've done was tip off the competition.

He had to trust his instincts.

A loud alarm bell clanged; the building shuddered and the huge presses rumbled to life. Soon they would roll off some 80,000 papers, neatly folded, counted, and bundled for the trucks to deliver everywhere the *Mirror* circulated throughout the state, outside of Seattle. Two hours later, after replating with updates, like sports scores from the east and midwest, they would spin off the big Metro edition. It would be delivered across greater Seattle, an area of three and a half million people.

He opened the door to exit the viewing platform and was hit with a wave of deafening heat as he descended the steel stairs of the catwalk to the floor. The head printer, who wore safety glasses and ink-stained ear protectors, nodded to him. They were old friends from Jason's time on the night-cop beat. They didn't attempt to speak over the noise as the printer handed him a damp copy of the next day's paper.

Jason nodded his appreciation, then left the pressroom.

Outside, he inhaled the quiet salt air as he stepped onto the loading docks where the delivery trucks were marshaled. Under the floodlights, he opened the paper to Nate Hodge's sharp dramatic pictures, his story, and the headline running under the paper's flag over six columns above the fold.

BABY SNATCHED, VAIN RESCUE BID
LEAVES MOTHER CRITICAL

A gull shrieked, sounding like a human scream.

Jason looked at his byline, then scanned the story and studied the photos for several long seconds before folding the paper under his arm. He walked to his car and considered the odds. Dylan Colson was probably dead. And his mother was probably going to die too.

It was a horrible tragedy and—God forgive him—a helluva story.

15

Jason drove along Denny Way toward Broad Street.

The Space Needle rose before him, reaching some 600 feet into the night, the red beacon at its tip pulsating like a fading heartbeat, he thought, before glancing south at the skyline rising over the metropolis.

Jet City.

Dylan Colson was out there somewhere.

Was he dead?

Had he been tossed into a back-alley Dumpster? Or buried in a shallow grave in a park to be discovered on some rain-misted morning by the proverbial jogger or dog walker? Or maybe he'd been put into a sack weighted with cinder blocks and dropped into Elliott Bay?

Anything was possible. There was no shortage of evil in the Pacific Northwest. It visited in many forms and Jason had seen them all.

Some up close.

He glanced in his mirrors, then changed lanes.

Maybe Dylan was alive. Maybe this case would beat the odds.

Who knows.

As he headed north on Aurora, light from the street-lamps flashed on Maria and Dylan. Their faces stared at him from the front page splayed on the passenger seat as he approached the Aurora Avenue Bridge, which spanned Lake Union. The bridge was the gateway to Fremont and Wallingford and the fringes of the small neighborhood where he lived in a huge nineteenth-century house that had been divided into apartments.

His place was on the third floor.

But he couldn't bear to go there right now; couldn't bear to climb the creaking stairs to his empty living room, his empty bedroom, his empty kitchen; his empty life where nothing waited for him but the tropical fish gliding in the tank and the half-eaten can of baked beans in his fridge.

It'd been a hard day. He dragged the back of his hand across his mouth. His throat was dry. He could always stop off at the liquor store, pick up something to get him through the rest of the night.

No.

He fought the temptation. One drink would lead to another, then another. And he knew where it would ultimately end. He wrestled his craving into submission, exhaling his relief when he turned off Aurora to a darkened, deserted back street and a small sign with the word *Ivan's* flickering in neon.

The little all-night diner was Jason's fortress of solitude, a place where he could endure the bad nights. Besides, he was hungry and the food was good, he thought after locking his Falcon.

Ivan's had a checkered linoleum floor and eight red

vinyl high-backed booths, six of which were empty tonight. Fourteen red vinyl stools, most patched with duct tape, stood before the Formica counter. The walls had dark fake wood paneling, dark fake brick. Above the cash register, next to permits, business cards, and phone numbers, was a 1990 *Seattle Times* profile of retired Navy cook Ivan Sulaticky's no-frills diner.

"A decent place for decent food for working people."

After taking a back booth, Jason took stock of the few nighthawks. An old man alone on one of the stools was staring down at the counter in front of him. At a front window booth sat an older couple: the woman was reading a fat paperback, the man was staring off into the night. In a booth nearby, a solo white-haired woman peered over her glasses at her crossword puzzle.

"What'll it be, pal?" An unshaven man in a white T-shirt, chewing on a toothpick, nodded to Jason through the pick-up window to the kitchen.

"BLT toasted on white with fries and a large glass of milk."

The man nodded and Jason heard the sizzle of bacon as he spread his newspaper over his table and went back to the story. He studied the pictures, then reread every word of every item on the abduction as he searched for answers.

Who would do this? And why? For money? As far as he knew, no ransom call or demand had come. Lee was a tow truck driver. Maria was a supermarket cashier. Not wealthy people. Was it random? An impulse crime? Or was it premeditated, executed by someone who'd been stalking them? Maybe someone

had a vendetta, or the Colsons had enemies, Jason
wondered as a plate thudded on his newspaper.

"Enjoy," the cook said.

"Thanks." Jason bit into his food. It was good. As he
chewed, he could see little sense in any enemy theory.
It appeared the Colsons were a well-liked, young, blue-
collar couple.

But they'd had previous problems. Problems that
could've been serious, from the way the neighbor had
reacted, refusing to talk about them. The supermarket
cashier said Maria had trouble conceiving. But how
could that be linked to what happened? It made no
sense. Then there was the way Grace Garner jumped
on him after the news conference.

He must've hit on something.

But what?

A secret?

Everyone had them.

Look at his old man. Before Jason was born, his old
man had been a Seattle cop. He had to quit the force
after only a few years. Jason never knew why. It was
something he never, *ever*, spoke of. Whatever
happened, it haunted his father. After failing to make a
go of it as a private investigator, he ended up working
in a brewery.

Then Jason's mother walked out on them when
Jason was a kid. His old man crawled into a bottle,
nearly taking Jason with him. Nearly destroying everything. Jason shut his eyes to the images of that time.

That was then.

His old man was doing better now. He was faithful

to his AA sessions, took early retirement from the brewery, and was a part-time private detective.

In many ways, his father was doing better than he was right now, Jason figured as he finished off his meal. It was rough with Spangler at the paper, seeing him fire Astrid. True, she had it coming, but Spangler was brutal about it. And catching the Colson story in the wake of Spangler's termination rage didn't help.

Jason had no one to turn to, really. After Valerie returned from Europe, they were together again. But it was never the same. While he'd quit drinking, he'd withdrawn. They only lasted about six months before Valerie said, "Jason, one of us has to say it: this is just not working. We've grown in different directions."

It was a fact.

So they agreed to go their separate ways without any bitterness. He remembered how she smiled, tears in her eyes, as she kissed him at the airport on her way back to Europe.

That part of his life was finished. Over. Dead.

Forget about it.

He reached for his milk. Despite everything, he felt a little better and was contemplating having a slice of apple pie. Could it be that he'd found hope by way of Detective Grace Garner?

Maybe he should call her right now.

He weighed the idea, reasoning that he needed to check on Maria Colson's condition before final edition. Jason pulled out his camera phone and began viewing some of the pictures he'd taken during the day, coming to a few of Grace Garner at the news conference.

He remembered how she had smelled mildly like roses when she got in his face today. She had the aura of a strong, bright woman, maybe a year or two older than him. She was attractive. Right, and she was probably married or had a guy, he thought, staring into her eyes.

He clicked to the next image.

Maria and Dylan Colson.

He was going to find out what happened to them.

No matter what it took, he thought later that night, as he continued staring at their faces.

In the darkness, they glowed from his camera phone like ghosts.

16

Detective Grace Garner sat alone in the placid light of the hospital cafeteria searching the cream clouds of her tea for answers.

Several floors above her, Maria Colson remained comatose, her condition unchanged. Perelli had insisted Grace take a break while he and Lee kept vigil, giving her time to study the status of the case.

Dupree should've called by now.

A new break had surfaced more than an hour ago out of Sea-Tac International, where a woman traveling with a baby was acting strangely while trying to board a flight to Los Angeles.

Dupree was on it.

And he should've called by now, Grace thought, staring at her phone. The cafeteria was okay for cell phones. "Surgeons are on them all the time, talking to brokers or booking tee times," a nursing supervisor had told her. Grace added sugar to her tea just as her phone finally rang.

"The airport dead-ended," Dupree said.

"What happened?"

"Turned out the mother was a nervous flyer who'd

been mixing alcohol and medication. She spooked some travelers when she said she'd had dreams that the devil was going to steal her son. Comparison of the baby's footprint with Dylan Colson's didn't match."

"So we've got nothing."

"This is solvable. With all the attention, something will break. What about there at the hospital, anything?"

"No, her condition hasn't changed."

"Forensics isn't done yet, they're still scrutinizing everything they picked up at the scene. They'll be going at everything all night, maybe they'll give us something."

"Maybe."

After Dupree's call, Grace looked at the time. It was coming up on, what? Fourteen or fifteen hours since Dylan Colson's abduction and nothing concrete had emerged.

The false alarm on the takedown, the alert, the intense news coverage, hundreds of tips to process, but nothing solid that brought them closer to the suspects. Words blurred as she flipped through her notes. All were fragments. Pieces of a thousand possibilities. Nothing stood out as a solid lead. Had she overlooked something? Had they done everything? Had they looked everywhere? What was she missing?

Initial background checks of the Colsons revealed nothing more than an old parking ticket issued to Lee. Maria was a churchgoer who attended mass every Sunday and did a lot of volunteer community work.

These were good, decent-living people.

Detectives and FBI agents were scrutinizing the

Colsons' circle of friends, neighbors, and social networks for any possible links, for anyone who may have lost a baby, or wanted a baby, or had a grudge against Lee and Maria.

They lit up the neighborhood to check databases against people with criminal records, or those whose names were with the sex offender registry. Nothing. They'd examined the Colsons' e-mail exchanges, Internet travels, and phone records. Scores of detectives were probing several other areas; they'd been going full tilt.

Dupree pointed to patterns in baby abductions and believed the odds favored a break arising from the way offenders traditionally acted. "They're often illogical in the time after the abduction," he'd told her. "They get tripped up on the getaway part because they don't plan it and they're irrational."

Irrational? Agent Dupree, whoever did this is insane.

Grace thought of Maria and Lee upstairs in the intensive care unit. Since the Lake City takedown earlier that day, Lee had never left her side, had never released her hand as he whispered prayers into her ear.

While observing them, Grace had, for a moment, let her emotional guard down. She had no one in her life to anguish over her. No one to miss her, should she lay dying. And the more she thought about it, the more it weighed on her. She looked at her hands. No rings. No strings. Nothing to complicate her life.

Wasn't that the way I always wanted it? Ever since that time? Knock it off. You've always been a loner.

That's the way you like it. You've got a job to do. Focus on it.

All right. She went into her bag and pulled out Dylan Colson's baby book with its soft blue, pink, and yellow flower motif. *Baby's First Year.* Lee had volunteered it from the house. Filled with Maria's journal entries about their son's birth, it was as close as you could get to a diary.

Maybe there was something here.

Again, she examined Maria's neat handwriting, intrigued by some of the passages. "To Mommy's Angel, no one believed we would have you, except me. I always believed you would come to me."

That was a strange way of wording her joy. What exactly did she mean? When she'd asked Lee, he explained that doctors told Maria long ago that she might never be able to conceive. But Maria never gave up hope and prayed for a child.

That's it?

Sitting alone in the cafeteria looking at the blue ballpoint ink that formed the words Maria had written in the time after Dylan's birth, Grace sensed there had to be more to it.

Maybe it had a bearing on the case. Maybe it didn't. But there had to be more.

Gently biting her bottom lip, she considered Jason Wade, the reporter from the *Mirror*. He was smart. Quick. Good looking too. Was she attracted to him? No. Stop it. Blame that on stress and the adrenaline rush of the case. Focus here, Grace. Wade seemed to have picked up on the same angle that was eating at her.

What was Wade's cryptic question again? She flipped through her notes. There it was, in her own shorthand: "I know this is a difficult time, but there may have been others for you and Maria?" Lee said he didn't understand the question, yet he called Dylan their "miracle" just like Maria had in the book. Here it was— "Today God granted me a miracle… my answered prayer."

She had to go back to Lee on this. Had to press him on it, she told herself, stepping into the elevator. As it ascended she reflected on the juxtaposition.

Lee was praying for his wife to live.

Grace was preparing for Maria's death.

Grace needed a dying declaration from Maria. She was the only one who could identify the people who took her son. Perhaps her final gift would be to help Grace catch her son's abductors.

To help solve her own murder.

Grace spotted Lee sitting on the couch in the lounge. Perelli was unwrapping a candy bar. He loved peanuts and chocolate. Lee was talking softly with Maria's aunt and uncle, telling them that he had to step out of Maria's room while the nurses tended to her.

"She's going to be all right, Lee," the older man was saying.

Lee nodded.

"We have to be strong," Maria's aunt said, following Lee's gaze to Grace, who signaled that she wanted to take him aside. His face sagged into dark whiskered lines as he joined her and Perelli at the far side of the lounge.

"Lee, I'm sorry, but I have to come back to something, I have to ask you this." She opened the baby journal to show him Maria's words. "What exactly did she mean by these words?"

Lee looked at her, then the words again.

"I told you, we had trouble conceiving. We were told it may never happen."

"Why, what was the reason?"

"When Maria was twelve she got hurt bad after falling when she was on a school camping trip in Glacier National Park. The doctors blamed her problem on her fall. But Maria wouldn't give up, kept praying, and Dylan—" Lee stopped to compose himself. "Then we had Dylan."

"How long were you trying for?"

"I—" He shook his head. "I don't know, a few years. I mean, we just wanted to have kids and we were told we might have trouble."

"Did the doctors say it was impossible, or just going to be hard?"

"Well, some thought the odds were against it ever happening but Maria refused to accept that."

"What did you do?"

"Kept trying."

"Did you tell people about it?"

"I know she told her friends at the supermarket."

"Did you consider other options?"

"Like what—adopting?"

"Yes, or surrogate, or in vitro, stuff like that?"

Lee nodded. They'd considered everything.

Two nurses rushed to Maria's room, faces taut as

they uncollared stethoscopes. Muted serious tones leaked into the hall when they swung through her door, monitoring equipment was beeping, they glimpsed staff moving quickly around the bed.

Lee stepped toward the door, but a nurse in green scrubs stopped him from entering his wife's room.

"Wait here, Mr. Colson, please."

"What the hell's going on?"

Grace found her cassette recorder in her bag, gripped it. "I want in there in case she says anything."

"No, Detective. I'm sorry. She's not able to say anything."

"What the hell's happening?" Lee asked.

More staff were rushing into the room. The door swung again releasing glimpses of urgency and words like *defib*, *epinephrine*, and *ECG*.

Perelli and Lee's uncle got him to the couch, where they waited. Some twenty minutes passed before a doctor, face red, approached. Lee stood.

"Maria went into cardiac arrest."

"Is she all right?"

"She's stable," the doctor said. "It was touch and go but her heart rate is normal and all of her signs are normal."

"Will she be okay?"

The doctor stared at Lee.

"Nothing's changed. She's still unconscious. As I'm sure Dr. Binder explained, she could still make a full recovery, or she may never regain consciousness."

Lee looked off, his shoulders fell, he put his hands over his face.

"She's in God's hands," Maria's aunt said.

The doctor nodded.

"Can I go back in to be with her, please?"

"That should be fine. Give it a moment so they can clear things up."

A few minutes later, a nurse let Lee into the room. Grace followed him. The room was dim. It was tranquil with the soft beeping and hum of the monitoring equipment.

It took a few seconds before Grace's eyes adjusted to the light.

All of Maria's hair had been shorn off. Her scalp was a web of stitches from the surgery. Her face was bruised. A large-bore IV line ran from her left arm, while a sensor clipped to her right index finger ran to a monitor. A clear oxygen tube looped under her nostrils.

Lee took her hand, then adjusted Snowball, the white stuffed polar bear, next to her; he'd bought it the day Dylan was born.

Grace heard him whispering to her.

"Wake up, please wake up. Don't leave me."

Grace turned to the window and looked at the twinkling lights of Seattle and the reflection of Lee Colson, on his knees next to his dying wife. Then Grace saw herself, alone, helpless, as she feared for Dylan and the worst.

Better face it, you could have a double homicide on your hands.

17

At that moment, across the city from where Maria Colson was fighting for her life, the television flickered in the darkness of Nadine's living room.

Casablanca was tonight's late-night classic.

A beautiful story about tortured souls in love. She sighed as the movie was interrupted by another stream of commercials. This time starting with an ad for cheap furniture—*nice-looking stuff*—pre-owned cars—*don't they really mean used?*—laxatives—*yuck, gross*—pre-planned funerals—*morbid*—Big Poppa Vinnie's Pizza—*yummy*—and the latest local news update.

Nadine leaned forward.

The Colson case was still the lead item.

So tragic.

But it was better than the movie and she didn't want to miss any new developments. Did that make her a horrible person? She hoped not. Wasn't everyone in Seattle drawn into the story? she thought as the images from earlier in the day replayed.

No trace of the baby. No lead on suspects. Frustrated detectives. Maria Colson remained in critical condition.

Watching Lee Colson's pleading broke Nadine's heart. What happened was terrible. Just awful. If only she could help in some way.

But how? She didn't know the answer to that question.

Casablanca resumed but without her interest. She'd lost sight of Bogart and Bergman. Instead she chewed on her thoughts and her fingernails.

She looked across the room at Axel in his recliner, taking in the outline of his hard, muscular frame silhouetted in the tranquil light. She only saw his face in the brief halo that blossomed each time he dragged on his cigarette. She liked his deep-set eyes, his strong jaw, and the fact he seldom spoke.

She felt safe with him, her protector.

Axel kept most of his feelings locked inside. She never knew what he was really thinking, only that he was smart, wise from his experiences. And that he had a lot on his mind lately.

So did Nadine.

They'd been so busy in the last little while.

Axel was expecting to close his business deal any day now and receive his payout. And he'd said that if things went the way he expected, there would be "a huge bonus" to go with it. Enough for them to first take a vacation, then buy that little house on the beach in Oregon, up the coast from Portland—*then get married*.

Nadine smiled.

Her dream was coming true. Finally coming true. They'd live happily in that house by the sea. It had been a long road for both of them, but it was meant to be.

It *was* happening.

Not a moment too soon either, she thought, taking stock of the living room with the sofa, bleeding stuffing through the torn fabric. And would you look at these walls with their surface fractures and unfilled holes left by the previous tenants. There was a faint urine-like odor in the carpet of the back room, which convinced her the previous people had also kept pets, which was against the rules. Some people were just so inconsiderate. And in some areas they'd left the electrical wiring exposed and frayed. Surely it was a building code violation, but she never complained.

No point in making a fuss.

They'd be gone soon.

Nadine was grateful it was a rental and none of this junk was theirs. But the mess was. She groaned at the takeout food cartons on the coffee table; at the sweater, the jeans, and other clothes scattered about, along with their business papers and wrappers from all the things they'd bought recently. Look at it. All of it was spread everywhere. They'd been so busy she hadn't had the chance to keep up. Things just sort of got away from her.

"I can't stand it. I've got to clean this up."

Axel's face glowed for a few seconds as he smoked.

She collected the plates, utensils, glasses. Heading into the kitchen she remembered to step around the treacherous floorboard with the loose nail that always popped up unexpectedly to snag her sock.

A small color television on the kitchen counter was tuned to a different local channel. The sound was low but Nadine had caught the tail end of another late-night news report on the Colson abduction.

Still nothing new.

Setting the dishes in the sink, she admitted she couldn't take her mind from the story. It was silly but she was obsessed with keeping up on details. Who wouldn't be? It was real-life drama, a hundred times better than any fake reality show.

She glanced to the top of the refrigerator where an AM radio was tuned to an all-news station. At the other end of the kitchen, atop the stove, she had another radio going.

Nothing new was being reported.

An hour earlier, when Axel went out to pick up some Chinese food for their late dinner, he stopped at a twenty-four-hour corner store for cigarettes and tomorrow's—actually today's—edition of one of the papers, the *Seattle Mirror*. It was opened on the kitchen table. Nadine sat down and read the stories.

Again.

She wanted to go through them once more in case she'd missed something. Tapping her red pen against the newsprint, she scrutinized the articles, concentrating on every iota that had been reported.

Sentence by sentence.

Quote by quote.

Word by word.

It was such a horrible thing.

If it had happened to her child she would just die. She drew a red line under a sentence. Of course she would do the same thing Lee Colson had done. She would beg for her baby.

But she would do more.

Suddenly, her vision blurred, her entire brain spasmed, and a wave of nausea rippled through her. As she recovered, her jaw tensed and she circled another sentence with dark red ink.

Yes, she would do more than beg for her baby.

Because she would be forced to act. Forced to take matters into her own hands. She gritted her teeth against her pain and drew another line under another quote.

But one thing she would never do was lie.

Lying was a sin.

Lying was destructive.

Lying concealed the truth and hurt those who needed it.

Nadine knew because she had been lied to all of her life.

This time her penstroke pierced the paper.

Lies. All lies. Lee Colson is lying.

Her grip suddenly switched as if her pen had become a knife. Her knuckles whitened as she raised it to stab Lee and Maria Colson, whose faces smiled at her from the newspaper.

Liars!

Nadine stopped herself.

What was that?

She thought she'd heard something. Something distinct from the radios and TV.

Nadine closed her eyes, lifted her face to the ceiling, and took a long, deep breath. Fine. She got up and walked out of the kitchen, leaving the newspaper splayed on the table, like a bleeding victim.

She needed to check on the sound.

Rubbing her temples, she padded silently down the long, dark hallway toward a closed door, then was struck by an odd thought. Lee Colson had come close to the truth on that business about miracles. Funny, wasn't it? Her hand hovered over the handle as she hesitated to listen. A moment passed, then, without making a sound, she entered.

Her heart swelled.

The room was bathed in soft light spilling from a lamp shaped like a circus clown. Its oversized mouth was agape, frozen in laughter. The air carried the pleasant hint of talcum powder and the soothing strains of a lullaby as bunnies and bears floated in a circular pattern over a handmade wooden crib.

Nadine lowered herself to gaze through its ornate spindles upon the child stirring on the mattress. Drawing her face near enough to feel his sweet breath.

Yes, miracles do happen.

"Oh sweetie, they're all lying. The news. The police. Lee Colson. Everyone. They're all against us. They want to keep us apart. They just don't understand that you're *my* baby. You are. I'm your mommy and I rescued you today."

Tears stung her eyes and she brushed at them.

"I saved you, and soon I'm going to take you far away to someplace safe where no one will ever keep us apart. Oh sweetie, I would die before I would let that happen. *I would.*"

DAY TWO

18

After waking, Jason fired up his laptop, got online, and compared the *Mirror*'s first-day coverage of the Colson story with the competition.

The *Post-Intelligencer* was reporting that investigators had "not ruled out anybody" as a possible suspect. A standard line but it played well. *We have that.* The Associated Press had a retired FBI agent, famous for his expertise in child abductions, armchair quarterbacking the case by doubting that this was a random act. "Somehow, in some way, there's a link between the Colsons and the suspects." *So? We've got a criminology prof saying the same thing.* And the *Seattle Times*, citing "sources," led with a report that Maria Colson's condition had taken a grave turn the previous night. *Got that too.*

Tension knotted in Jason's neck and shoulders as he stepped into the shower. Everybody was pounding hard on the story, he thought, but no one was leading on the story.

Not yet.

It was only a matter of time.

After showering, he reviewed what he knew, searching for a fresh angle to chase this morning. He was considering looking deeper into the Colsons' background when his phone rang. Wrapping a towel around his waist and leaving a watery trail on the hardwood floor, he took the call in his living room.

"Hi, Jason, it's Rosemary," the news assistant said over other lines ringing on the switchboard. "Sorry to bother you at home so early. Fritz told me to alert you if any readers called with anything worth pursuing."

"What's up?"

"I've got this woman on the line. This is the third time in twenty minutes that she's called. She insists on talking to you this instant. Claims she has something important to tell you on Dylan Colson's abduction."

"She give you her name, or her connection to the story?"

"No, she wouldn't give me anything like that, or leave a message."

"She sound credible, or certifiable?"

"Hard to tell."

"All right, put her through."

"I'll connect her. Just a second."

While waiting, he inventoried his apartment, the fireplace and built-in bookcases, the secondhand leather sofas, the coffee table heaped with newspapers. On one wall, Jimi Hendrix, his beloved rock god, gazed from a giant poster above Jason's thirty-gallon aquarium. The colorful fish gliding among the coral and bubbles kept him company. He was drawn to Detective Grace Garner's picture in the newspaper when the line clicked.

"Hello? This Jason Wade?"

"Yes."

"Jason Wade, the reporter who wrote the story about the baby being kidnapped?"

"Yes. Who's calling?"

Silence.

The caller ID display on his home answering system showed the newsroom switchboard number because the call was bounced to his apartment from the paper. He sifted through his desk for his small tape recorder.

"Who's calling?" he repeated.

"I don't want to say. First, I need to know if you protect sources. If you guarantee to keep names out of print?"

He found his recorder, connected the jack; the red recording light blinked. Relief washed over him for remembering to install new batteries.

"Yes, we do that sort of thing. Look, just who are you and what is it you want to talk about?"

"I have information on this case."

"What kind of information?"

"Critical. It's about who kidnapped the baby."

"You know who did it?"

"Yes."

He tightened his hold on his phone.

"Who did it?"

"I can't tell you over the phone."

"Why not?"

"It's complicated. I need to give it to you in a public place."

"Can you give me a hint about who it is?"

"No."

"Have you given your information to the police?"

"No."

"No? A baby's been stolen, his mother's dying, and you call me up to play guessing games. Come on, if your information has any validity, you would tell them, wouldn't you?"

"They don't understand how I obtained this information."

That stopped Jason cold.

"Have you called any other reporters?"

"Just you."

"Why me?"

"Your story is closest to the truth."

What truth? He didn't know what the hell this woman was talking about but he decided to go a step further. "All right, we'll meet at the paper at eleven. Go to security and—"

"No. I have to do this my way."

"And what's that?"

"I'll have my information ready to give to you in one hour."

"One hour?"

"Yes. Here are details on what to do."

19

Jason lived several blocks south of Woodland Park, on the fringes of Fremont and Wallingford.

After getting dressed, he made a few calls, then pulled his Falcon from his building, deciding Aurora Avenue to 85th Street would be the best way to go for his meeting. Along the way, he listened to "Voodoo Child," Hendrix's long blues jam, because it suited his mood, as he thought about the mystery woman he was going to meet.

She'd claimed to know who took Dylan Colson but refused to give him any details over the phone. She wanted to meet within an hour at a northwest park. She sounded halfway credible but it was impossible to gauge people in these situations. Odds were, this tip was pure bull and the woman was a wack job. But it was early and the park wasn't far, so he figured he'd follow it up. All it would cost him was an hour or so, he reasoned as his cell phone rang.

"Where are you?" Spangler said.

"On the story. Following up some leads."

"You see today's coverage in the *Times* and *P-I*?"

"Yes."

"Our stuff is good but not good enough. We're not leading."

"No one is."

"We have to lead. We need an exclusive today, do you hear me? Turn your radio down, do you hear me, Jason?"

He didn't touch the volume.

"I hear you."

"So what've you got going today?"

He hesitated telling him about the tipster just yet. In his short time at the *Mirror*, he had learned a few cold, hard facts about editors and how dangerous ones, like Spangler, reacted to wild tips. They jumped on them as if they were confirmed, then listed them on news skeds. And all day long other editors would talk about the tip as if it *were* a fact or an actual story being written, rather than a lead being checked out. And when the tip fell through, there would often be pressure to somehow resurrect or salvage the engrossing aspects of it, to shape it into a news story, to try to find other facts, which didn't exist, to support the notion of a story that originated as a false lead. Revealing long-shot tips in their embryonic stage was a dangerous thing to do.

"Well, Wade, what've you got?"

"There's a case status meeting of the FBI and Seattle Homicide squad this morning. I want to follow that."

"That's obvious. If they have a major break they'll tell everyone. What else you got?"

"I was going to door-knock in the neighborhood."

"Do that. Because for now, the Colson family is the story. I want you to keep pushing. Find out more about them. I get a sense from your stuff that there's a lot more going on with Lee and Maria."

"I'll keep digging."

"And while you're at it, keep this in mind. Everybody has a dark side. Everybody has secrets."

Jason agreed. Whatever it was, nobody had the full story on the Colsons, and on this beat he'd learned that there are always more than two sides to a story, that nobody is ever as bad as people think, and nobody is ever as good as people think.

"I want you to keep digging on the Colsons until we know absolutely everything there is to know about them," Spangler said. "I also want you to stay on top of Maria's condition. The instant she dies, I want to know, because then we'll have a murder, likely a double murder when they find her kid, and then this story will explode."

Sounded like Spangler was hoping for that outcome, which disgusted Jason, but he said nothing.

"Did you hear me, Jason? What's that crap you're listening to?"

"I heard you, loud and clear. That it?"

"Check in with me every two hours."

Sunset Hills Park, in northwest Seattle, offers a sweeping view of the Olympic Mountains and Puget Sound. Alders, Douglas firs, and big-leaf maple trees cover its steep slopes rising above Elliott Bay.

Jason parked, then walked to the designated meeting place and stood along the chain-link fence overlooking the hundreds of sailboats docked at the Shilshole Bay Marina. He inhaled the salt air and watched the gulls gliding in the clear blue sky.

He turned to inventory his immediate area of the park and neighborhood. Empty. Except for an old man on a distant bench who was reading a large print edition of *Ulysses* by James Joyce.

The park was beautiful, but Jason felt the clock ticking, felt seconds slipping away as he began to doubt himself for agreeing to come and stand here when he was under pressure to break news.

Then his cell phone rang.

"This Jason Wade?"

He studied the number ID display for incoming calls. It came up blocked but he recognized the voice of his female tipster.

"This is Jason."

"Did you come alone?"

"Yes." He scanned the park and vehicles parked nearby. "Where are you?"

"Out of sight. This is how I have to do this."

"Look, frankly, this is silly, and I don't have any more time to waste. Come to the point now, or else—"

"See the trash can to your right?" His hesitation agitated her. "You're not looking. Look."

Christ. She's near. Watching me.

"Do you see the trash can?"

He glanced at it. It was clean, practically empty.

"Yes, what about it?"

"There's an orange plastic bag in it. Do you see it?"

He stepped to the bin and saw the bag.

"I see it."

"The bag and its contents are for you. Good luck."

The call ended.

"Wait!" He swirled around, pricking up his ears for

anything, sharpening his focus for something to help him understand. With the exception of the old man reading, and the distant sounds of the marina, the gulls, and the bay, he saw and heard nothing to point him to the woman.

He used his pen to hook the handle of the bag. It was very light. He sat on an empty bench and looked inside. It contained a large, plain, sealed white envelope bearing the words "For Jason Wade, *Seattle Mirror"* in neat block letters.

He opened it and slid out the documents inside, which were on very small sheets of yellow paper. The first was text of a computer printout. Looked like some kind of summary or note:

Information Pertaining to:
The Abduction of Dylan Colson and Injury of
Maria Colson:

The following was developed through methods other than known senses, or traditional channels of investigation. Those behind the crime departed the scene with the child immediately in a vehicle in an easterly direction through the community. Their vehicle was seen by hundreds of people. But as nothing untoward was known to have occurred at this time in the community, the vehicle did not stand out, or register with nearly all of the witnesses. In fact, they do not recall seeing the vehicle. However, at several junctures of the vehicle's departure, there were indi-

viduals who encountered it. The vehicle is a van.
While it is difficult to ascertain witness recollection, one strong impression has emerged. A
woman was seen sitting in the passenger seat of
this van.

"What? What the hell is this cryptic bull?" Jason said
after reading it. "Everything in here is known to the
public. It was in the alert. What a stupid waste of time."
He flipped to the second page. As he continued reading,
he stopped breathing.

The woman's true name is Diane M. Fielderson,
born in the very early 1980s in a jurisdiction at
the U.S. Canada border, possibly Michigan, New
York, or Ontario. Caution: *Death stands over this
case.*

Death stands over this case.
*Man, what the hell is this cryptic crap? Strange,
weird bull,* he thought, biting his bottom lip and turning
to the final page.

It was a sketch, done in pencil, that depicted a
woman's profile, in shadow, in the passenger seat of a
van. Underneath the sketch was the line:

This woman abducted Dylan Colson.

20

"This is the shoe of Dylan Colson's abductor."

FBI Special Agent Kirk Dupree's attention was on the big screen overlooking the polished table in the conference room of the FBI's Seattle field office.

Grim-faced detectives from the FBI, Seattle PD, King County Sheriff's Office, Washington Highway Patrol, and other departments studied the image, as did off-site investigators who hooked up via a secure audio-video link, in Quantico, Salt Lake City, Chicago, Portland, San Francisco, Los Angeles, and Denver. They were joined on the link by Vancouver and Calgary city police, the Royal Canadian Mounted Police, and border agencies in the U.S. and Canada. It was now twenty-four hours since Dylan was stolen and the multiagency task force had kicked off its first case status meeting.

All on the same page, thought Detective Grace Garner.

Most of the Seattle people at the meeting had had less than two hours of sleep. They reached for coffee cups and doughnuts, taking notes as they examined the huge, blurred, blow-up frame of a white sneaker emerging from the van used to abduct Dylan Colson.

The image had been recorded on the security camera at Arnie Rockwell's hardware store. FBI and Seattle technical wizards had worked nonstop enhancing it and the quality they had produced was remarkable.

"The shoe we're looking at is solid evidence on the suspect," Dupree said. "The image lasted exactly zero point eighteen seconds in real time on the tape. By comparison, it takes an average zero point thirty seconds for a human to blink their eyes. So this work is outstanding. Paul, from ERT, will take it up here."

"Paul Cray, FBI Evidence Response Team," he said, raising his voice for the speaker phone. "As you can see"—Cray worked the slide so the shoe's image jumped back and forth repeatedly showing it touching the sidewalk—"where the shoe makes contact, there is a patch of dew-moistened street dirt. A thin layer, but enough to capture a partial foot impression. Everything but the heel, which creates a challenge."

Through their work with casts and photos at the scene, investigators narrowed the identity of the shoe. It was either a Suntour Glider or a near-twin knockoff, a Sunchaser Slipstream, Cray said.

"It is imperative that we confirm the precise model. In both cases the shoe is an Oxford-style women's casual sneaker, a canvas lace-up with a rubber outsole and traction pattern.

"The Glider retails for about forty-five dollars, is manufactured in Brazil, and is widely available in department stores largely in South America, Europe, and parts of the southern U.S.," Cray said. "The Sunchaser is made in Nigeria. It sells for about twenty-one dollars and is widely available in the Middle East, Eastern Europe, Canada, and the Midwestern United States."

"All that from one footprint?" a young King County detective said.

"We got a bit more," Cray said as the screen displayed a magnified image of the impression made by the shoe. "The outsole is rubber with a traction pattern. But see here, as we consider the circles, waves, and diamond design of the sole, you've got very distinctive characteristics. Unique."

Cray started clockwise, pointing to a slight gouge in the tip, some wear bars in the center, two nicks and cuts in the inside midstep.

"So what we have is like a fingerprint?" Grace asked.

"Exactly," Cray said.

"The problem is the Nigerian manufacturer's offices recently burned down. An FBI agent with the U.S. Embassy in Abuja is working on obtaining a crisp color image of the shoe from a distributor in Senegal."

"What's the ETA on that picture?" asked McCusker, a white-haired man who oversaw Seattle's FBI operations.

"The FBI agent in Nigeria e-mailed me this morning advising that we could have our image by tonight," Cray said.

"Good."

"At that point," Cray said, "we advise that we publicize the security tape image and the shoe's image in an appeal to the public to report anyone with shoes like this who may have come in contact with a baby, or a van like the suspect vehicle."

"It's a double-edged sword," said an FBI agent in Chicago. "As soon as you do that, your suspect ditches the shoes."

"But you stand a chance of getting closer to the suspect and the child," a King County detective said.

"You're also tipping your hand to your suspect and risk losing them," the Chicago agent said.

"All views hold merit. The shoe is strong key fact evidence that will ultimately have to withstand a court challenge. Paul, have you run it through ViCAP?"

"Yes. No footwear matches from other crimes in the country."

"In abduction cases like this, leads to an arrest typically come from the suspect's social circles. We'll launch a public appeal once Paul's team has confirmed the shoe and has obtained the image for circulation. Until then, and let me be clear on this, this is holdback. We must ensure there is absolutely no confusion on the shoe evidence, since we have two possible models." McCusker checked the time.

"Let's move along quickly, please. On the vehicle," McCusker continued. "We have a red 2002 Chrysler Town and Country minivan. We have nothing on the plate but a witness noted the rear door had a small mural showing the sun and trees. We're checking with airbrush artists, people who do custom paintwork with cars and vans."

They moved through the status. No ransom call so far. Nothing through the Colsons' Internet use or phone records that pointed to a lead. A run of all registered sex offenders in the region was ongoing. Criminal checks of neighbors and all of the contractors linked to the construction project at the Lincoln estate down the street were ongoing. The community was being canvassed again and again under the belief that someone had to have seen something.

Time lines for Lee Colson had been checked; as were his financial situation, his insurance policies, and business matters. At this point he was not a suspect and investigators had no reason to believe that he, or anyone known to him directly, had abducted his son. That did not rule out people in Colson's circles and social networks.

Investigations so far showed nothing criminal in Lee or Maria Colson's past. No drug debts, extramarital affairs, or run-ins with people who might have harbored a grudge against the family.

Shannon Tabor, the teenager who had been distracted from watching Dylan, was checked, as was her caller. No concerns there.

"Look, I think there may be something to the fact that Maria Colson had trouble conceiving," Grace told the task force before reading excerpts from what Maria had written in Dylan's baby book. "I've got nothing more than her journal here, but I just get a feeling."

"But she is Dylan's biological mother," Dupree said. "And Lee is the biological father. Hospital records confirmed it and we interviewed the doctor who delivered."

"I know, it's an intangible. They went through a rough period. According to Lee they'd considered adopting, or using a surrogate."

"But never acted on it," Dupree said.

"We need to investigate beyond their social circles," McCusker said, "to people they may have had contact with while looking into adoption or surrogates. Charlie"—McCusker checked his watch—"give us your take."

Charlie Paine, the FBI's profiling coordinator, cleared his throat before outlining a psychological portrait of people who abduct babies.

"The offenders are almost always women with a pathological need to have a child at any cost. They're mentally unstable individuals whose acts are fueled by fantasy, delusion, drugs, alcohol, trauma, or a combination of any of these things. They have usually lost a child by stillbirth, miscarriage, or accident, or simply cannot bear children. A child is paramount to their existence. They may see the replacement, or the filling of the void, as the cure-all to their psychological distress."

McCusker and the others took careful notes as Paine continued.

"Their desire to have a child evolves into a plan with months of detailed and careful preparation. A family or mother can be selected or targeted for any number of reasons, none of which could be logical. They can be surveilled and stalked, and the operation may be practiced over and over as part of the offender's obsession. The event can also involve a blitz attack, whereby the desperate offender simply acts when an opportunity arises."

"Sounds like our situation," someone around the table said.

"The fact violence was used makes it clear the offender in this case will not allow anything to prevent them from fulfilling whatever fantasy is driving them."

"Do you believe Dylan Colson is still alive?" Dupree asked.

"It's a possibility, depending on who else is involved. If one of the individuals is a violent sex offender, then that injects an entirely different dynamic into the scenario."

"Meaning?"

"The child would likely be killed and discarded within hours of the abduction. In such cases, you're seeing the work of a serial sexual predator who's likely offended before and travels extensively."

"All right, thanks, Charlie," McCusker said. "So, we go back to every woman who was in Maria Colson's birthing classes, or was in the same hospital around the time she had Dylan. We comb all hospital records, and go to hospital staff in Seattle and King County, and fan out from there, for women who've suffered stillbirths, miscarriages, or deaths of children under the age of two, over the last two years. We ask psychiatric services for help on serious cases of postpartum women. We check with clinics and welfare agencies about women who suddenly have a baby. Detective Garner will continue to keep a vigil for a dying declaration from Maria Colson, who remains our best hope on identifying the suspects, while we roll. Thank you, everyone."

"Remember," Dupree called out as the meeting closed. "As you knock on doors, keep your eyes open for Oxford-style sneakers."

"Kinda like Cinderella, only this time if the shoe fits, Cinderella is read her rights," Perelli said to Grace.

She didn't hear him.

She'd stepped away to take a phone call, her face creased with concern.

21

Jason had to check out his tip fast.

Some ten blocks after pulling out of Sunset Hill Park, he wheeled his Falcon into a secluded corner of a Burger King parking lot and began pressing numbers into his cell phone.

"Newsroom library, Nancy Poden."

"It's Jason. I need your help on something. It's urgent."

"Let me close up what I'm doing. Okay, what is it?"

"I need you to mine every databank we subscribe to, local and beyond, for everything you can get on a Diane M. Fielderson."

"Spell her name."

He did. Twice.

"Got a date of birth?"

"Approximate date of birth is early 1980s," he said, judging from the sketch.

"That's general. Specific would be better."

"I know. It's all I've got. To be safe broaden the date of birth from the late 1970s through the 1980s and narrow it to Michigan and New York, and Ontario, Canada."

"What're you looking for?"

"Anything and everything that matches the name. From news stories to property and divorce records, relatives, obits. *Everything*. From birth to now."

"This will be expensive. Is this related to the Colson story?"

"Yes, but Nancy, swear that you won't tell anyone about this search. It's a wild hunch."

"You're such a cloak-and-dagger guy."

"Humor me, Nancy, please."

"Sure, but you're going to owe me, buddy."

He had to be careful with this lead, given the circumstances by which it had come to him. Unsubstantiated allegations came with risks: moral, ethical, legal, you name it. And while he was wary and skeptical, his instincts urged him to chase this down fast.

Studying the notes and sketch, he sipped coffee in a booth at the Burger King, and decided on how best to pursue his tip. He wouldn't tell anyone about it. Not Spangler, not anyone. First, he would try to confirm any part of the information. If he could verify it, he could then develop it, then go to Seattle PD and the FBI and try to parlay it into a major exclusive.

But time was working against him.

He pulled out his wallet, fished out a worn, creased slip of paper bearing several penned phone numbers. His most dependable law enforcement sources. He started making delicate enquiries on the name without giving up a single detail of the context. He sniffed peripherally, politely asking if Diane M. Fielderson rang any bells with anyone in any way. *"Whaddya mean,*

Wade?" "Well, as in traffic tickets, charges, noisy party complaints. Anything. Does her name come up?" His sources promised to check and ask around and get back to him later.

Back in his Falcon, Jason turned the ignition to start for Ballard, then shut it off to follow an idea. He'd make one more call. *Be careful, you're playing with fire*, he warned himself as the line rang.

"Garner."

"Jason Wade."

"Jason, can this wait? I'm kinda tied up at the moment."

"A few seconds is all I need. I understand there was a case status meeting this morning. Anything new come out of it?"

"Things are still being assessed."

"What does that mean?"

Grace considered matters, then said, "The FBI's leading the abduction, you should be talking to Dupree."

"Is that a yes, as in, there is a development?"

"Look, ask Dupree. There might be something later."

"Like what? Do you have any breaks, like a suspect, or a name?"

"There may be an update later. Other than that, I have no information and don't you dare quote me. Ask Dupree, or the press office. Now, do you have anything critical you want to discuss? Did you dig up something, hotshot? Because I've really got to go."

The name Diane M. Fielderson burned from the tipster's pages on the seat next to him. Staring at them, he contemplated telling Grace about his lead.

"Jason, is that it?"

Don't tell her everything yet. He'd wait until he nailed it down.

"I've got a thing but it needs checking."

"You want to tell me about this 'thing'?"

"Ah, it's likely bogus, you know, somebody claiming to know something. I'll let you know if there's anything to it."

She waited for a beat.

"All right, well, like I said, there might be something later."

Jason spent much of the day in Ballard knocking on doors, talking to the Colsons' neighbors, trying to flesh out a profile. At times he would float Diane Fielderson's name with people in the community, which succeeded only in prompting shrugs and head shaking.

He went to the hospital to try to interview Lee Colson. The press pack keeping vigil there was told that Lee was not making any statements today. He'd refused to leave Maria's side. Jason secretly managed to get one of Lee's friends to ferry Diane Fielderson's name, scrawled on a page from his notebook, to Lee inside the hospital.

"Doesn't mean a damned thing to him," the friend confided later after coming outside for a smoke.

By the end of the afternoon, Jason was back in the *Mirror* newsroom. He was putting the final touches on his profile of the Colsons when, one by one, his cop sources got back to him on Diane M. Fielderson. And one by one, they told him that her name didn't register with anyone and didn't surface in any of their checks, not even as an alias.

He pondered his tip while he waited for a BLT in the paper's cafeteria. At least he was checking it out. Before he dismissed it, he'd check with Nancy Poden on her search. News librarians often put detectives to shame with what they could unearth, he thought, clearing the mess at his desk for a spot to eat.

He was curious as to why he hadn't heard back from her yet. Moreover, he was concerned that the secret documents from his tipster seemed to have vanished from the controlled chaos of his desk. What the heck? Where were they? He had just begun rummaging when his phone rang.

"Jason, it's Grace. A heads-up, there may be something later."

"Like what? Give me a hint."

"There may be an update, that's all I can say. It may come real late."

"Fine."

His stomach was growling as he searched used notebooks, ancient press releases, and news pages for the small yellow papers. He'd left them in a blue file folder on his desk and the damn thing was—he glanced toward Spangler's glass-walled office, where he saw him holding a blue folder and talking to Sonja Atley, the chief news librarian.

His newsroom line rang.

"Wade."

"Jason, it's Nancy in the library. Sonja found out about the search because of the—"

"Wade!" Spangler summoned him to his office.

"Got to go, Nancy."

After Atley left, Spangler closed the door and pointed to a chair. "Sit down." He rolled up the sleeves of his shirt. "I could fire you right now for what you did."

"What are you talking about?"

"You neglected to inform me of what you were doing. Of certain information you were pursuing. The search you requested just cost one thousand, six hundred, and forty-one dollars and seven cents and didn't yield a damned thing."

Jason followed Spangler's forefinger to the stack of database searches and the automated billing rates and said nothing.

"I don't give a rat's ass about the money. I just approved it out of my Metro budget to keep Sonja happy."

Jason swallowed.

"You failed to tell me about this, Wade. In my book, I have grounds to fire your ass."

"I wanted to confirm—"

"Shut up and listen. I called Rosemary at home, she said you'd received a tip this morning from a caller she'd patched to your home. I talked to Nancy Poden and found this on your desk." He held up the blue folder, opened it to the small pages and the sketch. "This is it, the tip and data you were secretly pursuing without my knowledge and at great expense to the company?"

Jason nodded.

"All of it?"

"Yes."

"Tell me everything."

Jason updated Spangler; he played his tape of the caller, told him about the park and how he'd acted on her information. Spangler let several tense moments pass in silence.

"We're going to run this story and sketch on the front page."

"What? I don't think we should do that."

"That's right, you don't think. Period. What you have here"—Spangler studied the file—"is a person who thinks they're a psychic. It's clear from the tone and syntax. We used to get a lot of this when I worked at the *Daily News*."

Spangler plucked a card from his Rolodex.

"Call this number. Ask for John Gordon Chenoweth. He's with a foundation that police go to when they quietly want to call in a psychic. He'll give you some on-the-record comments about the use of psychics in policework. Very respected guy with a highly regarded group."

"But the library search found nothing. The tip is unsubstantiated. I object to us running the story as it is," Jason protested.

"We'll hold the story until you talk to Chenoweth."

Relieved, Jason exhaled.

"Good; that will give me time to ask the FBI and Seattle homicide to respond to the name."

"No."

"*No?* Why?"

"Because they will not respond. They will urge you to sit on this, or kill it, and by then we will be overtaken."

"If you run that name and sketch, aren't we opening the door to all kinds of problems—maybe a lawsuit?"

"Let me worry about that."

"But it's likely a bogus tip."

"We don't know that. Besides, your tipster could've gone to the *Post-Intelligencer* or the *Seattle Times*. Right now, it's our exclusive. You call the foundation in New York. Chenoweth will give you balanced comments on valid and invalid psychic work."

"But with the time difference the New York office is likely closed," Jason protested.

"Quit stalling. Try reaching him now and Wade, be thankful you're still employed. Now move your ass!" Spangler ordered.

Jason could not reach Chenoweth in Manhattan. He tried well into the night, until they were pushing first-edition deadline; he notified the night desk.

"Vic, I couldn't reach a key source."

"You're losing your magic, kid," Beale joked.

"Just my mind. Look, hold my psychic exclusive until tomorrow."

"Fine, but I've got orders to let Fritz know."

"Sure."

Jason drove home, exhausted.

So exhausted he forgot to call Grace in Homicide.

Forgot all about the update she'd told him was coming.

DAY THREE

22

Flames lashed from the big steel drum in the backyard where Axel prepared to burn trash. He pulled a brown paper bag from the items heaped near the drum and studied its contents:

Nadine's white sneakers.

There they were. Wrapped in the morning newspapers with headlines and pictures telling every damned person in Seattle what the hell she was wearing on her feet when she grabbed the kid.

Stupid bitch.

Axel glared back at the house; he could hear the shower hissing and Nadine humming.

Humming.

All of his careful plans gone to hell and she was humming. Lost in her own fairy-tale world. Made him want to grab that two-by-four over there, march into the house, kick down that bathroom door, and—

Hold on. There's a way out of this.

He stared at the shoes and the flames. *Don't burn them. Not yet.* And the goddamned van. Common sense screamed at him to get rid of it. He would, but not just yet. He had to think. Consider the circumstances. This was not supposed to happen. He hadn't expected this at all. She'd destroyed everything.

So leave her.

No.

Their trail was too messy. Too many loose ends he had to take care of. But how? There was no time and there was too much heat. *Think it through.* But he'd never seen this coming. No hint of it. Certainly not when she'd started sending him letters. That was how they'd met. She was his pen pal during his last months inside.

"I ache for the chance to start over with a new man who needs salvation, redemption, and love, like me," she wrote.

She told him how she was alone in this world. No family. No friends. Just a single mom raising a new baby by herself after she'd fled her ex who would beat her after a few drinks. That was what she wrote.

Sure, whatever, he thought, after she'd sent him her picture.

She was a knockout. And that was no lie. Not like the desperate pigs who wrote to inmates. Nadine was the real thing. Actually, better-looking than her picture. And she had a fantastic body, which she put to good use as soon as he got out. Nonstop for three rainy days in a motel off of I-5.

At the start, when Axel first hooked up with her, things went according to his plan. Nadine Getch was what he needed on the outside. It was good that she'd had a kid because it was exactly what he needed her for. Not for that shit about salvation and redemption. *Give me a break.* He'd lied about that to string her along. And not for that happy family in a little house dream she was chasing.

That was actually kinda funny.

No, Nadine was perfect for his secret, longer-term setup.

He needed a woman he could manipulate. A woman who was vulnerable and somewhat simpleminded. The fact she had a kid made his plan even better. But there was no sign of her baby when they'd first met. Come to think of it, not even a picture. He should've pegged that as the first clue of trouble. Because back then, whenever he'd asked Nadine about her kid, she began to cry.

"It's a long story and it hurts so much," she told him, explaining how she'd gotten sick from her medication, from pills she took for the injuries she'd suffered from her ex beating on her. So sick that she couldn't take care of her baby.

She said she got a lot of good counseling and some money through a church group. The group had put her in touch with some people from a community shelter who were taking care of her baby until she got better.

"And I am getting better now that I have you," she told him late one night a couple of weeks ago. "I still see my counselors whenever I want to, and they let me visit my baby. They tell me I'll be able to bring him home soon. Then we'll all be together like a family. In our new lives, like we talked about."

The thing was, she always drove off alone to her appointments, which were at all hours. And she never wanted Axel to go with her. A few weeks back, he'd pressed her on it but she never really answered because that was when she'd returned from a session with some file folders.

And news.

"We can pick him up in a few days! Oh God, I'm so happy!"

This time she invited him to drive her to Ballard, where she directed him to park on a quiet tree-lined street. They waited as Nadine bit her nails, fidgeted, and scanned the neighborhood while eyeing a neat little two-story house several doors away.

"That's where my baby's been staying. I've been coming here almost every day to see him."

They sat there waiting for almost an hour with Axel growing impatient.

"We're early. Sorry, I'm anxious," Nadine kept repeating until a woman emerged, pushing a stroller down the street. "There! We have to follow her."

"Follow her? Why?"

"I'm sorry, this is embarrassing. I'm so excited. I messed up on the details. Keep a good distance but follow her. I forgot, we're going to do this wherever she's going. I thought it was at the house, sorry. Oh God, don't lose her! Oh God, this is really going to happen!"

Axel kept the van back half a block, puzzled and growing pissed. This whole thing was nuts, he thought, turning onto a street with several small stores. This didn't feel right.

"There! At Kim's Corner Store! Go there! Now!"

Then it all whirled before his eyes like a movie. The baby unattended in front of the store. Nadine jumped from the van and took the kid from his stroller. The woman they'd followed shot from the store and leapt onto the hood, clawing at the wipers, screaming, "My baby!" Nadine was clutching the bawling kid and screaming back at her.

"Get off! Liar! Drive! Get her off! She's a goddamned liar! He's my baby and you know it! Liar! Drive! Drive!"

Axel lurched the van and they roared away, clipping people in traffic, feeling as if the world must be watching them; thinking sure to Jesus he was now implicated in some bad shit that was going to put him back in prison.

He didn't know how, but they made it safely back to their house. He pulled the van into the garage out of sight and started working on finding an escape from the nightmare.

Before a police SWAT team showed up.

In the aftermath, the news reported that the woman, Maria Colson, was going to die. There were alerts going everywhere, the FBI was involved with every police force you could think of, there was video showing a fragment of the van, a psychic, a sketch of a woman, and evidence of Nadine's white shoes.

It had all gone to hell.

Sooner or later they were coming for them.

Axel had to find a way out. A way to turn it around because he had big plans and he was not going back to Coyote Ridge. No way in hell would he let that happen.

But he couldn't turn Nadine in to the FBI. Not with his record. No one would believe he was innocent of anything.

He was in too deep.

He looked to the house, listening to the shower. He looked at the flames licking from the barrel. He looked at her shoes in the bag, then the other items heaped by the barrel. He glanced toward the garage, knowing he had to get rid of the van. He just needed a bit more time.

He collected everything and headed into the house.

There was one way out.

Only one.

23

Stiff from two hours of troubled sleep, Grace Garner untangled her sheets, reached for her phone, and called the hospital.

"ICU."

"This is Grace Garner. Has there been any change in Maria Colson's condition?"

"No change, Detective."

"Is my partner there?"

"Detective Perelli is sleeping in the lounge. Would you like to talk to him?"

"No, thanks. Please tell him that I'll call later."

Grace went to her bathroom. She splashed cold water on her face while thinking of Dylan, the odds against him being alive, and how badly they needed a break in this case.

She slid on SPD jogging pants, an academy sweatshirt, tucked her hair under a Mariners ball cap, and grabbed her keys, phone, and change. Then she rode the elevator down to the lobby to get the morning papers from the boxes in front of her building.

The air felt good on her skin. The street was wet, early fog was lifting, and the boxes' spring-loaded doors clanged as she withdrew crisp copies of the *Times*, the *Post-Intelligencer,* and the *Mirror*.

As the elevator ascended, she found a measure of hope in the news. The late-night confirmation of the shoe impression evidence was the top story with pictures in the *Times* and the *P-I*. It could yield a solid lead. Stepping from the elevator, she looked at the *Mirror*'s front page and stopped in her tracks.

What the hell?

A story about a potential key *suspect* in the Colson case was lined above the fold in a Mirror Exclusive, by Jason Wade.

Suspect?

The item ran with a graphic of an anonymous note over an enlarged picture of a sketch with the headline: "The Woman Who Abducted Dylan Colson?" The sketch lacked detail, identifying the suspect only as Diane M. F.

Who? What the hell was this? She didn't have a clue about this.

She snapped through the inside pages. Nothing in the *Mirror* about the shoe. Nothing at all. Shaking her head, cursing aloud, she read every word of Jason's story, then reached for her phone.

The ringing jerked Jason awake.

"This is 'the thing' you were working on, Wade?"

"Who's this?"

"You promised to alert me before it ran. You gave me your word."

"Grace?"

"This is how you keep your word, Wade? Pulling a stunt like this? I thought you were different; that maybe we could establish some sort of trust. Maybe help each other. Turns out you're just a lying hack trying to sell papers."

"Hey! I don't know what you're talking about. All right?"

"You don't? Well, it's all over your front page."

He hadn't seen any morning papers.

"Just a minute. Don't hang up."

He rushed down the stairs to the lower-floor apartments. He didn't subscribe to Seattle's newspapers because he got them in the newsroom. This morning he stole the *Times*, the *Mirror,* and the *P-I* from the doorsteps of his neighbors, mentally promising to replace them.

The shoe evidence was news to him.

Man.

Then he saw the *Mirror*'s front page and his stomach twisted.

He picked up the phone. "Grace, I didn't write that story. I mean, it's my story, but I don't know what happened. I swear."

He could hear the anger in her breathing before she hung up.

Steeped in intrigue, the story outlined his call and how he'd picked up the tipster's envelope at the park. It left off the suspect's last name. A black bar obscured it in the reproduction of the note. The article quoted John Chenoweth, the expert with the psychic foundation in New York, and a retired Chicago detective who'd worked with psychics, giving the piece enough balance for skepticism. *Who wrote this? Where did this stuff come from?* He'd never called these guys. He'd never heard of the Chicago cop. Coming to the end of the article, he found his answer in the tag: (With files from Fritz Spangler).

As soon as he arrived in the newsroom he began hunting for Spangler. *You bastard,* he thought.

"He's in the morning news meeting, Jason," Rosemary said while taking calls coming through the news department's switchboard. "You've got twenty-two messages already this morning on your psychic story. Some producers with the daytime talk shows want to interview you."

"No, they don't. They want to use me to get to the 'psychic'."

"CBS News in New York just called too."

"Look, Rosemary…" He searched in vain for other news editors. Everyone was in the meeting. The few reporters on duty were working the phones on stories. "Have you heard why, or how, we missed this story?" He held up the *Seattle Times* with the shoe impression article.

"That one? Oh, they caught it late." She rummaged on her desk. "The night desk caught it on the fly for the fourth edition. Guess we missed most of the run, but we have it. See?"

She handed him a copy of the *Mirror*, the front page with the psychic story and the shoe evidence. The series of little stars near the date and price indicated a late-night replate to update the front page.

Spangler passed by him. "Helluva story."

"I want to talk to you."

Jason followed him into his office and tossed the *Mirror* on his boss's desk.

"When I left, you assured me that we'd hold this story until I'd reached Chenoweth and I confirmed the information with my sources. You betrayed me and burned my sources."

Spangler loosened his tie.

"I considered the circumstances, made a few calls, and decided we'd go with it. I wrote it."

"You could've done the courtesy of calling me."

"There was no time, and I couldn't risk you telling your sources."

"Jesus Christ, Fritz, either we're on the same team here or we're not!"

Spangler's eyebrows rose and his face tightened as he shut the door.

"Sit down, shut up, and listen. You obtained your information while in the employ of the *Seattle Mirror*. The company has ownership of any material you gather. And I, as management, have the authority to determine when and how the company will make use of it. I exercised my authority, which resulted in an exclusive with your name on it."

"But we've got absolutely no confirmation on that material. Zero."

"We took it as far as we could."

"Not as far as I wanted to go with it. The story was not developed."

"You seem to forget an expensive news library

search. The rest is up to the police. They now have a lead thanks to us." Spangler turned to his notes from the morning story meeting. "It was the right way to go under the circumstances. The Associated Press moved a hit on our psychic tip. We're drawing attention. Got crews from CNN, FOX, and ABC coming in—and CBS too, I see."

Jason looked toward the newsroom and shook his head. *All bull.*

"Today, I want you to go to the investigators, see if they can confirm our psychic suspect. Are you listening to me?"

"Your style of journalism sucks. It's dangerous."

"Excuse me? Did you just say you're resigning?"

Jason drew his hand over his reddened face.

"No."

"Good. I have approved the library to spend a little more to go to some private data firms to continue a full-court press in the search for Diane M. Fielderson. Now, I suggest you get to work."

Jason fumed for the rest of the morning and through lunch, which was a bowl of mushroom soup eaten at his desk. Every cop source he called couldn't help him. *Or wouldn't.* The news library made no further progress than it had the day before in attempting to confirm the existence of a Diane M. Fielderson, born in the early 1980s in the United States or Canada.

For a moment he considered calling his old man for help, now that he was working as a private investigator, but he didn't want to get him involved. Besides, something was gnawing at him. Something he'd over-looked or had forgotten at the outset of this psychic caper.

He tried to recall what it was, as he got fresh coffee from the newsroom kitchen. Passing by the photodesk, he was on the verge of remembering when he saw a group of well-dressed people huddled around his desk, then recognized Grace Garner, with her partner, Kirk Dupree from the FBI, and a couple of other guys in suits.

"Jason Wade?"

"Yes."

Jason's eyes went round the group meeting ice-cold expressions, including Grace's.

"We'd like the original note and sketch and all related original documents you cite in your article here, pertaining to Diane M. F.," Dupree said. "We'll also need a list of the names of all people who handled the original documents."

"I don't think I can give that up. You know, freedom of the—"

Dupree nodded to one of the men, who unfolded some legal papers.

"We've got a search warrant signed by a federal judge."

Newsroom staff had gathered around Jason's desk.

"I'm Fritz Spangler, Metropolitan Editor. Who are you?"

IDs were flashed, then Dupree handed Spangler the warrant. After reading it, Spangler said, "We've got federal privacy laws that prohibit police searches of newsrooms."

"There are exceptions that concern the material we're interested in," Dupree replied as he pointed to a paragraph, "as we have reason to believe that the immediate seizure of such material is necessary to prevent the death of, or serious bodily injury to, a human being."

"Well, we've published the sketch and the source's letter."

"Are you refusing to cooperate?" Dupree asked.

Spangler indicated his office and led Jason and the small group inside. He punched a number on his phone then put his call on speaker.

"Dixon, Niederman, and Bailey."

"Sarah, it's Fritz at the *Mirror*. Can you get Winston on the line?"

"He's in a meeting with a client, Mr. Spangler."

"Get him now, please. I've got the FBI in my office with a search warrant."

Fifteen minutes later, after the *Mirror*'s legal counsel, Winston Bailey, advised Spangler to cooperate, one of the FBI agents pulled on white latex gloves and placed the documents in evidence bags.

Jason looked at Grace, who looked away, her expression cold.

"By the way, you're going to be in tomorrow's paper." Spangler nodded to the newsroom.

The group turned to face the photographer taking pictures of the exchange through the glass walls of Spangler's office.

"Just so you know," Dupree said, "you've hampered the investigation into the abduction of Dylan Colson."

"How so, Agent Dupree?" Spangler folded his arms. "We've given you a lead."

"You've most likely given us a bullshit lead in order to boost readership, and you know it. Your presentation of this 'tip' gives it unwarranted credibility." Jason lowered his chin and smiled to himself as Dupree continued. "You've diverted attention from the first solid piece of evidence to emerge in this case. We'll be inundated with calls from every nutcase who thinks they have psychic abilities, or thinks they can identify this phantom in the sketch. There's no detail here. This could be you, me, or an alien. We've already put resources on this thing which are being drawn away from following up solid evidence on the suspect's shoe."

"If our tip is such a bogus one, then why are you here, huh?" Spangler asked.

"Unlike you, we confirm our information before deciding to make it public."

At that moment, Jason noticed Nate Hodge in the newsroom standing next to Danny Kwong, the photog shooting the police.

It puzzled Jason why Hodge was waving this morning's front page of the *Mirror* and his camera.

Then it started coming back to him.

The thing he'd forgotten.

Yesterday morning, before heading to Sunset Hill Park, he'd called Hodge to ask him to get there in advance of his secret meeting and set up. Jason wanted him to take pictures from a distance with the same powerful lens he used to shoot Seahawks games.

It was an ass-covering thing some reporters did whenever they met with sources in public places.

Since Jason hadn't actually met anyone at the park, he'd forgotten to ask Hodge if he'd actually shot anything.

Now he could see Hodge nodding to him, holding up the *Mirror* and his camera and nodding big nods, confirming that Christ yes, he had something to show him.

Right now!

24

Axel didn't have a lot of time to pull it off.

Forty-eight hours.

If he was lucky.

The way things stood, he was jammed tight by the situation—guaranteed to go down for it unless he tried something.

Anything, man.

His plan was his only chance.

Nadine was still in the shower when he returned to the house. He took her shoes and the other items into the room they used for storing stuff. He hid it all there among some sheets and blankets.

Then he sat at the desk in the room, a sheet of finished plywood atop two two-drawer file cabinets. He switched on his laptop computer, used his secret password to log on to the files he kept hidden on his hard drive.

As his computer beeped, he accepted that the FBI, with that shoe evidence and other stuff, would likely find Nadine. It was just a matter of time. But he could erase himself from the picture, or at least complicate the trail leading to him. He'd learned about police procedures from other inmates at Coyote Ridge.

His mind raced back to the store. Why hadn't he seen this coming? That she was lying about a kid, that she was a psycho? She had to be nuts. He couldn't believe the kid was hers. The whole time they were hauling ass from the store with the thing bawling he kept drilling her.

"Nadine, is this baby really yours?"

"Yes!"

"Bullshit! I want the truth, Nadine!"

"He's mine, I swear, Axel. The services people took him from me and gave him to the Colsons. When I got better they wouldn't give him back to me."

"Why not?"

"They didn't think I was well enough to take care of him. But they're wrong. Tell me that they're wrong, Axel!"

He glared at her in disbelief.

"Is this the truth, Nadine?"

"Yes, I swear. I had to rescue him. I'm sorry I didn't tell you everything, Axel. I needed your help."

Oh, he was going to help her.

He seethed as he worked on his laptop. This psycho bitch was not going to pull down his life's work, the grand plan he'd begun building inside for the last three years of his life.

It had gone well after he got out. He found a job at a wrecking yard. He had limited supervision, worked his own hours, and was paid in cash. He got the van through a friend of a friend through a side deal with a repo guy. He got a safe plate and a motorcycle. Neither the van nor the bike were registered to him.

He'd established his relationship and "ties to the community" with a single mother. However, on paper, Axel had passed off Nadine to the community corrections officer as Ms. Jane Carruthers, a secretary at a daycare center. He gave Axel a thumbs up for taking the correct rehabilitative path with such an upstanding and pretty young lady. More important, his CCO, an absent-minded white-haired guy, kept pushing back residential visits because he was being treated for some kind of cancer.

It didn't matter because Axel had listed three different addresses. All of them wrong. He kept promising his CCO that he would update his residential address as required.

The address thing was all part of living smart outside. In prison, other inmates taught you to stay out of all databanks. No credit cards. Never list a real address; use postal boxes, general delivery. It was what he and Nadine were doing with this place they were renting.

Axel had tried to be certain nothing tied them to the property. And he always ensured his fingertips were cut up with deep scrapes, or he wore bandages or gloves, something he could pass off to the work he did on wrecks. Keep yourself invisible, don't make it easy for anyone to find you. Keep your number unlisted, or use a public phone.

They must've done it right, or Nadine's stunt would've had the FBI on their doorstep by now. It must've bought them a little time.

Until now, the real deal Axel had been working on

involved an upcoming job meticulously planned by some guys inside. He was part of the project team. He had to first set himself up as being clean, then they would get him a new identity and a job repairing armored cars in Los Angeles. When the time came, he'd help the team pull off one mother of a heist.

Axel's cut was going to be $2.5 million.

Then he'd dump Nadine and her kid and head off to one of the South American or Caribbean countries that had no extradition deal with the United States and he would enjoy the rest of his life on the beach.

That was Axel's dream plan.

Nadine's move threatened to send him back inside. He could not allow that to happen.

The shower stopped.

He heard her hair dryer going as he continued working online with his files. The best thing he took out of prison was an extensive network of friends on the outside.

Axel could get expert help fast on just about anything he needed: forged passports, stolen credit cards, counterfeit cash, drugs, stolen plates, guns, advice on how to leave no trace evidence at crime scenes, how to make bombs, plot a bank job. He could contact brokers who handled every stolen item on the planet: cars, diamonds, art, guns, computer programs, postage stamps, trading cards, university exams, even plutonium.

Axel needed help now.

"Here's a scenario," he began an e-mail to a friend he trusted with his life. When he finished, he sent off two more to other trusted sources, seeking their help on his plan to turn Nadine's act around. The floor in the hall creaked.

"What do you think, honey?"

Axel closed his files and looked at Nadine standing in the doorway.

"My new look for our new life."

She grinned, buffed her head with her hands. Her hair was short and dyed a completely different color. She didn't look a thing like the woman who'd stepped into the bathroom.

He nodded.

"Whatcha working on, there?"

"Just keeping an eye on things."

"I saw you at the fire by the drum." She nodded to the back. "You get rid of everything?"

He nodded. "Everything we needed to get rid of."

"Good. I'm going to check on my baby. He's still asleep." She turned, then stopped. "I'm hungry, and I'm going to have a tomato sandwich. Can I fix you anything, hon?"

He shook his head.

After she left, he checked his e-mail inbox. One response already. Good. "Friend," it began, "the answers you seek will soon be on their way."

Good.

He closed his files, cocked an ear to the radio news in the kitchen where Nadine was humming again. The stupid bitch. Satisfied no new developments were being reported, Axel left his desk, went down the hall to the room where the kid was.

He entered.

The shade had been pulled down, washing the room with soft light.

Axel liked the sweet smell, the serene calmness. Tranquil like a funeral chapel during a wake, he thought, gazing down at Dylan Colson, who slept in the crib.

The light over the baby dimmed as Axel drew closer.

He stood there in silence, knowing that soon he'd have the information he needed to take the action Nadine had forced him to take. He looked at Dylan Colson, thinking it was too bad but it was out of Axel's hands. He was not to blame.

It was Nadine's fault.

25

Everett Sinclair couldn't let it go.

The bastard in the van who had cut him off had to pay.

But how?

Vengeance had consumed Sinclair during his business flight to Detroit. After landing, it was all he could think of during late-night meetings with executives and engineers in white hard hats. It was all he could think of as he inspected the retooling of the company's Canadian plant, which was a short drive across the Detroit River in Windsor, Ontario. And it was all he thought of now, during his first real break since leaving Seattle for this pain-in-the-ass emergency project.

Dammit.

The fact he had been diverted from pursuing restitution *on his terms* for the asshole's affront—the marring of his beautiful Jasper Blue Mercedes and the destruction of his $900 tailored charcoal suit—pissed him off supremely. He refused to wait a moment longer. He was launching a counterstrike now.

As his laptop beeped to life, Sinclair took stock of

his Windsor hotel room, his clothes strewn everywhere along with key reports. Was that the Tokyo file mixed with Boston and Pittsburgh? Sinclair's counselor had warned that he would experience aggression, disinterest, depression, and erratic behavior to compensate for the wound of the divorce.

This is the wisdom $200 an hour gets you. A bartender is cheaper and you can get hammered at the same time.

Sinclair had buried himself in work; on this trip across the continent, he had been disconnected from current events in Seattle, let alone the world. Hadn't watched any news. Unread copies of *USA Today*, the *Detroit Free Press,* and the *Windsor Star* were piled in the hall next to his room-service trays from a late-night dinner and a half-eaten breakfast. Why should he care about the world? The world didn't give a damn about him.

You're a lone wolf, Ev. Take care of yourself.

He looked across the river at Detroit, then began formulating his retribution strategy. He studied his laptop screen and the evidence he'd gathered. He clicked onto his pictures of the damage to his beloved 450SL, his suit, and began checking his summary of the incident, and spelling out his plan.

Now, by resolving things on his terms, he stressed in his e-mail, meant that he did not want police involved. And he did not want insurance companies involved either. Those pricks would find some way to blame him and jack up his rates, given the fact he had that old drunk driving record from his college days and that he also had a recent speeding charge and a red light charge against him. His life was stressful, but no one seemed to appreciate that.

So, no cops and no insurance.

Hell, he'd been beaten up badly in the settlement with his bitch ex-wife, he didn't want her getting wind of anything else she might use against him someday.

Nothing to make her suspect he'd hidden a large chunk of change in a numbered account in Aruba—the same place he'd tucked the cash he'd finessed through subcontracting side deals he'd arranged over the years.

Relax, he told himself. No one would find his "vault," as he liked to call it.

He was too smart to get caught. He was a guy who demanded respect. That was why he couldn't tolerate the insult of his wife cheating on him, or this asshole in the van.

He wanted the jerk responsible to pay. He wanted $1,000 for the suit, $5,000 for damage to the car, and another $2,000 for his anguish and costs. So, $8,000 total for the incident. All in cash, Sinclair wrote.

"I want you to track this mother down ASAP and shake the cash out of him. Tell him I'll sue his ass. Tell him that I'm going to see a doctor for a possible back injury related to the collision. Attached is all the evidence. Should be a slam dunk and take you less than two hours."

Sinclair gave one last check of the photos: his car, his suit, the time, street, location, and, oh yeah, the tight blurry shot of the van's rear bumper, showing some sort of custom artwork and the Washington State license plate. He had the plate for sure.

The bastard probably thought he'd gotten away with it. Sinclair hit the Send command on his laptop, instantly dispatching his e-mail to Don Krofton, the Seattle private investigator Sinclair had hired to successfully catch his whore wife banging that ex-Seahawk used-car salesman in Tacoma.

Just wait until the bastard in the van sees a hard-ass ex-Seattle cop on his doorstep with the evidence.

Oh, you're going to pay, asshole.

Big time.

26

Dental magazines were still arriving at the office of Don Krofton's private investigator agency.

No matter how many times she wrote to them, the magazine people still didn't get it, Michelle, the office manager, thought as she shuffled through the mail. The agency had moved in when the Vorax Brothers dental team moved out. It had been two years now and Michelle could still detect the antiseptic smell throughout the lavender rooms of the second-floor office.

Located in a south Seattle strip mall, the P.I. firm shared the same address as a pet store, Bandito Supremo Tacos, and Eternal Solace, a business that offered cut-rate classes for aspiring funeral directors. The building featured a carnival of smells, of which Michelle preferred Don's cigars. It also had its share of weirdos, like Bill, the white-faced operator of the funeral school. "You know, Michelle, I'm the last man in your life who would ever let you down." Bill's tired joke was always accompanied by his yellow-toothed smile.

Michelle went back to her computer when it beeped with a client e-mail.

"Oh God, not you again." She read quickly through Everett Sinclair's tirade slash investigation request, then shook her head before bumping it to Don's private e-mail address. She wondered how the boss would handle this one from Sinclair, the client who believed the world was out to get him and wanted "to sue the ass off of every bastard" who looked sideways at him.

Sinclair just had never gotten his head around the fact his wife awoke from her prolonged state of stupidity to realize he was not a human being, but a jerk posing as one. Why he felt entitled to take out his problems on everyone was baffling.

Michelle resumed filing invoices, hoping Don would pass on this one, counting on the fact that he was vacationing in Las Vegas with Lola, a twenty-four-year-old showgirl who found Don, a sixty-two-year-old ex-cop, a fascinating man. Maybe it was the fact he had just undergone a face-lift.

Michelle caught the phone on the second ring.

"Shell"—Don always called her that—"just read that one from Everett Sinclair."

"That was fast. Are you in Vegas, still?"

"Yeah, was checking my e-mail when this one came in."

"So you want to pass?"

"No. Give it to Henry."

"Henry?"

"Yes. I want to give him more time toward his P.I. license. File it as a claims investigation, run the background for him. Call him and tell him I said to contact the subject and take a soft approach on the client's request for direct restitution before hinting at litigation, insurance, or police involvement. The evidence is strong and should help."

"All right, boss. How's Lola?"

"Tanned and energetic. I'm taking her to a Shania Twain show tonight."

"You're a dirty old man."

"Got to live life while I'm alive. Help Henry get going on this one."

Michelle hung up and sighed. She responded with respectful courtesy to Sinclair's e-mail, then went to the agency's more powerful computer, which was linked to a number of federal and state databanks, and worked up the background.

Washington's Vehicle/Vessel Inquiry System held records on nearly seven million vehicles registered in the state and some four and a half million licensed drivers. Michelle studied the grainy photo of the license plate and Sinclair's notes. She'd say one thing for him—he was good at getting the goods on people. What was that plate number?

After scrutinizing her blurry printout showing the Washington State plate of the van that had damaged the Mercedes, she entered "575 QIO" to query IVIPS and waited for the response.

Don was a retired Seattle police detective. He started as a young beat cop, then worked up the ranks. Now he operated a small, private agency where he farmed out investigations to some two dozen former law enforcement types he knew.

After her husband passed away, Michelle, a retired Seattle PD clerk, joined his operation.

Her computer screen flashed.

IVIPS showed no records for her query. The first version of the plate didn't exist. Oh, she must've made a typo. She rechecked, right, then typed "575-QID" and, bang, her response came up with the name of the registered owner, address, remarks on the vehicle, title, and miscellaneous other data. She simply glanced at it without giving the data any consideration. She never took note of the details. After processing thousands for the agency, they pretty much all looked the same. She just passed them to the investigator.

She forwarded it along with Don's instructions to Henry, an old friend of Don's from his Seattle police days. Henry was a quiet man and a bit of a mystery. He'd been a Seattle cop years and years ago but for only a short time. He'd recently retired from working in a warehouse, or something like that, and was working on getting three years of experience under his belt so he could obtain his license and supplement his pension.

Maybe Henry would be happy to handle this one, Michelle thought, looking up his number, oblivious to the fact that she'd overlooked one key thing.

She had completely forgotten to check the registered owner's name through the online database for the Washington State Patrol and Criminal History Section to determine if the person who had crossed Everett Sinclair in Ballard had a criminal record. The system held data on arrest records and cases not open to the public.

And had she looked further, she would have noticed that the plate did not match the vehicle.

27

After reading his son's story on the *Seattle Mirror*'s front page, Henry Wade swelled with the usual wave of pride.

The kid had accomplished a helluva thing with his life.

Against the odds, Jay had worked his way out of the brewery, put himself through college, and had earned a good-paying, full-time job with the newspaper. Now he was writing about the city's biggest crimes.

It was a helluva thing for sure.

Truth was, his boy had inspired him to turn his own life around. Even if it had taken years. Long, painful years. He took stock of his empty house, confident that he had put his ghosts to rest. *Most of them, anyway.*

He rubbed his chin, reflecting on his own small achievements. He'd been faithful to AA. Over four hundred days sober now since he'd taken early retirement from the brewery. It gave him the strength to resurrect a dream. One that he'd buried a lifetime ago when he had to quit the Seattle Police Department after only a few years on the job. *Don't go there, don't think about that. Best to keep the past in the past.*

Stepping carefully around the locked rooms of memory, he came to his resurrected desire of working as a detective.

After all he'd been through, he'd managed to salvage it.

Hell, he was doing it. Maybe on a small scale, but he was doing it. Thanks to Don Krofton, a decent guy who didn't owe Henry Wade a damn thing. Nobody did, but Krofton had remembered him from the old days and took him on as a trainee to help him get his three years in to get his license. Krofton had given him a shot, first with some small files. A little surveillance. Checking court records. Confirming people worked where they claimed to have worked.

It was all going just fine.

Henry resumed looking over the state's study guide on the exam for private investigators. He flipped through his well-thumbed copy of the Washington State Criminal Code. A lot of it was coming back to him from the old days.

He'd used his pension and retirement package to buy a new top-of-the-line computer. He took courses to learn how to use it and the Internet. Got himself a cell phone and a few other high-tech toys.

Funny, he was living in the same house in the same blue-collar neighborhood near Boeing Field, south of the airport. He was driving the same old pickup and wearing the same workingman's clothes, but he'd traveled a world away from the life he'd left at the brewery.

At sixty-one, Henry Wade was a new man.

He peered into his empty coffee cup, went to the kitchen for a refill; the phone rang.

"Hi, Henry, Michelle at Krofton's. Are you available for a job today?"

"I am."

"As we speak, I'm sending the file to your e-mail."

"All right, hang on."

He sat before his computer with its high-speed access.

In seconds, he was reading Everett Sinclair's ranting request and looking through the photos Sinclair had attached. He took careful notes as Michelle relayed Krofton's instructions. She directed him to the results of her query of IVIPS, the state's database for driving and vehicle records.

After giving it all a quick read, he said, "Sounds good, I'm on it."

As his printer kicked to life, he filled his coffee cup and thought fondly of the guys at the brewery calling him Jim Rockford when word got out about his second career. He adjusted his glasses as he studied every aspect of the file, reading and rereading the details of Sinclair's note, until he noticed something.

Hold on.

He unfolded his street map of greater Seattle. Then retrieved the *Mirror* and reviewed the facts on the Colson case. *Just hold on. Let's look at the time Sinclair's thing happened. The location.* He consulted the map. The news stories. Sinclair's report.

A van. *A red van.*

According to Sinclair's report it was a van that had

clipped him while driving dangerously out of the Ballard area. The color. The timing. Still, something didn't look right. Hell, he should call this in to Seattle PD, or the FBI.

Wait a sec. Just relax there.

He kept checking the details. If Krofton cleared it, then it had to be just a coincidence. He didn't want to overreact here. Come across as a complete hysterical dope, especially while trying to get his license. He went to the IVIPS printout.

Maybe this is it. A clear mistake. Wasn't it? Sure looked like it. Look at the results of the query on the registered owner and the type of vehicle. This was a car, a Toyota Corolla. But look at what Sinclair stated. He was emphatic that it was a van.

Henry sat there staring at his pages, the map, and the newspaper.

Something about this one didn't make sense, he thought as he consulted his map for the best way to the address linked to the plate from the van provided by Sinclair. He collected the documents into a file folder, gathered his keys and jacket.

But before he headed to his pickup, he stopped.

He wouldn't go alone. Something about this one didn't add up. He reached for his phone and began dialing. He needed a second opinion.

It wouldn't take long.

Besides, it was probably nothing at all.

28

Nadine is four years old.

She's alone in the cold, dark basement while above her the floorboards creak.

Big Pearl is coming.

The basement door opens, the wooden stairs groan, Nadine trembles, and the dog chain jingles. In the darkness, Nadine picks up the bad smell coming off of Big Pearl. She hears the clink of an empty glass bottle joining the others in the pitch-black corner beside the furnace, sitting there breathing fire like a patient dragon.

Then the flashlight finds its target, trapping Nadine's small face in a circle of harsh light. It hurts her eyes.

"This place stinks like cat piss and you, Natty Nat."

Big Pearl grunts as she comes closer.

"No wonder your mama didn't want you. Nobody wanted you, why, you're nothin' more'n what people scrape from their shoe. You thank your lucky stars for Big Pearl. Now, git over here!"

Nadine recoils and the chain scrapes across the cement floor. She knows what's coming. Can feel what's coming even before it starts.

And it starts with her leg.

Big Pearl grabs the chain shackled to Nadine's ankle.

And pulls.

"I said, git over here!"

Big Pearl pulls on the chain, dragging Nadine across the cold hard floor as she pleads. Then comes the rush of air and the belt whistles down on Nadine with a whip-crack against her skin.

She spasms with pain.

"No, Big Pearl."

"You better thank me, Natty Nat."

The leather cuts into her flesh, Nadine bites her tongue. Tears stream down her face as the belt comes down again and again and again until finally Nadine says it.

"Thank you Big Pearl for teaching me right. Oh thank you."

And it ends with Big Pearl heaving and huffing and the stairs groaning as she leaves Nadine in the darkness with her spirit broken and her skin on fire. Nadine sobs and fumbles in the dark for her baby doll, naked and alone like her.

Nadine hugs her so tight.

So tight.

Her baby is the only thing in this world that she loves because it is the only thing in this world that loves her back.

29

In six clear frames a woman was placing an orange plastic bag into the trash bin at Sunset Hill Park, then walking away.

"These are all I got."

Nate Hodge clicked through his pictures on his large flat-screen monitor in the *Seattle Mirror*'s photo department. Jason Wade, Fritz Spangler, the FBI agents, and the Seattle detectives were standing over Hodge's desk, studying his crisp digital images.

Four of the photos were full-body, head to toe. The woman was Caucasian, mid-thirties, slender build with short brown hair. She was wearing a lavender fleece jacket, print top, and tan slacks.

On her feet: blue sneakers.

A cell phone rang; an FBI agent answered it and stepped away from the desk, talking softly. Another agent leaned closer to Hodge's monitor.

"Can you enlarge her face?"

Hodge zoomed in on the frame where the woman looked directly into the camera. "She never saw me," Hodge said. "I was nearly two blocks away when I shot these. I headed to the park as soon as Jason called me to set up."

"See if I've got this," Kirk Dupree said. "Jason told you he was going to meet a source at Sunset Hill and you get there in advance to position yourself to take pictures with a long lens?"

"We do it all the time when we meet an anonymous source," Jason said. "It covers us. Try to get pictures of everything. Never know when you might need the information."

"You happen to follow this woman and get a plate?" Grace asked Hodge, who shook his head.

"I couldn't stay. Got sent to Bellingham on another job, got back late and thought nothing of this until I saw this morning's paper. So what do you think?"

The FBI agent completed his close-up study of the enlarged version of the woman's face and pulled back. "We know her. She's been up to our office."

"Who is she?" Dupree said.

"Robin, her name is Robin somebody."

"Robin Dove." The agent on the cell phone had finished and tapped a white-gloved finger on a copy of the *Mirror* showing the reproduced note from the psychic. "ERT just called. This morning, before we came, they started comparing this note published here with other tip letters we've received in other cases. From the composition, syntax, the font used, they say it fits with previous letters from Robin Dove."

"Who is she?" Dupree asked.

The agent consulted his notes. "A Seattle housewife. Works part-time at a daycare. She believes she has psychic abilities. She usually contacts us, unsolicited, several times a year with details she 'feels' will help our investigations."

"And?" Spangler asked.

"Her information has never been useful," the agent said.

For Dupree, it all ended there. "Our warrant covers this material." He nodded to the photos and Hodge. "We want all of them. Your photo card and a statement."

Another agent joined the group after finishing a call.

"Things are piling up on the shoe. We've got leads to check."

"Let's go. We've wasted enough time here."

"Excuse me, Fritz." Rosemary the assistant approached, nodding to the TV crews at the far end of the newsroom. "CNN and FOX are here to talk to somebody on our psychic story."

Camera operators hoisted their cameras to their shoulders and began recording the white-gloved detectives. Dupree shook his head, then led the investigators out in a direction that took them away from the TV people. Spangler's face flushed and he turned to Jason, but the reporter had left with the investigators.

In the foyer, Jason managed to pull the group aside for a private moment amid the tall potted palms. All of them, including Grace, were poker-faced. He tried to gauge their reaction and a silent icy moment passed. Careful not to single out Grace Garner as a source, he tried to put out the fire Spangler had ignited on his bridge into the investigation.

"You guys have to understand," Jason said, "I didn't write the story in today's paper. Spangler did. I didn't think it was developed and I wanted to hold off until I checked it out. That"—he pointed back to the newsroom—"is not the way I do things."

"That's your fucking problem, Wade," Dupree said. "Frankly, ours is a tad more serious than you having an asshole for a boss. Let's go."

Jason returned to his desk, utterly defeated. Any hope of breaking news on the Colsons through police sources was dead. As far as the cops were concerned, the *Mirror* was the pariah paper on the case.

This sucks.

The morning paper, the sketch, and portions of the "psychic's" note now mocked him.

"The forces behind the crime departed the scene immediately in a vehicle with the child in an easterly direction through the community. Their vehicle was seen by hundreds of people… Death stands over this case."

Death stands over this case. You think?

All crap.

Jason crumpled the paper.

Look at Spangler over there basking in the bright camera lights. One leg half-straddled on a desk, his body half-turned so the newsroom, "his" newsroom, was framed behind him. Thinks he's Ben Bradlee, or Lou Grant.

He's more like Perry White.

Unable to stomach another second, Jason grabbed his jacket. He had to hit the street. He'd try working on the Colsons' background by going back to the neighbors. He rifled through his drawer for a pen, then found his notebook as his phone rang.

"Jay," his father said, "have you got a moment?"

He closed his eyes.

"This is a bad time, Dad."

"Son, I've got something that could be connected to your big abduction story. Need you to take a ride with me."

"Dad, listen, I don't have time." *To listen to your wild theories about this case. Every time I'm on the front page you call me up with advice.* "I'm sorry, I've got to go."

"Jay, I'll be in front of the *Mirror* in fifteen minutes."

30

Rolling his eyes and clenching his jaw, Jason headed to the newsroom elevator where he repeatedly jabbed the down button.

I don't need this, Dad. Not now.

First the psychic crap. Then Spangler screwed everything up, leaving him to face the wrath of every FBI agent and Seattle detective on the Colson case—effectively killing any hope he had of cultivating Grace Garner as a source. *Or something more.* Thank you, Fritz.

And now his old man wanted in on the Colson story.

Jason spat on the sidewalk as he paced in front of the *Mirror* building. Tapping his notebook against his leg, he searched the traffic until he spotted a familiar blue Ford Ranger pickup. His father waved from behind the wheel then double-parked, forcing angry drivers to honk as they wheeled around him. Jason stepped into the street and leaned into the open passenger window.

"I just can't do this now."

"Get in, it'll only take an hour. Tops."

"Dad."

"Come on, get in, son."

Jason muttered something, got in, and was catapulted back through his life. The interior was immaculate but the smell of cologne and hops, the desperation
of the brewery, mingled in the cab with Johnny Cash,
whose singing of "I Walk the Line" floated softly from
the Ranger's sound system.

"I see you're kicking ass on the big story."

"Whatever you want to tell me, please get to it and
get me back to the paper, okay?"

His father nodded and squinted into the traffic.

"I'm sorry, Dad, but this has not been a stellar
morning."

His old man shrugged it off. He understood.

"I caught an interesting little job this morning from
Krofton. You might want to look at it. It stays confidential, by the way."

He passed a file folder to Jason, who read quickly
through its few pages then put it on the seat between
them.

"So? You confirm an address, press the guilty party
for compensation in a hit-and-run fender bender. All
straightforward. How's it related to the story? And
where the heck are you taking me?"

"I think you're missing some key facts. The client
says the vehicle was a van."

"Sure but your information confirms it's a car, a"—
Jason consulted the file again—"a Toyota."

"But look at the client's note. He insists it was a van."

"Whatever. I still don't get it."

"Also, look at the time and location of the incident."
Jason did.

"See," his father said. "Location: Ballard. Time: the morning of the kidnapping. Vehicle: van. See where I'm going with this?"

Jason reread everything. Much more closely this time.

"Maybe it's a coincidence, Jay. That's why we check it out first, right?"

As the implication dawned on Jason, his old man winked, in the good way he used to wink at him long ago, before things went dark. Jason felt the tension melt as his old man's Ranger headed northbound on I-5. The road rushed under them like so many of the bad years. Jason wondered if his old man's ancient internal war flowed from something that happened a lifetime ago when Henry Wade was a Seattle cop.

Who knows?

His old man never talked about it. Ever.

As the Ranger gathered speed, Jason looked at him. Polo shirt, faded jeans. Tanned. Silver hair. Looked good. Then he glanced over his shoulder. The cab's back window was still bordered with stickers of the American flag, the brewery union, and the brewery's security parking decal. It was all behind them now. Best to leave it there.

According to the printout from IVIPS, the address for the license number Everett Sinclair took down was in a North Seattle community, tucked away in the Pine-hurst, Northgate, and Maple Leaf area. Easy to miss on the map, Jason discovered as he kept correcting his directions to his father.

They rolled by brick Tudor-style homes and bungalows that had gone up after World War Two. There were several vacant lots with overgrown shrubs and over-turned shopping carts. One lot had a discarded TV and a dryer with the door torn off. The house next to it had an eviscerated pink Pinto in the oil-stained front yard. Sidewalks seemed to be missing. Most houses had dirt patches for driveways. FOR RENT signs were common in front windows.

"There, Brimerley Lane. Turn left here," Jason said. "It's 444 Brimerley Lane."

A few houses on the street had well-kept yards, tended gardens, and flower boxes at the windows. The place they were looking for was at the far end and backed on to I-5. Except for the buzz of the freeway, the enclave was tranquil when they stopped in front of number 444. It was a light green bungalow sitting way back from the street. Not a bad-looking place, Jason thought when they arrived at the front door.

The doorbell's chime echoed through the small home. His old man nodded to the flyers and junk mail clogging the metal mailbox. A few moments later, Jason pressed the bell a second time.

No response.

They looked back to the street.

Empty.

Jason knocked. Hard. Loud enough to wake anyone inside who might be sleeping. He placed his ear against the door. Not a sound, not a bird, not even the scratch of dog paws on linoleum.

"Nothing," he told his dad, who nodded to the single-car garage.

It was at the end of a dirt driveway, at the side but back of the house, canopied by a couple of tall alders. Paint blistered its wood sides and double doors. Jason scanned the small backyard. A trash can, some lawn chairs. Nothing beyond that. His old man, shielding his eyes, was gazing into the garage window.

"There's a Toyota Corolla in there, color matches IVIPS."

His father scanned discarded papers in the trash can while Jason tried the side door of the garage. It was open.

"Let's go in," he said, "check the plate, then we'll leave."

Reluctant, his father glanced around.

"It'll only take a moment, Dad. And you dragged me all this way."

Jason stepped into the darkened garage and waited a few seconds for his eyes to adjust to the light. After finishing with the trash can, his father followed. Dust particles danced in the light shafts. The car took up most of the garage. Garden tools hung from the side; so did a hose, extension cord, a ladder. A bicycle leaned against the wall. Adult-size. Jason squeezed himself to the front of the car, noticing a fine layer of dust on the hood as he crouched down before the front bumper.

"It's gone. There's no front plate."

"No back plate either," his father called from the rear of the Toyota.

Jason had a mini-penlight on his keychain and used it to examine the screws that secured the plate. They had fresh scrapes.

"Don't touch anything!" his father said. "Let's get back outside."

They returned to the rear yard to consider the matter. "The address is correct. The car's correct. The plates are gone and witnessed on a van in Ballard," Jason mused.

"Obviously stolen," his old man said. "What do you think?"

Jason stared at the house and pulled out his cell phone.

"What's the telephone number for here?"

"Why? What're you going to do?"

"Just give it to me."

Jason called the number and could hear the phone ringing inside the house. With each ring he stepped closer to the rear door, staring at it. *It wasn't closed all the way.* He pulled out his pen and, using the capped end, pushed on the wooden door. It creaked open wide, allowing a small squadron of flies to leave while inviting him to enter.

"Hold it right there," his father said. "I think we should call Seattle PD."

Jason held up his hand to stop that idea. As the phone continued to ring, he called out.

"Anybody home?"

He waited for an answer. None came. He stepped close enough to poke his head into the house and was hit with a powerful smell that repelled him. *He'd glimpsed something. What was it?* Ignoring his father's calls to step back, Jason ended his call, covered his face and nose with his hands, and stepped inside.

In that instant, Jason glimpsed a pair of feet in white

socks, jeans, legs on the floor. His view blocked, he pressed on slowly, staring at the legs until they became a lower torso then evolved into something.

Something that was moving.

A huge mass, sort of quivering in unison. A furry, feverish mass that looked—*holy Christ*—*that's a big fucking ball of rats!* They were feeding on decomposing entrails splayed in every direction on the floor.

Was that a hand? Was that human?

The body was swollen, the head a pulpy mass, the face blackened and bloated beyond recognition.

Two huge rats scurried over Jason's shoes.

His scalp prickled, his skin tingled with gooseflesh. He crushed his hands to his face to prevent the stench from penetrating his nostrils as it reached the back of his tongue, working its way down his esophagus, triggering a small geyser of bile to gush up the back of his throat. He was paralyzed until someone clamped his shoulder, yanked him out of the house back into the fresh air of the yard just in time for him to vomit.

As he doubled over, he heard his old man calling 911.

31

Across the city in Ballard, Maria Colson's condition had deteriorated and her family was talking to a priest.

Detective Grace Garner bit her bottom lip and said a private prayer as she watched them. They were down the hall from the lounge where she'd taken her turn keeping vigil for Maria's dying declaration.

Come on, Maria. Fight. Lee needs you. Dylan needs you. And I need you to tell me who did this.

Grace was alone, reviewing printouts of tips and leads. She checked her watch when her cell went off, displaying the number for Stan Boulder, her sergeant.

"Grace, we've caught one in North Seattle."

"Is it Dylan?"

"No. An adult. You're the primary and this one's pissing me off already."

"Stan, I can't. It's not looking good here at the hospital. Her family's asking about last rites. I am going to be jammed up."

"Listen, this fresh one may be linked to the Colson case."

"What?"

"I can't go into it now."

"Do we know who the victim is?"

"No, but we know Wade made the find."

"*Jason Wade?* The reporter from the *Mirror?*"

"That's what's pissing me off. How did that jack-off find out?"

"He's a good digger and likes playing detective," Grace replied.

"Well, he's playing with fire. He faces obstruction, if he's holding back information on this case." Boulder paused. "I've got somebody from Vice relieving you now. The scene is 444 Brimerley Lane. You copy that?"

"Got it."

"Get rolling."

The sky had darkened as sector cars from the SPD's North Precinct sealed the bungalow on Brimerley Lane. Uniformed officers stretched yellow tape around the yard.

Officer Kyle Scheel, the first responding uniform, and his partner protected the primary scene inside, then escorted Jason and his dad to wait in the back of their patrol car. Scheel took careful notes, collecting initial statements and information.

Grace arrived, parking her unmarked Malibu amid the tangle of vehicles that had grown to include an ambulance, crime scene investigation vans, satellite trucks and press cars bearing station call letters and newspaper logos. A few residents came to the tape. Mothers kept small children close as they gossiped softly, their faces etched with curiosity, concern, and fear.

"Grace." Perelli waved her over to the responding

officers. After they talked, she started a case log in her notebook and coldly eyed Jason in the backseat of the car.

"I'll get to you later," she told him, then headed for the bungalow's back door with Perelli. Holding up the tape for her, he said, "The uniforms think they chased away most of the rats."

"Not the two-legged one in the car."

They tugged on white latex gloves and shoe covers. The usual gagging stench of a corpse that had been undiscovered for a long time was prevalent. The victim appeared to be a female. Maybe in her late twenties or early thirties, it was hard to say. Decomposition had distorted the face into a grotesque death mask.

A small pond of blood had spread everywhere, laced and smeared by the work of vermin. The bacteria that had built inside the corpse's internal organs had caused the body to swell and discolored the skin tissue. The rats had gone to work on the intestines, which were webbed over the corpse and pulled into every direction on the floor.

Fortunately the rats were gone.

Grace and Perelli sketched the scene and took notes. Using a small digital camera, Grace took scores of photographs of the victim without moving the body.

They looked for a purse, bag, or wallet, anything to suggest who the victim was, but found nothing. She would have to wait for CSI to process everything, Grace thought, taking more photos. Perelli looked around for a wallet or bus pass, anything that might indicate who she was.

"Nothing. At least the hands look good for finger-prints," he said. "Jaw looks good too."

Perelli moved to the mail and bills on the kitchen counter. "Could be one Dorothy M. Hall."

"What do you make of this, Dom?"

"Given the terrible state, I wouldn't put any money on a cause, but it sure as hell looks like someone wanted something pretty bad."

"And how did Clark Kent and his father, the private dick, really know about this place?"

"You don't buy the dad's statement, that he was fol-lowing up on a client's hit-and-run fender bender and took Junior along for the ride?"

"There's got to be more to their story."

Taking stock of the scene, Grace shook her head.

After they'd finished in the house, Grace went into the garage, careful not to further contaminate that scene. When she came out, she talked to David Tanaka and Al Sprung's crew from the King County medical examiner's office and Seattle CSI detectives about gath-ering evidence from the house and processing the garage for any other evidence.

In the backyard, Boulder approached Grace.

"I've got the team going hard on the canvass," Boulder said, paging through his notes. "Not clear who resides here. The property owner is Dorothy Mae Hall, who is eighty-nine, has a severe case of Alzheimer's, and lives in a nursing home a little west of the campus."

"Anything else?"

"Neighbors say over the years, they've seen a younger woman come and go, sometimes stay. They think she takes care of the place. Got people going over records. The 1998 Toyota Corolla in the garage is registered to this address to Dorothy Mae Hall."

"She's not our victim, you think?" Perelli asked.

"Only if the vic is eighty-nine," Boulder said.

"That's not an eighty-nine-year-old woman in there," Grace said.

Boulder nodded to the patrol car with Jason Wade and his father in the back.

"The discovery is tied to them, Grace. I want to know what they know."

32

Grace Garner stepped into the dirt driveway at the side of the bungalow and pointed a white-gloved finger at a uniformed officer.

Detectives were now ready to question Jason Wade and his father. Officer Scheel escorted them to Grace, Dominic Perelli, Stan Boulder, and FBI Special Agent Kirk Dupree, who'd just arrived and insisted on being present. They went to the backyard, to a shaded corner and a wooden picnic table that was in sore need of refinishing.

"How you holding up, Jason?" Grace asked.

"I'm fine. How much longer are you going to keep us? I need to get back to the newsroom."

Signaling that he was in charge, Boulder positioned his right foot on the bench seat next to Jason, invading his space as he stood over him. Boulder's jacket opened, revealing the butt of the gun in his shoulder holster.

"We'll keep you for as long as it takes."

"As long as it takes for what?"

"For you to tell us everything you know about this case," Grace said.

"We already told you everything." Jason's father

looked at her, then at Boulder, who was flipping through his notes.

From the picnic table they saw the medical examiner's team and the crime scene detectives working inside the house. From the thin line of sight they had on the front, Jason noticed the crowd had grown. He saw several lenses at the yellow tape, TV and still cameras trained on him and the others at the picnic table. Above them, a helicopter was approaching.

"Henry, I see you're working toward your three years for licensure as a private investigator in the state of Washington," Boulder said.

"Yes."

"You're with Don Krofton's agency."

"Yes."

"I know Don, he used to be on the job."

"That's right."

"Come to think of it, didn't you used to be on the job, Henry? Long time ago, like when Jesus was a toddler?"

Jason watched a shadow cross his old man's face as he turned away from Boulder's question and looked off at nothing.

"Yes."

Boulder's expression changed almost imperceptibly, with a trace of melancholy, as if he was attempting to place Jason's old man somewhere in a buried corner of his memory. A silent moment passed until Jason's cell interrupted it.

"Jason, it's Spangler—what the hell is happening?"

Boulder grimaced; the volume of Jason's phone was high enough for the conversation to be overheard.

"I can't talk now."

"One of our shooters at this homicide just called and says he sees you, *inside the crime scene?* What the hell is—"

"I can't—I—"

Jason's phone vanished from his hand. Boulder shut it off, then slid it into his breast pocket.

"Hey! Give me that!"

"You better think over how to report this," Boulder said.

"I'm going to report everything I know."

"You might consider holding back on publishing every detail, because the killer might be interested in knowing if they've made any mistakes."

"My job is to report the facts, Sergeant Boulder."

"I'm warning you not to fuck up this case any more than you already have."

"How? By reporting the truth?"

"Let's start there," Grace said. "What exactly were the circumstances that led you to this address?"

"I was investigating a hit-and-run car accident," Henry Wade said. "This was the address that came up for the plate the client provided."

"And why did you bring Jason?" she asked.

"The drive was a chance for us to talk. Father and son."

Boulder smiled after quickly analyzing the statement Henry Wade had given to the responding officer.

"Let's see, it's got nothing to do with Jason's story on the front page of his paper? Got nothing to do with the client's alleged hit-and-run involving a van that occurred in the same neighborhood and at the same time as when Maria Colson was run over and her baby son was abducted?"

Jason's father said nothing.

"Who's your client, Henry?"

"All of our investigations are confidential."

"Horseshit," Boulder said, "I'm going to take you back to when you filled out that application for your private investigator's license, the one that Don Krofton's agency had to sign before employing you."

Jason looked at Boulder, then Grace, for a clue as to where they were headed.

"That first question they ask you on the form there, see if memory serves, goes something like, 'Have you ever been found guilty of divulging confidential information obtained in the course of an investigation to which you were assigned?'"

Boulder grinned and nodded at Jason.

"I bet your agency has access to IVIPS—that's confidential. You're working for a client, Henry, and your boy here makes the find. It *appears* like something confidential got divulged here. He gets a scoop and you risk losing your license, as a trainee. Not the best career move for a man of your years, is it, Henry? But there's a way out of your predicament."

"What do you want?"

"Your client," Boulder said. "Don't make us waste time to get a warrant. Pass it to us now, so we can maybe try to catch a killer—or should we just leave that to you and Jimmy Olsen here?"

Taking in the hard faces of the detectives, Henry

Wade nodded. He'd thought about calling them from the get-go. Something to be said for first instincts.

"I want to cooperate. Let me make a few calls. My file's in my truck. Can I get it?"

"Go with him, Dom," Boulder said, then turned to Jason. "It's been quite a morning for you, hasn't it, sport? You got a little breakfast on your chin there."

33

In Detroit, outside an imposing twenty-first-floor boardroom, a young secretary, her face drawn with worry, rapped on the oak doors. Her voice a whisper, she said, "Excuse me. I'm terribly sorry, Mr. Sinclair—"

She had interrupted Everett Sinclair's key presentation on the final stages of applying the company's El Paso scenario to Detroit-Windsor.

"What is it? Can't you see I'm engaged here?" Sinclair snapped.

"Two gentlemen are here—"

"Who are they?"

"They're FBI agents and they want to talk to you about a major crime in Seattle. They asked for you specifically."

Sinclair's face went red. He was speechless.

In fact, he said little as he rode in the back of a Ford Taurus across Detroit to the FBI's field office in the Patrick V. McNamara Building downtown on Michigan Avenue.

The federal office complex takes up an entire city block and is under twenty-four-hour security. The two agents who located Sinclair escorted him into the elevator and pressed the button for the twenty-sixth floor. He feared his ex-wife had discovered his account in Aruba and had her lawyer contact the FBI. It took several attempts for the agents to convey to Sinclair that the urgency to talk to him arose from the Colson case.

"What's the Colson case?"

As they explained the connection to Krofton and how the agency was cooperating, Sinclair began to believe it might be all true. They were treating him with the utmost respect—but he was wary. He knew federal lawmen could be crafty, to lull you into a false sense of security before hitting you between the eyes with a surprise.

His Aruba account could put him away.

Sinclair kept his guard up.

They led him into a meeting room and immediately pulled up a screen showing detailed maps of the route he had taken through Seattle at the time of his accident. Then they put him on a conference call to Seattle with Homicide Detective Grace Garner, Agent Kirk Dupree, and Ted Parsons, a detective in traffic collision. They walked him through enlarged zone maps showing buildings.

As he recounted the events he realized a problem.

"I don't want my name in the papers. Can you guys arrange that?"

The agents said they would see what they could do. Their chief concern was finding Dylan Colson and the people behind the crimes—the homicide, the abduction, and the hit-and-run.

"So the van that clipped my Mercedes is the one involved in the kidnapping?"

"That's our belief," Grace Garner said.

"Is there a reward?"

"We don't know all the details, sir, only that we have a homicide linked to the abduction of a baby and the assault of his mother when she tried to rescue him."

"So there could be a reward?"

"Tell us again what happened, Mr. Sinclair."

Sinclair repeated the details and they pinpointed his route with times and commercial buildings. He had no idea why one agent kept ticking off certain buildings along the route, not understanding that those buildings had surveillance cameras.

"Again, can you remember anything distinctive about the van, other than how your car got damaged and your suit got ruined?"

Sinclair thought long and hard before it came back to him.

"A palm tree."

"Sir?"

"The van had a small palm tree painted on the lower rear section." He sketched the van's rear, showing a palm tree in the sunset.

34

The Seattle Metro bus driver didn't look at the woman boarding with the baby stroller and dropping her money in the fare box.

His eyes were on his side mirror and the lunatic in a Corvette eating off of his bumper. He didn't need this. Not after yesterday's double shift. First the punks smoking dope on his coach, then a sleeper missed his stop and started screaming hellfire and damnation at him. After waving the 'Vette around him, the driver cursed to himself and they moved on.

The woman sat on a bench seat, where she gave her baby a bottle, then smiled at the two people near her, the first a sweaty, pasty-faced man with hairy arms resting on his tin lunch bucket. His stomach strained his T-shirt, which bore a flowered circle with the words "St. Jude's School—Helping the Challenged."

"Cute baby." The man pushed back his thick, black-framed glasses. "Say Betty, that baby's awfully cute," he said to the woman beside him.

A worn library copy of *Gone With the Wind* lowered, revealing the acne-ravaged face of a middle-aged woman. Her life had been a series of tragedies, tended to daily with vodka-laced coffee.

The woman eyed the baby. It was sucking hard on its bottle but only getting air. The young mother was in a pink top, jeans, and open-toe shoes. Oblivious to the need to adjust the bottle. *Maybe she should enroll at St. Jude's and learn something,* Betty thought.

"She's a cute baby, Warren." The book went back over her face.

"It's a *he*. He's my boy." Nadine beamed.

The baby began fussing but Nadine's attention was on the scenery and her dreams as the bus lumbered along its route. The baby's fussing continued for several more stops. Eventually the child began whimpering until Betty could no longer let things go.

"Adjust the bottle, *he's* getting nothing but air."

"Excuse me?"

"Adjust his bottle, he's not getting any milk."

Nadine glared at her as the baby started to cry.

"Are you saying I don't know how to care for my baby?"

"No, just look at him."

"He's awfully cute," Warren said.

"You're calling me an unfit mother. Admit it."

"What?" The baby's crying intensified, exasperating the woman. "Oh, for heaven's sake." Betty leaned forward and adjusted the baby's bottle.

Nadine thrust her finger a half-inch from Betty's face.

"Keep your fucking filthy hands off of my baby, or I'll kill you."

The bus driver's head raised to his rearview mirror. "There a problem back there?"

Nadine rang the bell and stared hard at the woman. "Want me to tell him you've been drinking, *Betty*?"

Betty shook her head and pulled her bag closer.

Nadine grinned. "No problem," she called to the driver. "None at all." Then she pushed the stroller to the rear door and got off with her baby.

At the mall, Nadine bought new sneakers from a discount bin. Then she shopped a bit, picking up a few things for the baby and herself. Although she wanted to show off her son, no one really paid any attention to her.

That was fine.

Things would soon be different.

On the bus home, Nadine took pains to sit alone. There were so many creeps and sickos in the city. She didn't want any of them near her baby—didn't want to repeat the earlier episode with the fat ugly woman and the sweaty tard boy. It was a quiet ride.

She watched the storefronts flow by. The pizza shops, the hair salons, the appliance stores, funeral homes, the parks, and the neat houses with their beautiful trees and pretty flower gardens. The well-kept homes radiated love; looking at them, Nadine couldn't help but think that soon her life was going to be perfect.

Just perfect.

She revisited her dream plan. It was almost complete.

Once Axel sorted out all the arrangements for his

new job—which should be any day now—they would leave Seattle. They'd settle into a pretty little house, one with a big wraparound porch with hand-carved spindles in the railing. They'd have a big swing where she and Axel would sit on summer nights, sip lemonade, and look up at the stars.

They'd have a pretty yard with a big old shade tree in the back where their son could play. They'd buy him a baseball and a glove and a football and Axel would play catch with him. And on weekends they'd all go for drives into the country for picnics and ice cream, then pick wildflowers and wade in a stream. Birthday parties in their house would be special. Christmas and all the holidays would be perfect, like in the magazines she read at the supermarket checkout.

They were going to be the kind of family Nadine had always dreamed of having. Ever since she was a little girl. And they were going to live in the kind of house she'd seen a million billion times in her mind.

It would have a big fireplace where they would sit and listen to the rain on stormy days, or keep cozy on winter nights. Their house would have a big kitchen where she would make the best home-cooked meals ever, and it would have big bright rooms filled with light.

Filled with love.

Nadine blinked as she looked upon the baby.

It was all so close. Just days away.

When Nadine got home, she was relieved that Axel had not yet returned. Taking the baby into her arms, she called for him as they checked out every room. *Just to be sure.*

"Looks like Daddy's still not home."

Good. Because before Axel had left, he'd ordered Nadine not to leave the house until he got back.

"Mommy doesn't always do what Daddy says, does she? Mommy needed new shoes, some clothes, and some things for you too. Oh, what is it, angel?" The baby began to fuss. Nadine touched her nose to his bottom and frowned. "You got a stinky diaper."

After changing him, she fed him some strained fruit then put him down for a nap.

As he slept, she kept the TVs and radios turned on low, listening for any new developments on that horrible baby abduction. And she resumed cleaning, packing, and humming as she wondered how much longer Axel was going to be. He'd left for a few hours of work early that morning on his friend's motorcycle, telling Nadine not to touch the van. Apparently, something was shot with the carburetor or ignition thingy and he needed to get a new part. He also had some surprise things to take care of.

In bed that morning, she rolled over and watched him pull his jeans up over his muscular frame. One thing Nadine loved about her ex-con was his body. Hard from pumping iron in the yard. It drove her wild.

"How much longer, Axel?"

"A few more days, then we can leave, babe."

"Promise?"

"Promise."

"Axel." She grabbed the waist of his jeans. "Got time to give me a little more?"

"Always got time for that, babe."

Smiling at the memory, Nadine thought she heard him approach. She left her packing and stepped to the window. It was just a truck passing by. She looked to the garage; the way the sunlight hit the side window, she could see a patch of the tarp covering the van. Axel said they'd likely sell it to one of his friends and get a car for their trip, but to load some things into it for the big move.

She closed another cardboard box, taped it, then carried it into the spare room. She got down on her knees and scrawled on it with a felt-tip marker. Sitting back on her legs, she noticed Axel's desk and his laptop computer.

He'd been worrying so hard on his big business deal. Always keeping the problems to himself so she wouldn't have to worry. She blinked. *Hey,* she thought, *he's left his computer on. Funny.* He always shut it off. He'd been working so late into the night, he must've just forgot. She got up and approached the desk with a wicked little thought dancing in her mind. It lifted the corners of her mouth.

Why not snoop through Axel's secret business deal?

He'd been promising to tell her all about it when the time was right. She tapped a nail to her teeth and considered searching his system. She could do it and he'd never know.

Did she want to ruin her own surprise?

She was not sure. Her ears pricked up at the TV and a burst of dramatic music that signaled a news bulletin.

"This is Stephanie London at the Live Eye Satellite

News Desk with a breaking story. We go now live by satellite to North Seattle, where WKKR's David Troy is at the scene of a homicide. David, what can you tell us?"

Nadine stood before the set to watch the bright smile and tanned, handsome face of the reporter.

"Stephanie... there's been a homicide in that bungalow behind me. We know there is one victim inside. Don't know who. Or how they were killed. Or who made the discovery. Crime scene detectives are working on that as we speak. Stephanie, many of the homes in this area are rented here with multiple tenants and roommates. That sort of thing. A lot of people coming and going. People keep to themselves."

"David, we understand there is something a little intriguing about this murder. What can you tell us?"

"That's right, Stephanie. My sources are telling me that Seattle police and the FBI are present here. It's not common to have the feds present at a city murder. The reason for that, according to my sources, is that there are strong indications that this murder is linked to the abduction of Dylan Colson and the assault of his mother Maria in Ballard. Maria Colson is still fighting for her life in the hospital. That's it for now, Stephanie."

"David, thank you. David Troy from North Seattle, at the scene of a homicide police suspect is linked to the Dylan Colson case. We'll have a full report later. Now back to our regular programming."

Nadine's hand covered her mouth at the terrible news. It had to be just horrible for the Colson family.

"Oh well." She shrugged. "It just goes to show you how lying can bring your whole world tumbling down." Nadine resumed packing, humming softly to herself.

DAY FOUR

35

Several hours had passed since Jason Wade had discovered the woman's corpse in north Seattle.

The sun had sunk below the horizon and from the newsroom he could see the red and white lights of traffic streaming along Elliott Avenue, the ferries on the Bay, and the Olympic Mountains.

It was a different scene at his desk and the heap of newspapers, old press releases, empty paper cups. He plucked his notebook out of the mess and flipped to the page with his large scrawl.

Who is she? Who did it? Why? What's the link to Colson?

He tried Seattle PD again.

"Homicide, Beckwith."

"It's Wade at the *Mirror*. You guys confirm the ID on Brimerley yet?"

"We're hoping you and your psychic could tell us, Ace."

"There's plenty I'd like to tell your sergeant."

"I'll put him on."

"Come on, Beckwith. Seriously, anything on Brimerley?"

"Cool your jets, Wade. I'll check if we heard from the M.E."

The sound of Beckwith's hand clamping the phone was followed by his muffled exchange. Seconds later he came back on.

"Nada, pal. Zip. But when you find out, be sure to give us a ringy-dingy, okay?"

Jason hung up and ran his hands through his hair.

He'd calmed down since coming upon the murder scene, and the blood rush in his ears had stopped. But he couldn't push the images of the eviscerated corpse from his mind as he reflected on life, death, and what it all meant to the story he was writing.

Who was the dead woman and how is her murder tied to the case? Did she abduct Dylan Colson? Is there a link to the family?

His attempts to find out had failed.

After leaving Brimerley Lane, he'd gone to the hospital and managed to get a nurse to pass a request to Lee Colson. He came downstairs with his uncle to the cafeteria. Lee shook his head after he'd told him what had happened.

"I already told police, I don't know that neighborhood, or anyone at 444 Brimerley. I'm sorry for the family, but if it has anything to do with my son, I hope it leads to his safe return. That's all I have to say."

Now, as he wrote the last half of his story, Jason looked across the newsroom and saw Fritz Spangler—loosening his tie, stepping from his office, studying a yellow legal notepad—striding toward him.

"Wade, I've read your story. It's not strong enough."

"What do you mean?"

"You've go to hit it harder. Switch to first person. Take the reader into the murder house with you. Be graphic. Visceral even. I like what you told me about the rats. Use it. Make readers feel and smell the scene in all of its grisly horror."

"Isn't that crossing a line? I mean, think of her family. Think of kids who might read this at the breakfast table."

"Too bad. The woman's dead. And we're not the city's babysitter. This is our line drive out of the ballpark. No one can touch us. It eclipses our little hiccup with the psychic. If we're controversial, all the better."

"I think we're overreacting."

"We're in a circulation war. If we lose, it's the death of the *Mirror*. We're getting publicity you can't buy. Do you realize that all afternoon TV's been reporting how you made the discovery and calling for interview requests? They want you to describe what you saw for their viewers. They want to know if it was the psychic that led you to the house—isn't this great?"

"I haven't heard anything on this."

"That's because we've been screening the calls and refusing all interviews until tomorrow. We're going to make sure that people read about it first in the *Mirror*. We're going to maximize our news value here. We're going to clobber the *Times* and the *Post-Intelligencer*. The *Mirror*'s clearly out front on this story. I talked to the circulation people. We're doing up a poster card with your face flagging our scoop for every street box.

We're going to boost our pressrun by fifty thousand, possibly seventy-five. Write the hell out of this story, Wade. There's a lot at stake. Do you understand?"

He understood all right. The place had gone insane. Shaking his head, Jason reworked his article, as per Spangler's orders. He stopped short of turning it into a lurid, tabloidy account of "The House That Dripped Blood," or "Rats Ripped Her Flesh."

Scrolling through his work, he was reminded of the fact his old man was the reason the *Mirror* had this story. And that Boulder had threatened to take away his private investigator's license.

Hell, Boulder had even sniffed around at the old police mystery his dad kept locked away from the world. On the drive back to the paper, Jason took a chance and had pressed Henry on it and was shocked when he actually started to answer him.

"As a cop you get to know a lot of secrets about people. Some you wish you never knew but have to live with for the rest of your life."

"Like what, Dad?"

His old man just stared ahead.

"Just don't ask. Christ, Jay, don't ever ask me."

It ended right there with Jason wondering if Boulder knew, what with his talk to take away his old man's license. Because for an ugly moment at the scene, the stakes got pretty high for his old man.

Had it gone bad, it might've started him drinking again.

Fortunately, Krofton knew Boulder and stood up for Jason's dad. Calls were made. The agency explained things to Sinclair and calmed him down after his meeting with the FBI in Detroit. In the end, Krofton was cool with it all because he said it proved his agency was topflight in investigations, helping the police on a major case and all. It made the agency look good.

Jason had just begun polishing the last few paragraphs when his line rang.

"Wade."

"It's Grace Garner. You got a minute?"

For a second or two he guessed at the reason for her call. Maybe an ID had been made?

"Sure."

"Not over the phone. Someplace quiet for a face-to-face."

"Now?"

"Yes, it won't take long."

Pete Anthony's Grill was a twenty-four-hour Greek diner. Slivered into a south downtown sidestreet amid warehouses near the waterfront, it was almost out of sight.

It had a low, black-beamed ceiling, black oak paneling, dark hardwood floors, and lights that dropped down low, creating halos over each table.

Grace was alone in a back booth, private with high-back seats, stirring tea. After settling in across from her, Jason checked his watch, then ordered a Coke.

"What's this about?"

"You'll keep it totally off the record?"

"Depends. You called me."

"It has to be off the record. Nothing I say here is used. We never had this meeting."

"Fine."

"Your word."

"Yes."

"I trust you. After meeting your editor and everything that happened before and after, I still think we could work together."

"Did Boulder send you?"

Offense flashed in her eyes.

"No one knows I'm here."

He searched her face for any hint of an ulterior motive. Looking into her eyes, up close like this, was nice.

"Okay, what is it?"

"Look, I want to try to work together on this. You impressed the unit with the stuff you come up with. Sure, it ticks them off, but you dig. Today, with your dad, well… sorry about that."

"You're not playing good cop to Boulder, are you, Grace?"

"Would you drop that?"

"Got an ID on Brimerley?"

"No, that won't come until tomorrow. After an autopsy."

"Any idea who she is, her story, that kind of thing?"

"No."

"You guys find sneakers, like the kind you pulled out of the abduction in Ballard?"

Grace shook her head.

"Any trace of Dylan Colson?"

"Nothing yet, everything's preliminary, the CSI people are just getting started. Tell me, what do you think about the Colsons?"

Grace's question surprised him.

"I don't know. By all accounts they seem like fine, upstanding people. Why?"

Grace shrugged.

"How's Maria doing? She going to survive?"

"Family's talking about last rites with a priest. Don't you dare print that."

"Why are you asking me about the Colsons? What do you suspect?"

"I don't know."

"Well, how does this homicide factor into everything? You think someone killed your Jane Doe for her license plates?"

"Don't know."

"Well." Jason glanced at his watch. "It's been nice, Grace."

"Wait. I need to ask you something, a favor."

"You can ask."

"If you get a tip at the paper, will you consider sharing?"

"As long as you do the same for me?"

Grace nodded.

"As long as it doesn't risk my case. Listen, we may have something coming, like before, only bigger this time, and I want to work with you."

"What do you mean?"

"Something we need to put out."

"You want to use me."

"No. I want to work directly with you."

"Why?"

She looked at him for a long, lingering moment.

"Your reporting on this case is strongest and it's my feeling that the people behind the abduction and murder follow your stories closely."

Jason listened.

"Through you, I think we can communicate directly to them."

He stared at her, at the stress and intensity in her eyes.

"Jason, I'm risking a lot here. I'm a lead detective on a multiagency investigation with the FBI. This has to stay just between me and you."

"You won't even tell Boulder?"

"No. And you don't tell Spangler."

"Just you and me, Grace. Deal."

They shook hands. It was the first time they'd touched. Something passed between them as Jason detected the promise of a smile on her face.

36

The morning after Jason Wade found the murdered woman on Brimerley Lane, her nakcd corpse lay on a stainless steel tray in the autopsy room of the King County Medical Examiner's Office.

It was in the Harborview Medical Center, downtown near the bay. Posted on the wall outside the Chief M.E.'s office was a credo. Part of it went, "The innocent shall be exonerated; murder shall be recognized." Grace Garner considered it now as she looked upon the victim.

Female. White. Five feet five inches. One hundred twenty-one pounds. Approximately thirty years of age.

Who was she?

Her ID *still* had not been confirmed. Fingerprints taken from her corpse were being bounced through AFIS, the Washington Highway Patrol, and a number of other databases. Eight possibles had surfaced, none confirmed. To ensure a visual match hadn't been missed, Grace pushed for the prints to be reprocessed.

She also traced the Toyota's VIN number to point of purchase. It lead to a series of subsequent private sales that ended with Dorothy Mae Hall, the eighty-nine-year-old woman who owned the house.

Dorothy Mae Hall's profile offered no leads on family that would point to the murder victim. The possibility that aliases were used, or identities stolen, was one theory.

Crime Scene was going 24-7 processing the house, the car, the property for anything leading to Dylan Colson and the homicide. So far, nothing had surfaced that would place Dylan at the address

Grace needed the dead woman's ID so she could pursue its link to Dylan's abduction and his mother's looming murder. Their initial canvass was a bust. Neighbors did not really know the people at the Brimerley Lane house. Or so they said. And the victim's face was too disfigured for a photo to be of any use.

As she adjusted her surgical mask, hairnet, and latex gloves, Grace stared hard at the corpse.

Who are you? Why did your life end this way?

She grappled with her questions and her own private fears that rose each time she witnessed an autopsy—especially those of women her age. It didn't matter if they were a schoolteacher, a hooker, a lawyer, a nun, an abused wife, or a homeless heroin addict. The taking of a woman's life forced her to secretly question her own.

Would she die alone?

Would she die with no children, no family, just a lonely woman too terrified to connect with anybody? Unless she did something about it, that was her destiny.

Why?

Because she believed the school shooting was her fault.

Counselor after counselor had failed to purge Grace

of her guilt. After all of these years, she still blamed herself for that day. God, why couldn't she let it go? Maybe she needed to let someone into her life to help push the crap out. For a moment she thought of Jason.

"Ready, Grace?"

David Tanaka, the pathologist, and Al Sprung, his assistant, had suited up and were set to begin. The M.E.'s office had six other deaths to process that morning. An apparent electrocution, a suicide, an overdose, a gang shooting, an elderly couple who died in a house fire.

Given that the Brimerley case was a homicide linked to the abduction of a Seattle baby and the possible murder of his mother, Grace's client was the priority.

Big-time.

Tanaka, a short, intense man, and Sprung, who could be a defensive back for the Seahawks, had already put in long, hard hours. They had meticulously processed the body at the Brimerley house before it was placed into a body bag, put on a gurney, rolled into the van, and delivered to the center.

At the M.E.'s office the body was weighed and tagged. All of the clothing was removed, then the body was X-rayed and photographed. Grace's brow creased as she examined the woman's chest and the scores of wounds.

Stabbing.

Off the top, she counted forty.

"She's been in the house for two weeks at least," Tanaka said to Sprung.

"Two weeks for sure," Sprung agreed as they set out

to work. "The rats have cleaned out her stomach, so it's unlikely we'll get a clear idea of its contents and her last meal."

Grace didn't like witnessing autopsies. She didn't like the coldness of the room; the smells of ammonia and formaldehyde; the odor of organs, their meaty shades of pink and red; the popping sound when the calvarium was removed, opening the skull to reveal the brain and dura; or seeing the primary Y incision in the chest as the pathologist worked through the identification, the external and internal examination of the body. She tried to keep up with Tanaka and Sprung, who also consulted the X-ray.

"Here." Sprung pointed a rubber-gloved finger. "A piece of the blade tip broke off around the spine. Some of the wounds, a good number, actually, went right through her."

Tanaka showed Grace how the victim had fought back.

"See the defensive wounds on her hands, the deep gash in her palms. She tried to grab the knife."

When the autopsy was completed, Grace and Perelli met with Tanaka in his office. He had a spider plant and a huge print of Monet's *Garden Path at Giverny*. He consulted his computer and worked quietly, inputting data, checking charts and other files, before his chair swiveled.

"In my opinion, Grace, cause of death is attributed to one of at least seventy incised and stabbed wounds."

"At least seventy?"

"It is impossible to count and detail them all. But

I'll break it down. There are about ten to the face and head, ten to the neck, thirty to the chest and stomach area, and some twenty incised wounds on both her hands, defensive wounds. And, as I'd mentioned, of that number, I'd estimate twenty wounds were penetrating."

"Jesus Christ."

"Judging from the wound tracks, the cleavage, the thrust, I'd say your killer is left-handed. I'd say this was a direct-approach attack; not a blitz from behind, but a confrontational one. It would appear the victim put up a fight from the blood spray patterns. She would have sustained many of the injuries while standing, I'd say a third, judging from the entry points. The remainder would have been sustained while she was on the floor. Are you still looking for the knife?"

"Yes."

"Well, it's serrated, maybe an eight- to ten-inch blade, with a hilt that would have a pattern like this, see?" Tanaka drew three parallel lines. "Crime Scene might help there. And"—he pivoted to his computer and checked data—"I'd put time of death at approximately two weeks ago."

"But, David." Grace looked at her notes. "At least *seventy* stab wounds?"

Nodding thoughtfully, Tanaka stroked the shadow of a Vandyke on his chin.

"It's overkill. A frenzied attack. Indicative of someone whose rage is right off the charts."

Grace took a moment to absorb his analysis.

"I'm just trying to get my head around it and decide

if this woman is an innocent victim, or had some role to play in all of this."

Tanaka's computer emitted a soft pong. He turned to check his e-mail.

"Ah, this might help. Our Jane Doe now has a name," he said, pointing at his monitor.

Grace stood and stepped closer to Tanaka's monitor, jotting down the info from the AFIS coordinator. Fingerprints confirmed the identity of the homicide victim at Brimerley Lane as

Beth Ann Bannon. DOB 02/10/74
Height: 5 feet 5 inches. Weight: 126 pounds
Eye Color: Blue. Hair Color: Brown
Address: 6099 60th Street N.E., Seattle, WA

37

After leaving the medical examiner's office, Grace and Perelli stood at the side door of a neat-as-a-pin bungalow that was sheltered by a grove of mature trees.

Grace was about to press the buzzer a second time when a woman in a beige sweater and matching slacks answered.

"Yes, can I help you?"

"I'm Detective Garner, this is Detective Perelli. Seattle Police."

They held out IDs.

"Police?"

"Does Beth Bannon reside at this address?"

"Yes. Well, she used to. Is something wrong?"

"May we come in, please?"

Stepping inside, Grace estimated the woman to be in her forties. She had a kind, attractive face. Intelligent eyes. Her home was immaculate, with oak floors, a sofa and matching love seat in the spacious living room where they sat. The air was pleasant with the aroma of something in the oven. *Cookies?* It was a relief from the autopsy room.

"We need to confirm your name, ma'am." Perelli opened his notebook.

"Vanessa Harlow."

"And you are the homeowner here?"

"Yes. Please, what's this about?"

"And where are you employed?"

"At the university. I'm an administrative assistant in the history department."

Grace opened a file folder to a clear color image from Beth Bannon's driver's license. Not homely, not pretty either. Plain. The kind of face you'd easily miss in a crowd.

"Can you confirm for us who this is?"

"That's Beth." Vanessa nodded, her face growing pale. "I'm feeling uncomfortable and you're making me worry. Was there an accident?"

Grace exchanged a quick look with Perelli, then took a quick inventory of Vanessa's tasteful home and how it smelled of baking. Taking stock of this quiet, private woman whose friend was on a tray in the cooler in the morgue, her body covered with stab wounds; knowing the savage way she'd died; how the rats had traveled from the vacant lot to feed on her corpse; and how this case was linked to Dylan Colson, Grace moved closer to Vanessa and took her shoulder.

"There is no easy way to tell you this, but Beth's been killed."

"What? No."

"She was found murdered yesterday."

"*Murdered!* Oh God! I don't understand. Dear Lord. Why?"

"That's what we're trying to find out."

"No. Who would hurt her? This has to be a mistake!"

Vanessa turned away but did not leave. Her soft crying and the ticking of her grandmother's clock on the mantel were the only sounds in her house. Long minutes passed until the oven timer beeped.

Grace rose and switched it off as Vanessa collected herself.

"Vanessa"—Grace moved a box of tissues near her—"when was the last time you spoke with Beth?"

"About a week ago. She called me."

"What did she talk about?"

"She was worried about Dorothy. Dorothy Hall, the woman whose house she took care of. Dorothy's in a home. She's nearly ninety and very sick. Is that where you found Beth? In Dorothy's house?"

"Yes. So Beth was house-sitting for Dorothy?"

"They'd met a few years ago through Beth's church and became friends. That's when Beth kind of moved out of here to take care of Dorothy's house and things."

Perelli made notes, then asked, "Did Beth ever talk about Lee or Maria Colson?"

"Lee or Maria Colson? Colson? You mean the couple whose baby was abducted?" Vanessa glanced at her blank television screen.

The detectives nodded.

"Why? No, I don't think she knows them."

"Did she ever talk about financial problems, or debts?" Grace asked.

"No. Money was never a concern for her as far as I know."

"She use drugs or gamble?"

"Beth? No."

"Do you know if she had any enemies, anyone who would want to harm her?"

"My Lord, no. Beth's a kind, gentle person. An unassuming person."

"Tell us about her background, please."

"We met several years ago at the university. She was a secretary, a newlywed. But after her marriage failed, she was devastated and I invited her to move in with me. My husband died of a heart attack years ago."

"What about Beth's ex?"

"I think he moved back to Virginia. I think he's with the Army and may have been posted overseas."

"Can you get his name for us?"

"Yes, I think so."

"They have kids?"

"No."

"She remarry, or date? Any boyfriends?"

"No."

"Can you tell us a little more about her personality, her jobs?"

"She's always busy with her volunteer work, charity groups, works a lot. I think she helps at hospitals. I think she worked part-time with a temp agency. Before that, long ago, I think she worked in a law office, maybe a social service agency, and a bank. I liked having her as a roommate. We were good company for each other."

"Why did she move out?"

"Well, she didn't move out entirely. She got to know Dorothy through her charity work at the church and they became close. All of Dorothy's family had passed and it seemed Beth was Dorothy's only friend in the world. Dorothy loved her house on Brimerley and did not want it sold. She wanted Beth to live there and that's what she did. Sort of lived there and here, because, well, I liked having her here too."

Grace and Perelli glanced around.

"Vanessa," Perelli said, "we'd like you to write down a list of all the places where Beth worked or volunteered. We know that several years back she worked at the Eagle Pacific Bank because that's where she was finger-printed."

Vanessa took Perelli's notebook and pen and wrote down the names of businesses and organizations, putting question marks next to those she was not certain of.

"May we look in Beth's room?" Grace asked.

Vanessa said Beth hadn't been in it for months but got up and took them there. It was neat, smelled fragrant. A single bed. Some clothes, a photo album, cards, letters, papers, shoes. The detectives put on latex gloves as they looked through the items, deciding they'd get CSI to go through everything. Flipping through the photo albums, pages crackling from the lamination, Grace asked about Beth's marriage.

"Do you know why it failed, Vanessa?"

"Who knows the real reason, but I suspect it had something to do with the fact she couldn't have children."

Grace's head snapped up. She looked at Perelli, then back to Vanessa.

"She *couldn't* have kids?"

"I think," Vanessa said, "that's the reason she did a lot of volunteer work with hospitals and expectant moms. So she could be near babies."

38

Nadine is in her twenties.

She's pregnant and alone on the subway platform.

The ground trembles and her face is trapped in the intense headlight.

Should she jump in front of the train?

Nadine didn't understand. He said he loved her. Promised that they would get married. But when she told him about the baby, surprised him with the wonderful news that she was pregnant, her world stopped.

"Get rid of it."

That was all he said.

Get rid of it?

How could he ask her to do such an evil thing?

She refused. She was keeping her baby.

Her parents, well, the God-fearing people who'd raised her after Big Pearl died, were ashamed. "A child out of wedlock. It's a sin, Nadine. A horrible sin. You're not smart enough to raise a baby. You have to go away and give it up for adoption."

She went away and gave birth to a boy. A beautiful baby boy who filled her empty life with light.

His adoptive mother was so happy.

But Nadine had her own plans for her son.

Her baby.

Because she loved her baby and her baby loved her back.

He'll be mine forever.

Forever.

39

The answers were in there.

Somewhere.

Kay Cataldo, a senior forensic scientist with the Seattle Police Crime Scene Unit, downed the last of her cold coffee and studied the evidence inventory sheets for the umpteenth time.

Her team had been going flat-out, 24-7, at the support facility at Airport Way South, a former office and warehouse complex the city had renovated after the earthquake in 2001. It was also where the Washington State Patrol operated one of the state's busiest full-service crime labs.

Cataldo's small CSI unit worked with the Patrol's forensic people, the FBI, the scientists at the University of Washington, and the King County Medical Examiner's Office.

Boy oh boy, we appreciate the help today, she thought.

Since Dylan Colson's abduction, Cataldo had existed on what, like three hours' sleep a day? Now, with Beth Bannon's homicide and its suspected link to Colson, the pressure for CSI to process a mountain of material and yield a key lead increased by the minute.

"The people downtown wanted it yesterday," Cataldo's boss had told her, "but anything we get needs to be airtight for court. Just do your best, kiddo."

Glancing at the clock, she exhaled slowly.

Kay Cataldo was a thirty-eight-year-old mother of two. Her husband was a naval officer on a nuclear sub, gone for months at a time. She was a member of the PTA. After her family and work, she loved F. Scott Fitzgerald and Steinbeck. She had green eyes, wore frameless glasses, and walked at a brisk pace that made her white lab coat flap. Soft-spoken, Cataldo let her work do the talking for her.

She was an expert latent fingerprint examiner. She'd also, after many long nights and weekends, obtained two degrees in forensic science. The courts considered her qualified to give expert testimony on a range of physical evidence—which she did. In some forty cases and counting. She'd also served in several senior positions in national criminalists' associations.

Her workstation looked and smelled like a high school chemistry classroom. The corkboard above her desk held honors, certificates, the American Society Crime Laboratory Directors seal, snapshots of her at Disneyland with her husband, their seven-year-old daughter, and five-year-old son. Magic times. Cataldo blinked at them; missing them; thinking of Dylan Colson, Maria, and Beth Bannon, she dug into the work done so far and the work Cataldo's team needed to do.

They'd set other ongoing cases aside for Colson, which they were still processing. Now with Bannon, they had to process the house, garage, car, and property at Brimerly. Add to that Bannon's room at the Ravenna duplex.

Cataldo tried coming at it all again. In the Bannon case, they knew the what. Beth Bannon had been stabbed to death at a residence she'd maintained and where she'd occasionally resided. Plates from the vehicle registered to the address had been identified on the red 2002 Chrysler Town & Country minivan suspected in the Colson abduction. The van's rear door had a small customized mural showing the sun and trees.

It all stopped there.

Nothing on which to build a case of any worth.

Was there a link—a rock-solid link—to Colson? Nothing concrete on which to build a case had emerged so far. Nothing indicating a baby had been present at the scene.

What about Beth Bannon's murder? Any trace? Anything in the way of DNA? Well, so far, according to Tanaka, there was no indication of any sexual assault, no semen, no fluid or DNA transfer.

And they hadn't found the murder weapon.

Flipping through the pages, Cataldo came at it from another angle.

The answers had to be in here.

Somewhere.

The link to Beth Bannon's killer would emerge. It always did. And that should take them closer to getting to the truth behind Colson.

Be positive.

It was going to be hard. Neither Bannon's purse nor wallet had been found. In fact, nothing identifying her had been found in the house. It was as if it had all been collected. Strange. Fortunately, Bannon's ID had been confirmed through her prints taken from her job at the bank.

It was a start. It was something. But they had a long way to go and a whack of evidence to analyze. They were scrutinizing the carpets in the house and the car, doing some XRF work on elements found in carpet fibers.

Much of the world Cataldo worked in was microscopic, ruled by her scanning electron microscope-energy dispersion X-ray analyzer, which could find traces of critical evidence that were virtually invisible.

She came back to the analysis of blood-splatter patterns, and the findings. Bannon's blood was A-positive. No other types were detected. There were some foot impressions in the blood, but they either were not usable or had turned out to be Jason Wade's, the reporter who found the body. Without thinking he'd walked in the killer's steps. Obscuring the shoeprints, except—hold on, what was that?

Cataldo was reviewing crime scene photos she had blown up on her computer. *What* is *this?* She'd come to a shoe impression, one where Jason's shoe was only partly transposed over the killer's.

A couple of clicks on her computer and the underlying impression, a large portion of it, grew before her eyes on her big flat-screen monitor. Could be familiar. Could it be?

Cataldo switched back to an image of the shoe identified in the Colson abduction. *Do we have a match?*

Hard to say at this stage. The impression is not clear.
Cataldo made notes. *Not ready to swear to this yet, but
I'm liking this enough to ask the FBI for help.*

Right now, she needed coffee.

When she was on her way to the kitchen, Vic Tucker,
a senior scientist, unshaven and looking rough, passed
her a stack of files as thick as the Seattle white pages.
All of it concerned the house, the property, the car, or
Dorothy Mae Hall.

"Haven't slept in nineteen hours, Kay. Going to the
lounge. Could you double-check these, please? Give
them priority over the priority."

Cataldo would get back to the shoes shortly. Tucker's
files contained a lot of documents. Mostly bills.
Nothing special. Much of it had been dusted or scoped
and had yielded nothing. Cataldo took them to her
workbench and set out to review Tucker's work.

Because most of the CSI and forensics people were
usually exhausted, they checked and triple-checked
each other's work. It was a good system, she thought,
meticulously reviewing the papers in each file folder.

In this case, Tucker had gone through bills, invoices,
and junk mail. He had mistakenly included an empty
folder in the pile. He hadn't indicated a single thing in
his assessment notes on this folder. Maybe he made a
mistake. Fine. Cataldo flipped to the next file folder.

Hold it. What was that?

The empty folder opened and an image flashed by.
The manila folder was empty but there was something—writing or an imprint—on the inside. *Tucker
had cleared this one. Had not made any notes. He was*

too burned out and had missed this one. Had missed the evidence inside. Something—written? No. Cataldo's white-gloved fingers opened it wide. *Here it is. An image of some sort.* She turned the folder quickly. It had once held an envelope, a business-size envelope.

The envelope was missing.

But it somehow had left an impression, as if the ink on it had bled and created a ghostly reverse image of an address or something. Cataldo produced a mirror. The image was so faded. Darn it. She killed the immediate lights and used a direct, intense halogen to see the impression clearly.

The return address was for The United National Trucker's Newsletter. It was from—just a second, it was faded. There, St. Louis, Missouri.

Postmark blurred, but from St. Louis. Date was really obscured, but if Cataldo had to guess, looked like two years ago. American flag stamp. The "to" address was very faded, but she could just make it out.

Lee Colson
104 Shale Street
Seattle, WA

And as Cataldo read it, the significance rolled over her. *Whoa. How does Lee Colson's home address end up here? Wait, there's something else, a notation near it. A brief, handwritten note:*

Follow up with payment.

Cataldo stopped breathing.

Holy flying cow.

Tones sounded as Kay Cataldo's latex-covered forefinger pressed the numbers for Grace Garner's cell phone.

40

"**W**hy would anyone want to hurt Beth? It doesn't make sense."

Jason Wade gave the woman who'd phoned him time to compose herself as he looked at Beth Bannon's picture.

A few hours ago, Seattle Homicide had put out a press release identifying Beth Ann Bannon as the victim on Brimerley Lane. It came in the wake of his exclusive hitting the streets, his account of how he'd found Beth Bannon's corpse.

It was lined across the *Mirror*'s front page.

His story, and the press release, led to a squall of radio and TV bulletins as reporters scrambled to learn more about Beth Bannon and how her murder was linked to the Colson case.

The *Mirror* was getting a lot of calls.

Some complained about Jason's "disgusting story." Some offered condolences for Beth Bannon and wanted to send flowers. Some, fans of TV cop shows, had advice for the police. None of the callers really knew much about anything.

Until now.

The woman on the line had identified herself only as Sylvia, a former bank teller who'd worked with Beth several years ago. She'd called him, asking for any more details on the murder while he pushed delicately for information on Beth Bannon's background.

"I know this is a terrible tragedy, Sylvia, but what more can you tell me about her?" he asked.

"She was a deeply sensitive person, very quiet."

"Was she married?"

"Divorced."

Jason made a note to get the records.

"And her husband?"

"Military."

"Did she have a boyfriend?"

"I don't know," Sylvia replied.

"She have family?"

"I don't think she had any living relatives at all."

"What about her connection to the house and home-owner?"

"I don't know anything about that."

"I see." Jason tapped his pen on his desk. "Sylvia, do you think Beth's connected to the Colsons in any way?"

"I don't know."

"Do you know if she was ever pregnant, or had kids?"

There was a long silence.

"Sylvia?"

"Beth couldn't have children."

"Oh?"

"I think that was the reason for her divorce."

Jason took rapid notes.

"Did she want children?"

"More than anything, at least that's what she told me."

"Then she must've had some connection to the Colsons. I mean, there has to be something, right?"

Several moments passed.

"Sylvia?"

"I don't know. I really don't know anything. I've just been speculating. Guessing. I'm very upset, please don't print anything I've told you. I think I've said too much."

The line went dead in his hand.

He stared at Beth Bannon's face, the woman he'd found desecrated in a North Seattle home. All he knew about her life was in the inked lines jotted on one page of the spiral-bound notebook sitting atop today's *Mirror*. He'd called Grace, but she had nothing. Not even a hint of something more.

"Keep in touch," was all she'd said.

So much for working together, sharing and caring and all that bull.

Jason drove out to the house in Ravenna. Vanessa Harlow was not talking to the press. He'd talked to friends and neighbors, the staff at the nursing home where Dorothy Hall resided.

Zip.

He'd called the Colsons' relatives, friends at the towing company and supermarket. No one had heard of Beth Bannon. And nothing had surfaced from the news library's search directories and databases. No hits so far.

Back in the newsroom, Jason continued studying the news release and Beth Ann Bannon staring back at him from the color head-and-shoulders shot police had released from her driver's license. A friendly, vulnerable-looking woman.

He chewed over his call from Sylvia. Beth couldn't have children. It led to a divorce. She wanted children. Man, that had to be it. The pieces were there. Why was she killed? Why were the plates stolen and used on the van that took Dylan?

Beth Bannon's murder remained a mystery.

"What the hell are you doing sitting here, Wade?"

Fritz Spangler approached his desk just as Jason's phone began ringing.

"Get your ass on the street."

"I've been out."

"Go back out. You can't break news sitting there. I want Bannon's life story by today's deadline."

The phone continued ringing.

"Excuse me, I have to take this."

"Jason, it's Ann Chandler in classified, just got a strange message for you from a public phone, according to caller ID. Want to hear it?"

"You bet, thanks."

"The caller said to tell Jason Wade to meet her at the south end of the food court by the pizza place at the mall off of Jackson in one hour for information on Beth Bannon."

"This person leave a name, number, or anything?"

"Nope. Just a nervous-sounding woman. I'd put her in her thirties."

"She sound crazy or drunk, Ann?"

"Not at all. Sounded pretty sharp, actually."

Jason slid on his jacket and headed to the parking lot. Some forty minutes later, while approaching the mall's main entrance, he saw his face in the card placed in *Mirror* boxes, promoting his story. Whoever wanted to meet him would have no trouble spotting him.

The food court was crowded but he managed to find a seat at the appointed spot. After he had waited for some ten minutes, someone from behind touched his shoulder.

He turned to find a woman in a white ball cap, dark glasses. His pulse picked up. She was pushing a stroller with a little girl. Jason was not great at the ages of toddlers but put this one at two, maybe.

What the hell's up with this? he wondered.

The woman had an attractive figure. Early thirties. At their table, she removed her hat and glasses. She was striking. Light hair, beautiful cut, smooth skin. She had to be fairly well off, he figured.

"Thank you for coming."

"Sure."

"I apologize for this secrecy stuff." She had a pretty smile. "I don't live in this area at all. Anyway, I won't take much of your time."

"I don't have much."

"I saw the horrible thing that happened on the news yesterday," she said. "It came out this morning that it was Beth and I read how you had found her, *my God*. I've been wrestling with this and not thinking too clearly. My husband has no idea that I'm doing this."

Silence passed as she tried to sort out her thoughts.

"I knew Beth."

Jason let her fill the silence.

"Beth had a secret life."

Jason hesitated.

"A secret life?"

"Yes."

"How do you know?"

"My daughter and I were part of it."

41

The headline linking the murder in North Seattle to the Colson case was lined across the front page of the *Seattle Mirror*.

The corner store clerk repeated herself.

"Will that be everything, sir?"

Axel pulled his attention from the paper and bought a Coke, Twinkies, copies of the *Times* and the *P-I*, which he'd struggled not to read as he walked back to the house. He was on fire to know what the *Mirror* had from its reporter, Jason Wade, who'd discovered the body.

How the hell could they connect the murder to the baby?

Axel shut the door to his workroom, where he devoured every word, exercising self-control until the part about the plate forced him to sit up.

The license plate?

Jesus.

The pages rustled as he tossed them aside and tromped across the yard to the garage. *What the hell happened? The license plate was linked to the homicide? How?* His keys jingled as he worked one into the case-hardened steel lock to the garage.

Dust specks swirled in the light spilling through the gaps of the rickety wooden walls as he raised the huge canvas cover at the van's rear. Bending his knees, he squatted to examine the license plate.

Reality hit him like a blow to his stomach.

He didn't recognize this Washington State plate. It was not the good plate—*the safe plate*—that his friend had given him when he first got the van. He looked toward the house.

What the hell did Nadine do?

He snapped the canvas back. More dust swirled, forcing him to spit and blame himself for not checking the plate after Nadine had grabbed the kid. How could he be so sloppy?

How could she be so stupid?

He returned to the house seething. *What the hell did Nadine do?* He had to work faster to end this. It couldn't go on like this. The heat was now so intense it was burning him up. At any moment the police would be at the door. They were coming. He could feel it.

His pulse thumping, he returned to his desk, firing up his computer, going online, searching for the answers, for the solution that would save him. He needed a little more time to pull this off.

Nadine's humming floated from down the hall in the baby's room.

And there she went again. Humming.

She's insane.

Her humming mocked him. He'd paid an enormous price to salvage what was left of his sorry life and that psycho bitch was destroying him.

Humming while she did it.

Just keep humming, darlin'. Axel's going to fix everything just right, you'll see. He looked toward the closet where he'd hidden her white sneakers and other things.

Just wait.

He turned up the volume on the small TV in his office. Channel 77's Live Scene Team had a breaking news bulletin. A woman's face appeared on the screen. Looked like a driver's license photo. Details were in the ticker crawling across the bottom of the screen. *North Seattle Homicide Victim Identified as Beth Ann Bannon.*

"Chuck Lopez reporting for Channel 77's Live Scene Team."

Beth Bannon? Who was that? He didn't know a Beth Bannon.

A knock sounded on his door. Nadine was standing there, holding Dylan Colson in her arms.

"Hi, honey. Oh, look. See, daddy's working hard."

Concern creased Axel's face as he eyed the TV, then Nadine.

"We're sorry to disturb your work." Her attention swept his desk, his computer, newspapers, and notes. He glared at her as she held her thumb and forefinger close together. "We just have one teeny tiny question."

He waited for it.

"When are we going to leave, Ax? I'm packing some things and was curious. Are you close to finishing your big deal thingy?"

His breathing came harder, flaring his nostrils.

"We're all really excited to get to our new—"

"Nadine," he cut her off. "Who's Beth Bannon?"

"Who?"

He indicated the TV with the victim's picture filling the screen.

"Her?" Nadine shifted the baby in her arms, her attention razor-sharp, eyes going to the TV then to Axel's computer, resuming her subtle inventory of his work. "She's just another liar. A real bad one."

"What do you mean?"

"Axel, I don't want to talk about it. Not in front of our baby."

He was trying to consider what he should do here when his computer beeped. He had a new e-mail, but he ignored it for now.

"You didn't answer my question, Axel. How much longer?"

"Not long."

"Good. I believe you. I know you love me. I know you're going to keep your promise and take us far away to start our new happy life. Because you'd never lie to me. Right?"

"Sure, babe."

Nadine smiled.

"I'll let you read your e-mail and get back to work." She closed the door.

Alone again, he opened his e-mail. It was long and detailed. Reading it, his stomach lifted. It was exactly what he needed to know. And there was more.

A phone number. But it was bear-trapped. Coded. Meaning he had to adjust each digit in a certain direction to decipher the true number. Starting with the area code.

This was good.

If he hurried he could pull this off.

42

The Malibu's V-6 growled as Grace wheeled it from the support building's lot on Airport Way.

After assessing Kay Cataldo's discovery, it took Grace and Perelli about one second to take their next step.

Confront Lee Colson.

Dark clouds had rolled in from the Pacific as the Chevy cut across Seattle heading for the hospital in Ballard. Perelli's nose was in the file Cataldo had flagged and copied for them. "It ain't looking good, Gracie." Perelli closed the folder to stare at the traffic and trouble ahead. "Not one bit."

Grace admitted that the new evidence had hardened her attitude toward Lee Colson. But it was inevitable. As with most homicides, the whole story never emerged at the outset. Nobody ever told the truth the first time. Cases were never as simple as they are on TV. There were always complications.

She glanced at the skyline, gleaming against the silver-gray clouds, letting go of the thread of optimism she'd held for this case. Guess she was wrong to think this one would somehow be different, just because a baby was involved. Taking stock of the city she asked herself the same question she'd asked every fifteen seconds.

Where's Dylan?

At the hospital they badged their way up to the intensive care unit. Maria Colson's condition was deteriorating, Agnes Filby, the detective who was keeping vigil for a declaration, informed Grace.

The duty nurse directed them to the hospital chapel, where Colson's relatives were clustered in the hall.

"Lee's inside talking to Father Orsen. He needs time alone with him."

"We need to talk to Lee now," Grace said.

The colors from the stained glass window were vivid and in sharp contrast to the somber air, redolent with the scent of candle wax and the wood polish used on the oak pews. Colson, his head bowed, was nodding as the priest spoke softly, stopping when the detectives interrupted them.

"Excuse us, Father." Perelli displayed his ID. "We need a moment alone with Lee."

Anticipating the worst for Colson, the priest stood.

"Perhaps I should stay, for Lee's benefit?"

Perelli gave his head a small shake, telegraphing that no, they hadn't found Dylan. "It's not like that." Perelli held up the file.

"We just need a few minutes," Grace said.

Father Orsen nodded, touching Colson's shoulder.

"I'll just be outside with your family, Lee."

Grace waited until they heard the soft bump of

the chapel door, then began flipping through her notebook.

"Did you find my son?"

"No, Lee, everyone's doing all they can."

"I think I'm going to lose my wife." Colson cupped his face in his hands.

Perelli and Grace exchanged glances. This had to be done.

"Lee, we need to be certain about some things relating to Beth Bannon and need your help. Do you think you can help us?"

"I don't know."

Perelli placed a large color photocopy of Bannon's driver's license photo on the pew, the same picture released to the press that morning.

"Do you know her?"

"No. I already told you."

"Is it possible that you may have met her in some capacity?"

Colson shook his head.

"What about the location of the homicide on Brimerley Lane in North Seattle? Do you know the address, or would you have had reason to ever be in the neighborhood?"

Perelli placed a photocopied page of a Seattle city map on the pew.

"I know the city, I've never been there. I don't know anyone there."

Grace looked at Perelli, then at Colson.

"Lee, look at me and think about your answer. Again, do you know Beth Bannon, or the address?"

Colson's whiskered face tightened with worry lines. He glared at both detectives, his eyes rimmed red with anguish.

"For the last goddammed time, I told you, no! Now why the hell are you asking me these questions when you should be out there looking for my son?"

The chapel door cracked and one of Colson's uncles stuck his head in. Perelli raised his hand, signaling the relative to back off.

The door closed.

"Lower your voice," Grace said. "We're going to show you something."

Perelli placed an enlarged photocopy of the reverse image of the envelope, with the evidence inventory and case number along the bottom.

"Tell us about this, Lee. It's your name, your home address, and a personal note about a payment."

Colson stared at it, blinking, thinking. He looked at Grace, then Perelli, as if expecting them to provide an answer.

"We found this in Bannon's house, Lee," Grace said, "so I'm going to ask you again: do you know Beth Bannon?"

Colson swallowed hard.

43

Across the city from where Grace and Perelli were questioning Lee Colson, Washington State Patrol criminalist Jim Wood was processing the 1998 Toyota Corolla from the murder scene.

The car was clean and Wood started wrapping up his work with a sense of defeat because he'd failed to extract a single piece of helpful evidence, other than the fact that someone had removed the plates.

Big deal. We already knew that from that reporter from the Mirror.

It was when Wood came to the last items on his list that he hit on something. He was helping Kay Cataldo's crew at the Airport Way facility and like everyone else assigned to the Colson case, he'd been going full bore.

But he'd taken Dylan Colson's abduction personally, because he and his wife, Ruth, just had their first child six months ago. Wood took the long hours in stride. He was used to functioning on little sleep, just like he'd gotten used to the whine of the jetliners landing and taking off next door at Sea-Tac International. Actually, he was deaf to them as he worked on the Toyota, a process that had started at the scene and continued when the car was moved to the garage.

At Brimerley Lane, Wood had followed his meticulous routine. He'd examined the Toyota in the scene environment, then covered the car, had it placed on a flatbed and transferred to the garage at Airport Way, where he processed it for any fingerprints, hair, fiber, trace.

He'd started with the usual areas inside, like the door handles, rearview mirror, seat-belt buckles, windows, dash. For the exterior, he processed the gas door, gas cap, trunk, windows, hood, support posts, wheel wells.

Through his efforts, Wood pulled usable latents, but after quick examination, eliminated them.

They belonged to Beth Bannon and Dorothy Mae Hall.

Frustrated, Wood went a step further. Something he'd learned from working cases with border agents. He put the car up on the hoist and examined its undercarriage, beginning with the bumpers.

That's when he got a hit.

A combination of patent and molded prints in the grime of the inner front bumper, protected from the elements, from car washes, rain, and wear. They were new, not among the elimination set for the Bannon homicide.

"What do you think, Kay?" Wood stood over her shoulder.

Cataldo blinked at the large flat-screen monitor displaying magnified prints. She studied the arches, whorls, and loops and confirmed what she'd suspected.

Nothing fit with the elimination set from the Bannon garage scene, the kitchen, or the Ravenna location. Yet they were familiar. She went to a different computer drive.

Wood's eyes widened as he recognized the file of elimination prints taken from the Colson home in Ballard. Cataldo's monitor displayed a split screen, enlarging a print from Ballard and the new print from the car. Automatically, Wood and Cataldo, expert analysts, began comparing all the minutiae points.

They quickly began counting up the clear points of comparison where the two samples matched. Most courts required ten to fifteen clear point matches.

In no time at all, Cataldo had jotted down twelve and was still counting, knowing that one divergent point instantly eliminated a print. By the time she'd compared the left slanting patterns from the last finger, they were up to nineteen clear points of comparison.

It was a match.

"Your print on the car belongs to Lee Colson," she said.

"Wow. And the hits just keep on coming."

Cataldo considered the mounting evidence.

"Lee's envelope is in Beth Bannon's house. His prints are on her car." Cataldo shook her head. "Lee, Lee, Lee, what the heck is going on?"

She reached for her phone to make a call.

She knew Grace's number by heart.

44

Grace found Lee Colson's face in the rearview mirror as the Malibu's wipers slapped against the drizzle. She and Perelli were taking him to headquarters.

"I don't understand why you're doing this, now," Colson said to the mirror. "Tell me, what's going on? You found my son. That's the truth, isn't it? You didn't want to tell me back there, you need me to ident—"

Grace watched a rivulet meander frantically down the windshield before the wipers got it.

"No, we're still looking for Dylan. It's just that we have a few new things we need to be clear on."

"What new things? Tell me! Did you find my son?" She didn't turn her head.

"It's best we talk downtown."

Colson's distraught face betrayed little, Grace thought, stealing glimpses of it as she drove, not sure what to think of him since taking Kay Cataldo's second call. The fact was, hard evidence was mounting against him, forcing Grace to suspect that maybe Colson had been playing everyone. Part of her didn't believe it.

The rest of the ride was subdued, aside from the rhythmic beating of the wipers and the hiss of the Chevy's tires.

No one spoke at headquarters as the elevator ascended to the Homicide Unit on the seventh floor, where Grace led Colson into an interview room.

It was stark and smelled as if something stale had refused to leave. One of the chalk-colored cinder-block walls held a window with mirrored glass that reflected the barren table, metal chairs, and Lee Colson's haggard face when he sat down.

"Coffee?"

He shrugged.

A moment later, she set down a mug with the phrase "Nothing but the truth—the whole truth" engraved on it. A long-standing joke from a long-retired old-school detective. *"Sets the tone nicely for our guests, don't ya think?"*

FBI Special Agent Kirk Dupree entered; a chair scraped on the floor as he turned it, sat on it backward, rolled up his sleeves, nodded at Colson. Perelli's shadow crossed over them as he entered, slapped a file on the table, and sat down. Colson took stock of the faces eyeing him, as the small room seemed to swell. Perelli removed Beth Bannon's color blow-up from her driver's license and spun it around for Colson.

"Let's start from square one again. Do you know this woman?"

"No."

"Have you ever met her, or do you think Maria might have met her in some capacity?" Grace asked.

"If she did, I'm not sure she would've told me. How would we know this woman?"

"That's what we need to clarify."

Perelli slid CSI's color enlargement of the envelope impression before Colson. "What's this personal note doing at the location where Beth Bannon was murdered, huh? *'Follow up with payment.'* Payment for what, Lee?"

Colson stared at it, then shook his head.

"I told you I just don't know."

Next, Perelli displayed a photo spread of the 1998 Toyota Corolla.

"This car familiar to you?"

Colson shrugged.

"I'm a tow truck operator, thousands of cars and trucks are familiar to me."

Perelli then slid an enlarged photo of the car's front bumper, showing the shadow impression of where the plate was.

"You see here, the plate's missing. You know from the news stories the plate from this car, from the Bannon residence, was identified as being on the van we suspect was used in Dylan's abduction. You follow me?"

Colson nodded.

"What we want you to tell us is how this is all connected to you."

"I don't know."

Grace studied Colson's body language, his facial expressions, his breathing, how he focused his eyes, the frequency of lip licking, swallowing, every muscle tic and twitch.

Dupree eyed Colson clinically as Perelli rolled his sleeves up, revealing a series of tattoos from his time in USMC. "Semper Fi" blazed from his forearm.

"This is the time to tell us what you know, Lee," Perelli said. "What happened with Beth Bannon? And are there other people involved?"

"God, I don't know."

With crack-whip speed Perelli's hand slapped down hard on the table, making Colson flinch.

"You're lying!"

Perelli then displayed half a dozen graphic photos of Bannon's corpse splayed on the kitchen floor. Streams of dried blood oozed in all directions, intestines appeared as if they'd exploded from her stomach. Colson shut his eyes and turned away.

"Were you banging her?" Dupree asked.

"What?"

"Were you screwing Beth Bannon?"

"I don't even know her, I swear."

"How does she fit into this?"

"Don't you know? Why're you asking me?"

"What does 'Follow up with payment' mean, Lee?"

"I told you, I don't know."

"Was Beth somehow part of a plan to raise a reward, split it with you for your business, huh?" Perelli said. "There have to be others, who are they?"

"I don't understand any of this. I think maybe I need a lawyer."

"You *think* you need one. Before we get to that, just hold on."

"You people don't make any sense. I just can't believe this."

Grace was uneasy but knew this was critical because Lee's answers were not consistent with the evidence connecting him to Bannon. It was disturbing because her instincts had ruled Lee out.

Dupree broke his silence and kicked things up.

"Things just got out of hand, right?" he said. "You didn't count on Maria jumping on the van. She wasn't supposed to get hurt. It was just supposed to be a clean grab. Raise a reward, return your baby, and later cash in for your business. Let's see, last we checked there's what? Something like twenty-three thousand put up."

"Which brings us to the next question, Lee," Perelli said. "Where's the baby?"

Colson shook his head, eyes stinging, biting his bottom lip.

"You bastards!" He stood. "You stupid bastards! My son's abducted in broad daylight, my wife's going to die. You come at me like this as I'm discussing her last rites with a priest, and you think I had something to do with the whole thing because I want to own a fucking tow truck business. I can't believe you!"

Perelli stood eye to eye with him, invading his space.

"Your prints are all over the car. We can't believe you!"

"What?"

"There are a lot of things that just don't add up here."

Colson turned to Grace, his eyes pleading for her to

believe him. She opened a folder and slid an enlarged photo of the fingerprints found on the front bumper.

"These are your fingerprints, Lee." Grace stared hard into Colson's face, searching for the answers, but it was a vain pursuit. His shoulders dropped; he turned away and groaned.

"Know what?" Perelli shoved a stick of gum into his mouth. "We're going to give you a little alone time, to think it all over, look at the pictures. Maybe something will jog your memory."

The detectives joined Boulder and McCusker, who'd been watching and listening from the other side of the mirrored window.

"What do you think?" Boulder said.

"I don't know what to think," Grace said.

"What about the canvass on Bannon?" McCusker asked.

"We got people out canvassing and recanvassing," Boulder said. "We still don't know much about her. She was house-sitting, had a series of clerical and administrative jobs. Kind of a quiet, mousy type. A churchgoer."

"Grace, what do you think?"

"Could be circumstantial."

"But his prints on the car? And the plate was stolen from the car and put on the van—that's what brought Jason to the find."

"We're starting to draw a lot of pressure from upstairs to get a break on this thing. Baby gone, mother dying, and now a murder. We need a point on the board for our side," Boulder said.

"Go back on his original time line, take it back to cover the M.E.'s estimated time of death. Go hard again on the night before the kid was grabbed. He was out on a call in the north, remember? See if that means anything, or nothing. Double-check e-mail and phone records, see if Lee or Beth or Maria ever talked to each other."

"What do you think?"

"Could be circumstantial, could be a noose tightening," Perelli said.

"I don't know," Grace said. "I just don't know. My gut is not clear on him."

"You believe Lee, Grace?"

"It just doesn't fit."

"There's one thing we're going to do to find out," McCusker said. "We've already made arrangements, set it in motion, so it should move fast."

45

"Beth Bannon had a secret life?"

The woman sitting across from Jason took her time answering. She blinked several times, thrust her face into her hands and exhaled. The baby in the stroller was content, chewing on the drool-slicked ear of a rubber bunny. The toy's molded grin beamed at Jason.

"And you were part of this secret life?" he continued.

The woman cleared her throat.

"I'm scared to death," she said. "With what's happened, and my doing this. It's dangerous for me meeting you like this. I know it's crazy but—oh God. I'm terrified."

"Take it easy."

She nodded.

"You have information on the case?" Jason asked.

The woman nodded. Jason began regretting how he'd forgotten to alert the photo desk. He was out here alone, no pictures to back him up this time.

"Why didn't you just call me?"

"I needed to know if I could trust you. I needed to see your face to find out if I could trust you. I needed to do this in person so that I could be certain you understand."

"Understand what?"

"What it is I know about Beth and how it relates to me."

"Why not go to the police?"

"I just can't."

"Why?"

She gazed at the streams of shoppers in the busy mall, oblivious to them.

"It's so complicated. It could ruin our lives if things were misunderstood."

"What things, please?"

"I'm sorry. Listen, you can't use my name."

"You haven't given me your name."

"You have to understand, even my husband doesn't know I'm doing this. Swear to me you won't identify me in any way and in anything you write."

"I won't identify you in any way just as long as you help me verify whatever it is you tell me."

After giving his condition consideration, she bit her bottom lip, then opened her bag, a Gucci bag, found her Gucci wallet, then caressed the baby's head.

"This is Emily, our daughter. She's our world. The center of our universe."

Then the woman showed him Emily's birth certificate. Emily Ann Montgomery. Then her own driver's license. Joy Montgomery.

"See? I am her mother."

Somewhat puzzled, he nodded.

"A few years ago I thought my life was over. My

husband and I were boating. I collided with a small boat while water-skiing. I broke a lot of bones in my pelvic area. The doctors told me I'd never have children."

Joy's attention had traveled back to the event.

"It nearly destroyed me, my husband, our marriage. There was the guilt over the accident and its consequences. At the time, we were planning our family. Our business was excelling, our investments were taking off. I couldn't understand why this was happening. We're not bad people. We didn't do anything wrong, so why us? We went through a lot of counseling, support groups, church groups, everything."

"What about in vitro, surrogate, adoption options?"

She nodded.

"We examined them all. In vitro was out for us."

"So adoption was how you got your daughter?"

Joy smiled at Emily and nodded.

"So how is this tied to Beth Bannon and her murder?"

"I'm coming to that. First, how much do you know about adoptions in Washington State?"

"Not much."

There were several types of adoption, she said, those that went through public or government agencies and those arranged through licensed private agencies.

"We learned quickly that with public or private agency adoptions you were scrutinized and assessed, and there were waiting lists that could take years."

She paused to reflect.

"This all compounded the anguish, the stress. There are so many laws and regulations. There are preplacement assessments, which are unbearable because every aspect of your life is examined. Your beliefs, everything. You worry to death, thinking, what if you were not deemed suitable? And in some cases, it was the birth parent who had a say on an adoptive family."

"And you went through all of that."

Joy nodded.

"It was horrible. We did everything we were supposed to do. Took the courses; at one agency we submitted to lie-detector and drug tests. We're decent, law-abiding people who just wanted a child. But it went on and on, and it was not getting us any closer to having a baby."

"Aren't there, like, independent adoptions too?"

Joy nodded.

"It's how I met Beth Bannon. One night I went alone to a church-sponsored support group for, well, people like us."

"Why did you go alone?"

"My husband had given up. The whole thing was taking a toll on him, the business, on us. Our marriage was really straining. That night after the session, I had barely made it into the hallway when I lost it, just completely lost it. I remember it was in a high school and I'd slammed my back against a locker and slid to the floor utterly lost and devastated."

"Kinda hit rock bottom."

The woman blinked and nodded.

"Then this young woman, Beth Bannon, appeared. She began consoling me. We went for coffee and talked. We opened up to each other. She said she couldn't have kids, was alone in her life, and even considered becoming a nun until she had a temp position with a small law firm that handled private adoptions."

Jason began making notes as Joy continued.

"Beth told me how she'd learned about the process, but more important, about the anguish of childless people who ached to be parents. She was so compassionate. Understanding. She said the law firm closed after the lawyer passed away, She went on to another job, secretary at some company, but she'd decided she wanted to keep helping people who needed to adopt, that it was a secret calling that gave her life meaning."

"What do you mean?"

"Well, she told me she was kind of like an unlicensed facilitator who helped connect people who yearned to adopt with pregnant women who could not give their baby a good home."

"Like a black market, or something. Isn't that illegal?"

"No, it was all done legally. Beth just helped connect people."

"Did she get a huge fee as a baby broker?"

Joy shook her head.

"No, she was a good person. Beth never asked us for a penny."

"Really?"

"Swear to God. She told me that she did this secretly, that she went to support groups, clubs, hospitals, looking for people who wanted a child. That's how she found me."

"What happened after she found you?"

"She linked us to a young girl from a farm family in California, who'd just arrived in Seattle to stay with an aunt. Beth knew of her from church. The girl was in no position to raise a child and agreed to let us adopt. The decree was signed and that's how we got Emily. We gave Beth and the woman money for expenses, but I think Beth gave her entire share to the girl."

A few moments passed in silence as Jason took notes.

"Tell me again how Beth Bannon found pregnant girls."

"She told me that she had confidential contacts who helped find girls and connect them with adoptive parents. Sometimes it all happened in a matter of weeks, depending on when the mother was due."

"Did you ever meet the Colsons?"

"No. I don't know them. First I'd heard of them was through the news. Then when I heard the news just now about"—Joy hesitated—"about what happened to Beth, I couldn't live with myself without someone knowing that she was an angel, the angel who saved our lives by helping us find Emily."

Jason looked hard into Joy's eyes.

"You should go to the police."

"No, it's complicated, that's why I'm telling you. You have the information. But swear to me you'll keep our name out of the paper, for Emily's sake."

"All right. But tell me, Joy, who would want Beth dead? Was it an adoption gone wrong? A young mother who changed her mind?"

Joy shook her head.

"I don't know why anyone would want to harm her."

"What do you think her connection is to the Colson case? The plate in the abduction led to her place in North Seattle."

"I don't know, you'd have to ask Lee Colson that question."

"I already did. He says he doesn't know Beth Bannon, that her murder's got nothing to do with his family or the case."

"And you believe him?"

"What do you mean, Joy?"

"Everyone's got secrets, Jason."

46

Grace Garner returned to the Homicide Unit's interview room alone, sat across from Lee Colson, and searched his exhausted, worried face.

"Lee," she began, "what you're telling us doesn't fit with the evidence."

"I want to see Maria."

"I understand. I just called Swedish. Her condition's stabilized for the moment. Listen to me, we need to rule you out as having any possible involvement in any crime here."

Colson started shaking his head.

"I just— What the hell do you want from me?"

"Will you agree to take a polygraph?"

Colson stared at her.

"It's only a tool, but it'll help us. It'll help everyone."

Colson looked at his hands. Rough, callused, workingman's hands, a father's hands, gentle when he played with his son, Dylan. God, he would do anything to hold him again.

Anything.

Colson raised his head to meet himself in the

mirrored glass, clearing his throat for the benefit of the detectives he figured were on the other side of it.

"I've got nothing to hide. If it'll help find Dylan, I'll do it."

Grace nodded.

"I have to tell you certain things first, because the law requires it."

"What things?"

"You have the right to remain silent…"

Jarred Sandel, four years out of Yale, was with Stein, Brewster and Follis, a midsize firm specializing in criminal law. He'd been following the Colson case and had agreed to represent Lee Colson during the polygraph. The initial fee would come in at just under two thousand dollars.

After receiving the call, Sandel juggled appointments and immediately hurried to the Seattle Police Homicide Unit. He met with Colson, then was briefed by the investigators and Paula Florres, who was with the King County Prosecuting Attorney's Office, before again meeting in private with his client.

Sandel flipped through his yellow legal pad and his extensive notes, then assured Colson, "Lee, the results of the polygraph will be inadmissible. The evidence they have is all circumstantial. Try to relax and tell the truth. Then they'll cross you off their suspect list."

Suspect? How had his life come to this?

Because of urgency and resource availability, it was decided between the Seattle Police and the FBI that the Bureau would conduct the Colson session.

FBI Special Agent Bob Heppler got the call.

Six feet five inches tall, he was an imposing figure, but when people spoke with him for the first time, their unease usually evaporated.

Heppler's blue eyes twinkled behind his frameless glasses and he had the calming demeanor of a gentle giant; one that was more in keeping with a Little League coach or a sheriff from a sleepy town who knew everyone's name, rather than that of an FBI polygraphist.

While Heppler was known for putting his subjects at ease, he was legendary for helping the Bureau clear some of its biggest investigations. In three separate instances, suspects ultimately confessed to him.

Bob Heppler was a master of his craft.

Prior to giving the FBI nineteen years "and counting," he had been a polygraph examiner with the Central Intelligence Agency. But he never went into the details of his time there.

Heppler was a devout Mormon, active in his church. He and his wife had raised four daughters and put them all through college. They were contemplating retirement property in New Mexico when McCusker reached him at home. It was Bob's day off, but the boss needed him to come in.

"Be there in thirty minutes, sir."

Upon arriving, Heppler met with Grace, Dupree, and the lead investigators on the Colson abduction and Bannon homicide. The detectives confidentially revealed to him every aspect of their cases in order for him to prepare to examine his subject.

Then Heppler met with Lee Colson and his attorney, explaining the process of "preparing Lee for a polygraph examination." Heppler's polite, pleasant manner contrasted with the magnitude of what awaited Colson, as the agent familiarized him with his machine.

The polygraph would use instruments connected near Lee's heart and fingertips to electronically measure respiratory activity, galvanic skin reflex, blood pressure, pulse rate, breathing rate, and perspiration, recording the responses on a moving chart as he answered questions.

"I'll ask the questions and I'll analyze the results," Heppler said. "When I'm done, I'll give the investigators one of three possible answers: the subject is truthful, the subject is untruthful, or the results are inconclusive."

Heppler had given his little preparatory talk many times.

"I'm fully aware and expect you to be nervous." He smiled, making notes with an FBI pen as he conducted the pretest interview, then discussed pretest questions.

About an hour later, Heppler positioned Lee in a comfortable chair moved from the floor's reception area and began connecting him to the instrumentation of his machine, making a point of sharing how he was trying the new versions of the Trustline and the Factfinder models of polygraphs.

The examination began casually with routine establishing questions and Heppler went over various areas repeatedly, as the ink needles scratched the graph paper, then it pinballed between mundane questions and hardballs.

"Why have you agreed to the examination, sir?"

"To help find my son, Dylan."

How the hell had his life come to this? His son stolen, his wife dying, a woman murdered, and police suspecting him. How does your life come to this?

"Lee? For this next aspect, I'd like you to answer only 'yes' or 'no.' All right?"

"Yes."

"Are you involved in any way in your son's disappearance?"

"No."

"Have you ever harmed your son?"

"No."

Heppler's glasses had slipped down his nose as he made notations on the graph paper.

"Have you ever harmed your wife?"

"No."

"Do you know Beth Ann Bannon, the woman murdered in North Seattle?"

"I—don't know. I—"

"Answer yes or no, please."

"No."

"Have you ever had occasion to visit the residence on Brimerley Lane where Beth Ann Bannon was murdered?"

"No."

"Have you ever had reason to touch the vehicle, a 1998 Toyota Corolla, associated with the crime scene?"

"I don't know."

"Answer yes or no, please."

"No."

"Did you ever encounter Beth Ann Bannon on a professional or social basis?"

"No."

"After your marriage, did you ever have sexual relations with anyone besides your wife?"

"No."

"Did you ever have sexual relations with Beth Ann Bannon?"

"No."

"Are you employed as a tow truck operator?"

"Yes."

"Do you desire to establish your own tow truck business?"

"Yes."

"Do you have the financial resources to realize your desire?"

"No."

Heppler made tiny indecipherable notations on the graph paper.

"Did you and your wife endure a long period where you believed you could not have a child naturally?"

The chart needles tremored.

"Yes."

"Did you once tell someone that you would do anything to see that you and your wife had a child?"

"Yes."

"Did you ever meet Beth Ann Bannon?"

God, he was going round and round with the same questions, Lee thought.

"I honestly don't know."

"Answer yes or no, please."

"No."

"Did you know Beth Ann Bannon longed to have children of her own?"

"No."

"Did you arrange in any way to have your son abducted?"

Tears were stinging Colson's eyes.

"No."

More notations and a pause.

"Did you harm your wife?"

Colson did not answer. Ten seconds passed. The needles scratched. Ten seconds. Heppler, watching the graph, repeated the question.

"Lee, did you harm your wife? Answer yes or no, please."

"No."

"Do you know Beth Ann Bannon's friends or associates?"

"No."

"Do you know why your fingerprints are on the 1998 Toyota Corolla found at the murder scene?"

The needles swiped the page.

"No."

"Do you know how your home address with a personal note naming you came to be in the residence where Beth Ann Bannon was murdered?"

"No."

"Did you kill Beth Ann Bannon?"

The needles swayed wildly.

"No."

Heppler's questions followed the same pattern and

rhythm deep into the afternoon. It wasn't until early evening that they finished and he began disconnecting Lee from the polygraph.

Grace, Dupree, and the senior investigators had watched the process unseen from the other side of the mirrored window.

"I won't have the results analyzed for several hours," Heppler told them when they debriefed in another room.

"What's your gut tell you, Bob?" McCusker asked.

"It tells me to analyze the results carefully."

After Heppler had left, Sandel emerged.

"Is my client under arrest, or charged with anything?"

"No, we'll take him back to the hospital to be with his wife," said Grace.

During the drive, Grace searched Lee Colson's face in the rearview mirror of her unmarked Malibu and wrestled with her suspicions.

Is he involved? Is there more to this?

She gazed across Seattle as dusk settled over it and lights sparkled throughout the city. Glimpsing Colson, she knew in her heart that sooner or later, she was going to learn the truth about Lee Colson and Beth Bannon.

Her only hope was that when it came, it would not be too late.

47

"It's time, Nadine," Axel said.

Yes. It was really happening. Her dream was coming true.

She was in the kitchen feeding the baby. Axel had finished working on his computer and was gripping a suitcase.

"I'll bring the car to the side, so we can start loading it," he said.

After she'd finished in the kitchen, Nadine washed the baby's face. Then she grabbed some of the things she'd gathered earlier and followed Axel outside.

In the darkness, they packed the small Ford they'd rented for the trip. The air was so still, as if the world had stopped to hold its breath. Nadine's heart began beating faster as she went in and out of the house fetching more bags to put into the car.

She'd put Dylan on the soft grass where he could watch. As they packed, she stole glimpses of him, her angel, then Axel. Her man, their protector. Her hero. He seemed to be watching her more intently now, underscoring what was at stake and how far they'd come together.

No need to worry.

Nadine's dream was coming true.

Everything was almost perfect.

She had her baby, she had Axel, and they were going far away to start their new life together. She looked up at the stars and her heart swelled. She took Dylan into her arms and told him how it was going to be.

Repeating her dream. Every detail the same.

Like a comforting prayer.

They were going to move into a beautiful little house with a big wraparound porch with hand-carved spindles in the railing. They'd have a big porch swing...

After Nadine put Dylan in his car seat, she concentrated on making sure she didn't forget anything. Everything had to be perfect. They were so close to the life she'd yearned for, *the life she was owed.* Soon they would leave this city of lies for the shores of paradise, just like an old song she knew.

Going through the house, Nadine dragged her forearm across her moist brow as she started a final inventory to ensure nothing was overlooked.

Passing Axel's office, she stopped.

His computer was still not packed. It was open and running, a few papers spread over his desk. *Isn't that like a man, messy, forgetful,* she thought, walking around his worktable. Should she close it up? Maybe he was doing a few last-minute things. She began to read—

"Nadine!"

She stepped to the window and saw him looking up at her.

"What are you doing up there?"

"Making sure we have everything."

"We're done."

"But your computer?"

"Get down here, I want to show you something. Hurry up."

Joining Axel outside by the car, Nadine glanced around for Dylan.

"Where's the baby, Axel?"

"In the garage, come on."

"The garage?"

"Come on, I have a surprise for you."

In the few steps it took to reach the garage, Nadine's eyes went to the door, closed but unchained and unlocked. She puzzled over Axel's surprise. What could it be? And why did he move the baby to the garage?

What was Axel planning?

Her stomach fluttered as she stepped inside and under the harsh light of a naked hundred-watt bulb. In an instant, she saw the tarp had been removed from the van. And she knew.

She saw Dylan in his car seat, tiny hands balled into fists, working on his eyes as she inhaled the fumes, felt the vapors, the overwhelming pungent, choking odor.

Gasoline.

She sensed Axel behind her, heard the door close.

48

Jason Wade was running out of time.

He sat at his desk staring at his monitor and the story he'd drafted. This thing was a ballbuster. As promised, he'd kept his word and kept Joy Montgomery's name out of it. But the piece was based on her revelations about Beth Bannon's secret life as some sort of guardian angel baby dealer.

It was dynamite stuff.

Exclusive.

He would kill the *Times* and the *Post-Intelligencer*. But he couldn't use it. Not the way it was. He needed a second source to back him up and so far his efforts to find one had failed.

The newsroom clock was sweeping his deadline closer.

Lights across Elliott Bay blinked as dusk fell over the city and he picked up his phone to call Grace Garner. It had been ten minutes since he'd tried to reach her. Where the hell was she? He'd left messages on her office line and cell phone. Even tried paging her through communications.

No luck.

All right. He took a deep breath and analyzed his situation. He needed Grace to work out a deal. If she'd confirm police either "are investigating" or "would investigate" what the *Mirror* had learned about Beth Bannon's life, his story would have official validation.

A green light.

And if he didn't reach Grace?

Plan B.

He'd go back to the supermarket girls, Pam and Candice. Push them on his Beth Bannon angle. What was it they'd told him? He flipped through his notebook. Maria had *"a hell of a time getting pregnant... one time the doctor told her she'd never conceive.... Maria was baby crazy... Lee would do anything for her."*

They might know something more.

But there was a risk his exclusive could be repeated back to the competition if they were trolling the community for leads, updates. The supermarket cashiers could say: "Oh, yeah, the *Mirror* called us and they said there was something about Beth Bannon dealing in babies."

Stealing thunder.

It happened.

"Wade!" Fritz Spangler had returned from his late meeting upstairs on circulation and staffing levels. "Print off whatever you've written and meet me in my office. I gotta take a whiz."

Minutes later, Spangler's expression tightened as he finished reading Jason's draft.

"I want this on page one of tomorrow's paper."

Spangler jabbed an extension for Beale, the night editor. "Vic, Metro's got a Colson story coming for front and you're going to want to line it."

After hanging up, Spangler clicked his pen and began editing the piece.

"This takes the Colson tragedy to the next level. It raises disturbing questions. The implications are huge and we're out front. Damn, this is evocative of that California case where the guy killed his pregnant wife after cheating on her."

"But you're going to let me get a second source before we go, right?"

"We have to go with it now."

"But we need a second source. I've been calling all over the place. Look at the time, we're going to miss first edition."

Spangler checked his watch, then said, "We're walking a tightrope with it the way it is, I know. But until you hear more, this is what we do." His pen tip touched Jason's notes and rearranged grafs, changed words. "We'll frame it as a situational and weave in your exclusive as speculation from the community, rather than confirmation. It's safe, still powerful, and keeps us in front."

"I don't know."

"What's to know? Just do it. Listen, the mother's knocking on heaven's door. We've got a murder mystery with a baby broker. The kid's missing. The old man's not looking good in light of what you've dug up here."

Jason was weighing everything against the deadline

when Spangler flipped him a business card of someone based in Manhattan with several crossed-out and penned-in numbers.

"This will help. Call him, get a few quotes, it'll firm up the piece."

"Clay Wilson?"

"He's a retired homicide detective who wrote a textbook on homicide investigation. I'm surprised it's not on your desk. Wilson consults and lectures. Larry King's had him on a few times. Call Wilson, lay out what you have, and he'll give you great quotes on theory. If you get him now, you've got time to fix the story for page one. I'll call front and buy you more time."

After striking out in New York, Jason reached Wilson at his cabin on the shore of Broken Heart Lake in northern Ontario near the Minnesota border. Clay Wilson agreed to be quoted. After listening carefully to everything, he asked Jason a few questions, then gave him his theoretical analysis.

"This casts a suspicious light on everyone connected to the case. I would go back to Lee Colson's time line and any evidence while continuing to build a resumé on the murder victim. It is unlikely that the Colsons' family history, with respect to children and the victim's activities, are entirely coincidental."

With an eye on the time, Jason took rapid notes.

"Finally, if the lead investigators have not already done so, I would think they would request Lee Colson submit to a polygraph examination. It's SOP."

Jason worked fast, rewriting the story, making his

deadline with no time to spare. He ran his hands through his hair and tried to concentrate on the next steps when his line rang.

"It's Garner."

"Grace, I've been trying to reach you, listen."

He told her everything he'd dug up on Beth Bannon's secret life as a baby broker, then requested her to confirm what he had, thinking that he would rewrite the story for later editions, making it even stronger. But her response caught him by surprise.

"You've got to delay running that story."

"What?"

A tense silence passed and Grace dropped her voice.

"Please, Jason. Hold it for one day."

"I can't." He glanced at the clock. "It's too late."

"I thought we had a deal? A deal to work together."

"Christ, Grace, what is it? If you've got a major break and want me to hold a story I enterprised, then you have to tell me everything."

He could hear her grip tightening on her phone as a drop of sweat trickled down his back.

"Later this afternoon we learned about Beth Bannon's past too, through recanvassing and a call to our anonymous tipster line."

"Then we're good. I don't understand."

"There's much more that you don't know. Prior to that, CSI confirmed some key fact evidence at the Brimerley scene."

"What sort?"

"Damning."

"Damning against who?"

"All I can say is that we're continuing to talk to Lee Colson—"

"Jesus, Grace—you're looking at Lee for this?"

"It's preliminary, with a lot of loose ends that we've got to sort out. Your story is one major piece—you run that now, it could damage our case."

"Did you charge him?"

"No."

"Does he have a lawyer?"

"Yes."

"Did you polygraph him?"

"I can't—"

"I think you did, Grace. I think you hooked him up to a lie detector and he failed and you've got questions about your evidence and Beth Bannon's link to this. Am I right?"

Jason looked at the clock, calculating time to deadline.

"He agreed to a polygraph," Grace said. "We're looking at the results. We're not done yet."

"And you've got damning evidence?"

She didn't answer.

"Damning evidence against him? Against Lee Colson?"

"Jason, none of this is on the record or usable. I swear, you cannot use this. Do you understand? I'm risking my case, my job. I could be charged for jeopardizing the case, Jason! Do you understand?"

"I understand."

"Swear to me."

"I swear, so what do we do?"

"Hold your story for one day, and I'll do all I can to confirm much of what I told you and give you more, if I can. That's my word."

"Grace, this is out of my control."

"I'm not censoring you. If you run the Beth Bannon stuff it'll damage the case."

"It's not my job to help you make a case, it's my job to report the truth. Besides, how do I know the other papers don't have what I have on Bannon?"

"You're the one who found Beth Bannon, no one's as deep into this story as you."

"I don't know what I can do."

"Jason, we just need some time."

After ending the call, his fingers trembled as his hand hovered over his dial pad, poised to punch in Spangler's number. A million images burned through his mind: Spangler calling Vic Beale on the night desk, pagination calling downstairs, the pressmen rolling in the newsprint, the typesetters aligning the presses, alerting the floor, trucks waiting on the loading docks told of a delay. Overtime that would cost thousands.

A murder case possibly lost because of his story and promises broken.

Jason swallowed hard.

Stress, exhaustion, fear, and—*Oh Christ*—he punched the number, catching Spangler as he was preparing to go home. His reaction spilled from his office into the newsroom.

"You want me to hold the story! Why should we hold it now?"

Spangler shot to his door and yelled to the night desk. "Vic, hold up on Wade's story. We have to talk!"

Spangler's and Beale's attention bored into Jason as he struggled to explain that it was critical they hold off running his story. Rubbing his chin, licking his lips, he told them that he'd just heard from a source close to the investigation that there'd been a development.

"What development?" Beale said.

"They are looking hard at Lee Colson."

"What? Then why can't we report that, right now?"

"Because I made a deal we'd wait. They've just polygraphed him and are waiting for the results. They'll give us everything—*exclusively*—if we hold our Bannon stuff tonight."

Spangler tossed his pen across the room.

"What the hell are you doing, Wade? You talk to me first before you go making any goddamn deals with the Seattle Police Department!"

"I don't have time for this." Beale grabbed Spangler's phone and made a call. "Yeah, Chuck, it's Vic, kill the Colson item. We'll replate. Yes. Replace it with Gloria Lambert's story out of Olympia—" Cursing leaked through the receiver, loud and clear. "I know. Just do it, Chuck."

"Son of a bitch!" Spangler ran a hand across his reddened face.

"I'll let you sort this thing out," Beale said. "I've got a paper to publish."

"Get the hell out of here, Wade," Spangler said.

That night, Jason sat alone in his apartment with the lights off, except for the calming, soft blue glow of his aquarium. He watched his fish glide in the bubbling water as he sipped ginger ale. He sat that way for a long time, until he felt the last of the adrenaline coursing through him subside.

Then he took a long hot shower, occasionally thinking of Grace Garner, grappling with his feelings for her and what had been at stake for both of them.

He had to admit, he didn't know if he would have done what he had if it was another cop. Like Boulder. Had she bested him in getting him to hold a story he'd enterprised? Had he allowed her to do it? Or was it all simply true, that they were working together to find out who was behind the murder and abduction?

His eyes closed.

He was too tired to know anything anymore, other than what his gut told him.

Odds of them ever finding Dylan Colson alive just got worse.

DAY FIVE

49

Ice cream.

A big, heaping bowl of butterscotch ripple with some nuts, maybe a dollop of whipped cream, and a cherry.

That was what Lou Rifkin was thinking, sitting on his couch before his big screen and a pissed-off John Wayne in the after-midnight movie, *The Searchers*.

Lou's wife had hidden the carton in the freezer behind the cold cuts. She'd gone off to bed. Their son was out. The Rifkin home was quiet, the lights were low, and Lou was thinking he should just go to the kitchen and help himself to some of that butterscotch ripple.

It was the first night of his vacation. He deserved to celebrate with a little treat. Sleep in tomorrow, contemplate the fact he was five years from retirement as a machinist at Boeing.

He glanced at his stomach and dismissed his wife's worries about his waistline. Ellie worried about everything. The ice cream was for Dex, their son the drummer, who turned twenty this Sunday. Dex was supposed to move to Century City, California, with his band, Point Blank, next month.

Lou would believe it when it happened.

Right now, he wanted ice cream and as the lawful owner of this abode, he was going to help himself. He grunted his way to the kitchen, stuck his head in the freezer, poked around the pork chops and rib eyes—then stopped.

What was that sound?

Outside.

Yelling?

Lou put the carton on the counter, glanced out the huge window over the sink that opened to the night.

It sounded like yelling.

Keeping an ear cocked, he got a bowl and a spoon, worked the lid off the carton, then looked at the far reaches of his yard. The huge double-size lot had a stand of trees on the north corner that rose above a line of shrubbery.

There it is again. Sounds like a scream.

Maybe it was a cat up there at the Madison place. Or a party. The property adjoined his, but the Madison yard was a huge isolated lot at the end of the lane, protected by trees and a neglected hedge that formed a massive green wall around the place. They'd let it go to hell ever since they'd started renting it, what, eight, nine years ago. Seemed like new people moved in every six months. Lou paid no attention to the comings and goings of tenants. Nobody did really.

Except Ellie. A few months back she'd said, "I think some weirdos moved in to the Madison place this time."

"El, it doesn't concern you, just mind your own damn business."

Besides, Lou was thinking now, as he scooped a ball of butterscotch ripple into his bowl, *we never see or hear much from them. Let's keep it that way.*

Now there it goes again.

Screaming. Has to be a damn cat, or something.

Licking the spoon, Lou froze.

Brilliant yellow flashed through the bushes.

Fire.

His neighbor's garage was on fire.

Lou reached for his phone and reported it to the 911 dispatcher, then scrambled to get on his sneakers, but decided on his work boots.

"Ellie! The Madison place is on fire! Get up, Ellie!"

Lou's heart rate increased. At work, he was the department's deputy fire captain. He'd also been a technical engineer with the Army Reserves. He knew what to do. He grabbed two long garden hoses coiled on hooks in his garage, hoisted them over his shoulder. He snatched heavy work gloves, then trotted double-time to the Madison property.

Flames glowed inside the garage.

Jeezus.

"Fire!" Lou yelled to the house, kicking the rear door. He'd been on the property years ago to help with some roof work. He went to the exterior water faucet and connected his hose. The rusted tap squeaked, the pipe gurgled and rattled with water as he hauled it to the garage, hoping he'd have enough pressure to douse it.

Through the grimy window, he could see the flames rising in the garage. *Take it easy,* he told himself, *it's only a building.* As he hit its weatherworn wooden planks with a blast of water, his skin prickled.

Someone was screaming.

Inside the garage!

He couldn't tell if it was a man or a woman; the screams were muffled as the fire roared.

"Help!"

Through the window Lou saw a vehicle inside. A dark van reflecting the fire. The garage doors were unchained, unlocked. Lou opened them and a wall of fire lashed at him, forcing him to the ground. The garage was engulfed, flames rolled up the interior walls and across the ceiling.

Above the roar, someone was screaming hysterically for help. Using the lid of a metal garbage can as a shield, Lou worked his way to the van's rear, got the door open, items spilled to the ground, some of them igniting.

Through heavy curtains of smoke, ash, haze, and burning embers, Lou stepped closer, struggling to see to the front of the van, which was also burning. The choking heat sucked the air around his neck, forced him to keep blinking to protect his eyes; he feared they would melt.

The pleading continued, Lou's stomach twisted when he saw the top of a baby's car seat and made out the shape of an adult in the front.

The adult's hair was catching fire!

Lou stepped back and doused himself with the hose; then, fighting the inferno, he climbed into the interior, crawling through the back, determined to reach the car seat and the person engulfed in smoke who was choking, coughing, gagging horribly.

Pain shot over every part of Lou's body. His gloves ignited, his skin seared, started blistering—*God, I'm being cooked alive*—Lou would die in seconds if he did not retreat.

His hands burning, his lungs filled with choking smoke, he made one desperate grasp for the baby's car seat before smelling gas and thinking, *The van's gas tank,* just before it exploded.

A deafening roar-thud put Lou flat on his back, staring up at the stars, his skin sizzling, sirens wailing, hand gripping the heat-warped car seat.

Am I alive?

No more screams.

Just the howl of an all-consuming, purifying inferno.

50

At that moment, in her hospital bedroom, Maria Colson's eyelids fluttered.

Lee was the only person in the room with her, but was concentrating on the television suspended from the ceiling, watching late-night news reports, scanning channels, hoping that maybe, just maybe, he would find a miracle.

His anguish deepened with each passing moment, because there was no sign of Dylan, because Maria was dying, because of the polygraph.

Because the police suspected him.

Why?

How could his home address and fingerprints be linked to Beth Bannon's murder and to the van used in Dylan's abduction? He didn't understand. What did Grace and the FBI know? What did the polygraph show them? He'd told them the truth.

Hadn't he?

Was he certain of his answers? He was so tired. So afraid. His attention was jolted as Beth Bannon's face suddenly stared back at him from a news report. An older story. Recycled news. Nothing new.

Lee looked at her.

That face. That car.

Did he know her?

Had he met her?

He wasn't sure.

What if he failed the polygraph? They had that letter. They had his fingerprints. *Dylan. Where's Dylan?* He couldn't think. He changed the channel, landing on a jittery live aerial news shot of a burning building.

"—a fire—this is breaking news—a death or deaths, unconfirmed reports of a fatal residential building fire in Seattle tonight... despite a neighbor's effort to douse the blaze—no other details."

"Dylan!"

Lee's head snapped to Maria. She was sitting upright—her open eyes circles of fear, her face a mask of horror.

"Dylan!"

Maria stared at nothing. She was in a trance-like state, fixated on her last seconds with her baby—replaying at the speed of light images of *a blackbird hitting her bedroom window—a portent of death. Lee on a call in North Seattle—nightmare fears of being childless—Dylan's crying all night—taking Dylan to the store—leaving him with Shannon—the van, the woman, oh God she's stealing Dylan—the stroller, the door handle—pounding on the van, she's stealing my baby! The hood—the woman staring back at me— you're stealing my baby!*

He's my baby! MINE!

"No! No!"

"Maria—"

Lee and two nurses were calming her, comforting her. A doctor uncollared his stethoscope and checked her. The room filled with concern, more staff and hope.

"She's okay, right?" Lee's voice was breaking. "She's coming out of it, she's going to be okay. Right? Somebody?"

Amid the chaos of people tending to Maria, one of the night nurses ushered him out of the room to the lounge, sitting him down on the sofa.

"Yes, Lee, it's very good, but we have to stabilize her, check for any serious damage, run tests."

Lee raised his shaking hands to his face. Maria was alive. She was going to make it. He glanced around. All of their family had gone to the cafeteria. He was alone. But happy. So damn happy.

He wouldn't lose Maria.

He stood, smiling, hands on his hips, not knowing where to go or what to do. The nurses coming out of Maria's room were smiling too, their eyes shiny as they flashed Lee a thumbs-up. It was a miracle. His body trembled with adrenaline and exhaustion.

Now he and Maria could fight this battle together.

They would find Dylan.

Lee turned to see Detective Garner and FBI Special Agent Dupree arrive. And they were not alone. They'd come with Jarred Sandel, Lee's lawyer.

No one was smiling now.

51

"Lee, the polygraph results were inconclusive," Grace Garner said. "We'd like you come downtown with us so we can talk a bit more."

"*Now?* Maria just woke up. I don't want to leave. I can't!"

"She's awake?"

Taking in the activity around Maria's room, Grace shouldered her way to her side. Maria's face was swollen, her eyes were clouded with fear. Nurses tended to her as Dr. Binder assessed her condition.

"Excuse me." Grace pulled Binder aside. "Can she talk?"

"She's weak, but lucid."

"What's she saying?"

"Her immediate recollection is tethered to the final moments of her son's abduction."

"I need to talk to her, right now."

"I'd rather we give her some time—say a few hours."

"I need to talk to her now."

Binder considered Grace's request. "A few short questions, as long as I'm present."

Grace nodded and rummaged in her bag for her recorder and her notebook as Binder cleared the room.

Grace took the chair next to her. "Maria, I'm Detective Grace Garner. Do you know what happened?"

Maria's head rolled from side to side as if to deny the tragedy, to push back time and erase it.

"Maria?"

"Dylan! She's taking Dylan!"

"Who?" Grace exchanged a look with Binder. He nodded to continue. "Who, Maria? Do you know who took Dylan?"

Her head rolled back and forth.

"Do you know her name?"

Her head shook negatively.

"Why are you taking him? Why?" Maria cried out.

"Can you describe her, did you see or can you remember anything unusual about the woman who took Dylan?"

Maria groaned, her head moving from side to side.

"Give him back. He's mine. Please give him back."

"Maria, do you recall any details about the woman who took Dylan?"

Her eyes shut tight. Her face contorted as she sobbed. Mindful of her condition, Dr. Binder decided to end the interview.

"We'll continue assessing her, Detective. Perhaps in a few hours you could try again."

Grace inhaled deeply and turned for the door.

"Tattoo."

She stopped cold.

"She has a tattoo on her hand." Maria, her voice raw, tapped the back of her left hand, touching the clear tube taped there. "The woman has a tattoo of a butterfly."

"A butterfly." Grace sketched in her notebook and held it up. "Here, like this?"

Maria's head shook.

"Spiderweb."

Grace glanced to Binder then to Maria.

"Butterfly caught in a web. Tattoo of a butterfly in a web, here."

Maria tapped the back of her left hand.

"Oh God! Give me back my baby. He's mine. Lee! We have to find Dylan. *Where's Lee?*"

"Easy. Easy. You're doing fine." Binder pressed the call button to summon a nurse as he leaned forward to comfort Maria. He turned to Grace to signal that time was up, but the door was already closing behind her.

Special Agent Dupree was talking with Lee Colson. After calling the Homicide Unit, Grace pulled Dupree aside, out of earshot, and alerted him.

"We've got a lead on the primary suspect. On the back of her left hand she has a tattoo of a butterfly caught in a spiderweb."

Dupree made an urgent call to run the details through the National Crime Information Center's computer and the ViCAP database. The bureau also had experts on tattoos used by gangs, occultists, satanic groups. And they had contacts with tattoo artists across the country.

Through the Justice Department, they'd query the Federal Bureau of Prisons—check inmate records, put out a call for help to all state and local authorities.

"It's a start," Dupree told his duty agent before hanging up and returning to update Grace, who was pressing Lee Colson about the new information.

"Think hard, Lee. Have you ever met a woman with that kind of tattoo on the back of her left hand?"

"No."

Grace's expression threw a silent question to Dupree as to whether to believe Lee. They were interrupted by a nurse at the station holding up a phone. Grace took the call.

"It's Boulder. Take this address down and haul ass to it."

"But, Stan—"

"Looks like we've got the van. Torched."

"Is it empty?"

"Looks like two fatalities inside."

"Two?"

"Adult and a child, a baby."

A baby.

Grace's reflex was to look at Lee Colson, but she turned away.

"Oh goddammit, Stan."

"I know, Grace. Just get the hell over there and get to work."

52

Jason's first waking thought: Morning had come too fast.

Groping for his alarm, he tried to shut the damn thing off until he realized it was the phone.

"Jason, this is Rosemary at the paper. You said to call you if I ever heard anything big on the Colson case over the scanners."

"What're you hearing?"

"They've found the van. Burned in a garage with two dead people, I think. There's a ton of chatter on the radios, all happening now."

"Where?"

Jason took down the address, reached for his pants, checked the time. 2:18 A.M. Every deadline had passed. *Okay, we're working for the* Mirror*'s Internet edition and tomorrow's paper.*

"What about that new guy on nights—Dan— where's he?"

"Gone to a domestic standoff around Dunlap and Holly Park. Whacked-out ex-hubby says he wants to end it all because of a custody fight."

"All right, get a shooter rolling to the fire. Wake

them up, tell them I'm on my way. You monitor the radios and call me with updates on my cell."

He got dressed, got into his Falcon, and sailed along traffic-free expressways listening to Hendrix's "Midnight Lightning." By the time he arrived, firefighters had doused the blaze, the air was heavy with the smells of smoke and ash and the growl of the pumpers as crews continued pouring water on the aftermath. Revolving lights from the tangle of emergency vehicles lit up the blackened remains of the garage and the charred skeleton of the van.

He took in the situation and the usual telltale signs of a tragic fire: the crime scene tape cordoning the area; beyond the garden hose, evidence of the panicked effort to help; then the bright yellow tarp draped over the van's interior.

The death flag.

As best as he could tell, few other news crews had arrived. He saw the WKKR van—those guys cruised the city nonstop. He didn't see the camera, although he spotted an ambulance, doors open with paramedics treating a distraught man. *That guy has to know something.*

"I'm Jason Wade from the *Mirror*. Can I talk to you, sir?"

Lou Rifkin stared at him as a female paramedic tended to his hands.

"Can you tell me what happened?"

Rifkin's Adam's apple rose and fell. His eyes were large and turned to the ruins, as if he were still searching the fire when he said, "I did my best to save them. I did everything."

A shadow crossed Jason's notepad and he met the stone-cold face of a uniformed Seattle police officer with Rifkin's witness statement affixed to his clipboard. He eyed Jason's press tag.

"You step back, we're not done here."

"Sure."

Moving away, he spotted Grace Garner's unmarked Chevrolet Malibu among the police vehicles. Then he saw her among the plainclothes detectives, huddled in front of the house comparing notes. He leaned against a fire truck and she acknowledged him with a subtle nod. After the detectives had dispersed, she approached him.

"You're fast," she said, watching as more crime scene investigators in white jumpsuits entered the house.

"Is it true? This is the van and you've got two victims?"

"It's definitely the van."

"And the victims inside? One is Dylan Colson, right?"

She looked at Jason with his pen poised over his notebook.

"We have no confirmation on the identity, or number of victims."

He closed his notebook, took stock of who might overhear, then lowered his voice.

"Does this story end here?"

"I can't say."

"Can you say who lives here?"

"I can't confirm that yet. It appears to be a rental and the people here kept pretty much to themselves."

"Well, what can you tell me?"

"Not much."

Disappointment settled on his face.

"Grace, I've gone through hell already holding a story on this case. I've cooperated and worked with you. I think you owe me."

"*I owe you?* Dammit, Jason. Look"—she nodded to the yellow tarp aftermath—"it's going to take time before we can process that van to confirm who died. At this point, we only have one witness account. And it's shaky at best. We honestly don't know much at this stage. Have you ever seen the corpse of a fire victim? You can't even distinguish gender at first. So give me a break. This isn't all about you."

He ran his hand across his face and stared at the yellow tarp trying not to dwell on the fact Dylan Colson's little corpse—or whatever remained of him— was under it.

"Spangler's leaning on me, I'm sorry."

"Grace." Dupree was holding up shoe covers and latex gloves. "They need you inside."

"I have to go."

Kay Cataldo met Grace at the front door. After Grace slipped on shoe covers and gloves, Cataldo led her through the house.

"Please walk in my steps," Cataldo said, quickly recapping the preliminary inventory. "We checked after the responding officers and it appears there are no other victims. The house is empty. But we've found something critical."

Grace took stock of the place as they came to the stairs.

"Up here."

Cataldo led her to a bedroom and a desk with a laptop computer. Next to it, there was a single sheet of paper, already sealed in a clear evidence bag. The page was a computer printout.

TO WHOEVER FINDS THIS:

I am sorry for all of the pain I caused. I have asked God to show me the answer and I have decided to go to Heaven with my baby.

Please do not hate me,

Nadine Getch

53

By the strobe of emergency lights, Grace Garner cursed God in a secluded corner of the yard, where she had gone to be alone to study her notebook and the words she'd copied from the suicide letter.

"I have decided to go to Heaven with my baby. Please do not hate me, Nadine Getch."

Grace flipped to a color printout of Nadine's Washington State driver's license. The address came up as a P.O. box in Seattle. Her date of birth put her at thirty-two years old. Two bottomless black wells of sorrow stared from her face.

Grace reviewed Nadine's license status. It came back clear. They had run her information through the Washington and National Crime Information Centers.

No hits.

They tried the WASIS, Washington State Patrol's Identification System. Nothing. They checked for any outstanding warrants or summonses for Nadine Getch. Nothing came back.

No fingerprints on file, no criminal record.

They still had more local, state, and out-of-state

agencies to check. And they still needed to positively confirm who died in the fire. An autopsy would take time. Maybe dental records to match the remains. Was Nadine Getch even a true name? Grace wondered, coming back to who clsc was lying out thcrc undcr thc smoldering ash.

Dylan Colson.

Why kill a baby? Why, goddammit? Why?

She searched the stars for the answer, battling her sense of utter defeat. She'd lost this one. But why? Why? It just couldn't cnd likc this.

It could.

And it does, she told herself. *It just does. That's how things work in this world.* Grace knew that firsthand. Amid the lights, the drone of fire trucks, the funereal, smoky air of crime scene work, she was hurled back through her life, to the truth.

The truth of that awful day. The reason Roger Briscoe came to Mr. Lorten's English class with a gun and plans to kill everyone.

The firecracker pop. Screams. Terror. Panic. Grace approached him, not afraid because she knew the truth as she inched close enough to look into his eyes.

"Roger, please put the gun down."

"No."

"Please. Why are you doing this?"

"You know why, Grace."

She did.

The night before, after she'd broken it off with him, he told her that she would live to regret it.

"What are you going to do?"

"Wait and see. And remember, it'll be all your fault, Grace."

After it happened, the counselors had absolved her of guilt. But she could never forgive herself. She was haunted by her failure, the same sickening sense of failure that overwhelmed her now as she stared at Nadine's picture and the ashes, the evidence of another defeat.

I'm so sorry.

Her cell phone rang. The number came up for Perelli, her partner.

"How're you doing, Grace?"

She hesitated to catch her breath.

"Fine."

The silence that followed screamed her lie. But they let it pass until Perelli said, "You know, we've got to tell the Colsons now, brace them for the worst before word gets out."

"I know. I'll leave for the hospital soon, like in ten."

"You did good work, Grace. Don't forget that. We were getting close."

"It doesn't mean much now."

"I know it's small consolation, but your reluctance to suspect Lee played out. But he did meet Beth, that's why his poly was inconclusive."

"The towing company found something?"

"Just got it confirmed. They went nonstop through old records, like you'd quietly requested, and they found some kind of note going back some seven months. Turns out Lee had serviced Bannon's Toyota. Explains his fingerprints on her car."

"What about the envelope with his home address and the notation about payment?"

"She mailed a cash payment later. It was confirmed by a note the shop found, that Lee brought in cash she'd mailed to his home."

"So what's the connection to Nadine here?"

"We're still working on it, but it has to be through Beth."

"Well, none of it means jack shit now, does it, Dom?"

"Stay focused, Grace. Sometimes we win. Sometimes we don't. But we never, *ever*, surrender."

"I'll remember that when they bury the baby."

"Grace, you listen to me and stay focused."

"Thanks, Dom."

David Tanaka and Al Sprung from the King County Medical Examiner's Office were working with the CSI people and two investigators from the Arson Unit, photographing and picking over the charred remains of the blaze where it had cooled. On her way to see them, Grace saw Jason trot to the crime scene tape and wave her over.

"Grace," he said, paging through his notes, "I just talked to Lou Rifkin's wife before they took him to the hospital."

"This'll have to wait."

"No listen, everyone knows that at the time of the abduction in Ballard, witnesses reported seeing a woman and a man."

"So? That went out in the alert the other day."

"Ellie Rifkin told me just now that she's pretty sure

a woman and man rented the house. The Madison place, she called it."

"You got a question?"

"Your victims, are they male and female?"

"We don't know. And we're well aware of the suspect descriptions from before. We put them out, remember? We're trying to confirm a few things. It takes time."

"What's that?" Jason's pen pointed to Grace's clipboard and the page with Nadine Getch's driver's license and photo.

Several tense moments passed with Grace staring into Jason's face before she came to a decision. *What the hell.* She pulled him aside between a fire truck and a marked Seattle patrol car.

"I'm going to show you something, but you cannot print any names without confirming with me first."

"What is it?"

"Swear."

"I swear! What is it?"

She showed him Nadine Getch's information.

"Who is she?"

"We think she's the one who took Dylan and we think—" Grace glanced around as firefighters hauled equipment to the garage. "We think she killed Dylan in a murder-suicide."

Jason stopped writing.

"The baby's dead?"

"All indications are pointing to a murder-suicide here."

"Christ. Oh no. I have to call it in."

Her hand moved fast, stopping his from reaching his cell phone. "Jason, you just swore that you'd wait until I confirmed with you."

"All right, yeah, what about Maria Colson, Beth Bannon, and Lee?"

"Maria Colson has recovered."

"Recovered? When?"

"Look, there are a lot of loose ends and we're working on them. I gave you this name so that you can dig into her background on the QT. It's most likely an alias. Still, *do not publish anything until you talk to me first, got it?*"

"Detective Garner?"

Kay Cataldo, a surgical mask under her chin, was approaching carrying a brown paper bag and a sheet of paper, which Grace signed after receiving the bag.

"What's that?" Jason asked. It was the size of a small grocery bag, the top folded closed. "What's in there?" he asked, walking alongside Grace to her car.

"I can't release that information."

"Grace?"

After getting behind the wheel, she placed the bag carefully, almost reverently, on the floor of the passenger side.

"Is it evidence?"

She nodded, then turned her ignition.

"Something I have to show Lee and Maria Colson."

She drove off, leaving Jason guessing about the contents. He watched the taillights of her Malibu until they vanished.

Then he pulled his attention to the crime scene investigators working on the human remains covered by the yellow tarp in the middle of the blackened ruins.

The death flag.

54

Of all the things she faced as a detective, telling parents their child was dead was the duty Grace hated most.

A piece of her died every time she did it. For despite all of her training, all of the grief counseling courses she'd taken, it never got easier. Each case was different. Sometimes people collapsed in her arms, or punched walls, or screamed.

Or just stood there in numbed silence.

And what Grace was going to do now, *had to do now*, broke all of the rules. But on her way to the hospital, over her cell phone, her sergeant assured her that it had to be done.

"I think it's cruel, Stan. It's bad enough that we failed them."

"It's hard, but it's critical at this stage of the case for identification purposes. CSI says there's not much to go on."

Dawn was breaking when Grace arrived at Swedish in Ballard. Perelli met her at the emergency entrance.

"Lee's with the chaplain and Dr. Binder in the chapel."

The early morning light colored the stained glass as Grace and Perelli entered. Seeing them, Lee Colson stood. He embodied exhaustion and anguish as his mouth began forcing out words no father should ever have to speak.

"Is my son dead?"

The chapel's hanging wall fountain gurgled for several long moments as Grace steeled herself.

"Lee, there was a fire involving a vehicle that we have confirmed as the van used in Dylan's abduction. We have indications that two people were killed in that fire."

"Just tell me."

"You have to listen to me carefully. We have no confirmation on the identities of the victims. We believe one is an adult—"

"And the other one?"

"The other appears to be a small child. I'm so sorry to have to tell you this way."

White flashed in Lee's mind, blinding him. He saw nothing, felt nothing, heard nothing but the blood hammering in his ears. He'd been bracing for his wife's death.

And now his son's.

How much more was he supposed to take? A raw, deep-pitched, agonized groan filled the chapel and was swallowed by the sound of the flowing water.

"Lee, listen to me, we don't have all the answers yet and until we know everything, we can't be sure of anything. You have to brace yourself for the worst but be strong for Maria."

Lee buried his face in his hands and stayed that way for a long time. As the water bubbled, the chaplain, doctor, and detectives sat in respectful silence while Lee gasped for air.

"How long before you know?"

"Everyone is doing all they can as quickly as they can, but we have to do it right."

"Who did this?"

Grace exchanged glances with the others as she placed Nadine Getch's driver's license photo in Lee's hand.

"Do you recognize this woman?"

Grace scrutinized his reaction, trying to read his body language. His breathing quickened, flaring his nostrils as he glared at Nadine.

"No. Maybe yes. Dammit, I don't know."

"Take it easy, Lee. Take it easy. Do you know where you met her? Can you tell us anything about her?"

As Lee shook his head, his face tightened, his breathing quickened.

"She did this! This woman murdered my son! Who is this stupid bitch? She better be dead, because I'll fucking kill her!"

The photo fell to the floor as Lee Colson broke down.

It was a long time before he pulled himself together, at least to the extent that he could accompany Grace and the others to the elevator where they ascended to his wife's room.

They would tell Maria Colson the worst thing in her life.

With the elevator humming like a dark chorus, Grace adjusted her grip on the brown paper bag and swallowed.

Maria Colson was alert, pacing next to her bed. She looked at the people who'd entered her room, including Special Agent Kirk Dupree. Her hopeful, fear-filled eyes searched for a sign of her baby.

"Did you find him? Is he okay?"

"Maria," Lee said, "something's happened."

"I heard the nurses talking about finding Dylan. It was on the news. Then they said that my TV's broken. No one knows anything. Tell me they found him, Lee."

Her words carried hope but in her heart, Maria knew when Lee sat on the bed. He took her hands. His were big, callused from his hard work, and they were trembling.

"We have to prepare for the worst."

Struggling to understand, she began shaking her head.

"Maria, they found the van. There was a fire and they think two people are dead inside. A woman and a— and—and oh honey, I'm so sorry—our baby boy…"

"No. Lee. Oh no! *No!*"

Maria's mouth went dry, and her scream ripped into the hearts of everyone who heard it. Lee's strong arms held her so tightly they kept her from falling off of the earth.

Dr. Binder exchanged glances with a nurse. Little could be done for Maria now. A sedative could be administered, but despite Binder's protests, the Seattle

Homicide Unit had to do something more. Lee held her for several minutes before Grace stepped forward.

"Maria"—she adjusted the table that reached over the bed—"do you recognize this woman?" Grace put Nadine Getch's photo on the table.

Maria nodded and sobbed into Lee's chest. "She's the one who took him."

"Are you certain?"

"I'll never forget her face and the tattoo and her hand."

Grace looked at Dupree and Perelli.

"Do you know her? Have you ever seen her before?"

Maria shook her head.

"It's my fault! I'm a bad mother. I never should have left Dylan outside the store."

"No, Maria," the chaplain said. "You must not blame yourself."

Grace placed the paper bag on the table.

"Forgive me for doing this, but we're trying to confirm things." Grace swallowed. "We believe the fire was deliberately set. There was an explosion. It caused a great deal more damage than there usually is in a fire of this nature."

Grace glanced around the room at the others who knew that *damage* was a euphemism. Grace cleared her throat. "What I want you to know is that it may take a long time to confirm identifications. Do you understand?"

The Colsons stared at the bag, then at Grace, who was tugging on latex gloves.

"I'm going to show you items we've recovered from the scene."

Maria's hand covered her mouth.

"You cannot touch these items, but I want you to examine them and tell me if you recognize them, please. It's very important."

With utmost respect and care, Grace reached into the bag for a baby's shoe. It was blue and its toe was singed. Then she set down a blanket, its edges blackened. Next came an infant-size T-shirt, blackened extensively by fire.

The items smelled of smoke.

Looking at them, Maria's heart slammed against her ribs.

She seemed to slip out of her body. She saw herself reliving her fears of not ever being able to have a child. She saw herself giving birth to Dylan in this very hospital. She saw herself waking in the night to the thud of the bird slamming against her window in the hours before Dylan was taken from her.

Why?

Why am I being punished?

Maria's hands shook as she struggled with her need to hold these items. They were blurring before her eyes as someone kept repeating her name. Her body was quaking; Lee's arms held her together for she felt as if she were literally coming apart.

Dr. Binder protested any further questions.

Grace rolled the table a few inches away from Maria so that her tears would not fall on the evidence. "Maria, can you positively identify these items?"

"These are Dylan's. I dressed him in them the morning we went to the corner store. This is what he was wearing when he was taken from me."

55

Leaving the scene, Jason beat the morning traffic and got to the *Mirror* just as the sun was rising.

The newsroom was empty.

In the quiet, contemplating the crime, he thought of Dylan Colson's tiny body, likely burned beyond recognition, and hoped that the baby hadn't suffered.

Why did this happen? Who was Nadine Getch? Why did she do this?

He vowed to find the answers. Maybe it would provide Seattle a small degree of consolation. He ran his hands across the stubble of his face while settling in at his desk, his adrenaline flowing, his head throbbing from caffeine deficiency.

He needed coffee.

But first he got his notes into his computer. As he finished, his cell phone rang.

"Jay," his father said, "I couldn't get you at home."

"I was called out. What're you doing up at this hour?"

"An old buddy tipped me on the Colson fire. You know about it?"

"That's what I was out on."

"I want to help you."

"But, Dad, Boulder threatened your license if you did more on Colson."

"Well, Stan plays rough, but that's fine. I've talked it over with Don. He says the agency's good as long as whatever I do relates to the client file, because it was my client who flagged the van and the plate."

That was true, but Jason was hesitant to accept his old man's offer and wasn't sure why. Maybe he was protecting him, or maybe he was still resentful for the hell his old man had put him through for most of his life. Maybe he was too damn tired to know.

"Son. I've let a lot of wasted years pass between us."

Got that right, he thought, squeezing the phone.

"So let me help."

Keep the past in the past. I need all the help I can get.

"All right. I have to know everything I can, as fast as I can, about this person." Jason dictated details of Nadine Getch to his old man.

"Good. I'll pull out all the stops. Krofton's got plenty of police friends. We can move pretty fast. I'll get right back to you."

"Okay."

After the call, Jason headed for the newsroom kitchen, surprised by the aroma of freshly brewed coffee. *Who's here this early?* Rounding a corner he nearly bumped into his answer. Spangler was holding a full mug with the New York *Daily News* logo.

"Rosemary called me this morning. TV's all over this fire. What have you got?"

"It's the van used in the abduction. A suspected arson with two dead inside."

"Is the kid one of them? Is it a murder-suicide?"

"I don't know. Nothing's confirmed yet."

"Bull." Spangler undid his collar button and loosened his tie. "They know. Have you worked another deal with your cop friends? Dammit, I'm disappointed in you. You've been out there since the get-go, and come back with nothing?"

Maybe it was exhaustion or adrenaline, or the sadness washing over him, but Spangler had crossed a line and Jason couldn't take any more.

"You're an asshole. Dylan Colson's likely been incinerated by a lunatic and you continue to spew moronic orders at me."

"Who the hell do you think you're talking to?"

"I know how to do my job, so just back off."

"Hey, don't you walk away from me, Wade. Now, I'll cut you some slack because you've put in long hours, but you'd better get a grip, pal."

"I'm sick and tired of swallowing your shit."

"You listen to me. You're riding Seattle's biggest story and we need to lead. I know the value of police sources, but we've already pulled back stuff for your cop friends. No more goddamm deals. We're not going to get beat on this story. So, tell me, is it the kid and his kidnapper?"

If Jason told Spangler that Grace suspected it was Dylan and Nadine Getch, he'd no longer have control of the information. He'd lose the chance to flesh it out, to leverage more exclusive data from Grace.

He needed to buy a few more hours.

"They don't know who's dead, they're sifting through the crap. There was an explosion. Seattle PD will release more later. Besides, we've got all day before final to work on this."

"We *do not* have all day. TV and radio will feed on this live every few minutes. It's started already. We've got to be in the mix now."

"You want something now?"

"For our Internet edition. Three hundred words. And later, by tonight's deadline, I want to know everything. Do you understand?" Spangler didn't wait for an answer. "Get busy."

At his desk, Jason downed nearly half of his mug of black coffee in one gulp, then tore into the first of two stale jelly doughnuts someone from the night crew had left in the kitchen.

That was breakfast.

Twenty minutes later, he'd finished a taut news item that began:

By JASON WADE, *Seattle Mirror*

Detectives fear that Dylan Colson, the Seattle baby stolen from his mother in their sleepy neighborhood, was killed in an early morning fire that also claimed the life of the woman suspected of abducting him.

He was satisfied that he'd nuanced his short hit so that it was speculative and did not betray specific details Grace had shared with him. After filing he checked his e-mail. His father had sent him a copy of Nadine Getch's driver's license.

He looked out toward the city, thinking there was one person who might have information on Nadine.

He grabbed his jacket and headed for his Falcon, hoping to beat the morning rush hour.

56

Nothing's a fact until the evidence says so.

Kay Cataldo had returned from the scene to her lab on Airport Way knowing that Colson was the number-one priority in all of Seattle.

In all of Washington State.

The answers were in the evidence and much of the evidence was in her hands. It was her job to help the King County Medical Examiner's Office close the case.

David Tanaka called from the M.E.'s office. "We're going to need a bit more time."

They were having major problems with the human remains because they were in bad shape. They'd located part of an adult lower jaw and pieces of an upper jaw. A forensic odontologist was working on them, preparing to expedite a comparison on a dental chart, should they make any progress toward identification.

Tanaka said that there was carbon monoxide in the blood of the adult, indicating that, at the time of the fire, the victim was alive—consistent with the witness account. But the bones of the adult were in pieces, making it difficult to analyze the ischium-pubis index, which, Cataldo knew, would establish the sex of the victim.

"And what about confirmation of the child, Dave?"

"We don't have much to go on. We're still working on it."

Meanwhile, Arson had confirmed the fire had been intentionally set with an accelerant. Unleaded gasoline. Available everywhere.

Fingerprint people were analyzing every decent latent found at the scene, comparing them to the Bannon homicide. Phone records were being reviewed, along with utility bills and other sources of information. A hair sample taken from the crib matched Dylan's, confirming he had been in the house.

But the homicide was going to take time to confirm because of the condition of the remains. The explosion had left little to analyze. The scene had been shredded and burned. The van appeared to have been jammed with belongings, as if there were plans for a move, or a long vacation.

Was that indicative of a suicide?

The note was puzzling. A computer printout. So far they could not locate anything else written by Nadine for comparison. That made it difficult to gauge if she had in fact written the note. There was no trace of the computer or the printer in the house.

Was it among the debris?

"But why?" Grace Garner had asked Cataldo at the scene. "Why write a suicide note and pack away the computer and equipment? Why bother?"

"Why steal someone's baby in broad daylight?" Cataldo said. "This is not supposed to make sense."

Grace conceded the point. Experience had taught

them that the explanations for many suicides were often taken to the grave by the victim. But the circumstances of the fire pointed to another critical aspect of the case: the male suspect associated with Nadine.

Where was he? Who was he?

The fingerprint people were not having much luck finding latents in the house that pointed to anyone.

Cataldo took a deep breath, released it slowly. She'd never had a case like this one.

Never.

Another glance at her own family and she got back to work as her phone began ringing again.

"It's Tanaka. Kay, we've got something and it is not at all what we thought."

57

It was a large, two-story frame house hidden from the street on a professionally landscaped, tree-lined lot in the Lake Forest Park area of Seattle.

A basketweave bricked walk invited him from the street to the door. Clutching the folds of her thick robe, Joy Montgomery gasped when she answered the doorbell.

"Jason Wade! Good God!"

"I'm sorry to bother you."

"How did you find our address?" She pulled him deep into the yard behind a garden shed. "Please, you have to go, my husband's in the shower, I have to drive him to the airport."

"I need your help on the Colson case. There was a fire."

"I saw it on the morning news."

"Do you recognize this woman, Nadine Getch?"

Joy studied Nadine's picture. She had blonde hair, a pretty face with hazel eyes that were hooded like they were half-dead. Joy covered her mouth with her hand.

"Have you ever seen her before?"

She continued looking at the picture, not answering.

"Joy, please. I need your help."

"I already told you everything I know. Now please go."

He knew she was not telling him the truth.

"Joy."

"I think I made a big mistake going to you," she said, shaking her head.

"Why?"

"It's so dangerous now. Beth's dead, the baby, the fire. I'm afraid."

"I understand, but it's over. Please, I need to find some answers. Just help me, then you should think about going to the police if you're afraid."

She shook her head.

"Why not?"

"If we talked to police they may look into how we got Emily."

"You told me it was all legal."

"Maybe part of it wasn't. I'm not sure. It was complicated and if they start looking into it"—Joy looked to the house—"if they ever took her away…"

"Joy, please. Think of the Colsons. I'm just asking for information about Nadine."

She looked at him, then looked at the picture.

"I know you know something. Please, help me, then I'll go and I won't use your name. I swear."

Her glance flicked up from the picture and she took a deep breath.

"About seven or eight months ago, I was at a support group to talk about our positive experience with Emily. The group was anonymous, like AA. Beth was there."

A glossy fingernail tapped Nadine's face. "And her too. She was there, at the back, not many people saw her."

"You're sure?"

"Yes."

"Did you talk to her?"

"No, but I think she was sitting with Beth."

"How do you know it was her?"

"Look at those eyes. I remember thinking they were creepy, like she was dead inside, the way they looked right through you."

"Why didn't you tell anybody about her before?"

"I never thought of her until now."

"Where was this support group meeting?"

"At a community hall, near the hospital in Ballard."

"Swedish?"

Joy nodded.

"Do you remember anything else?"

"It was raining."

"Wait a sec, you say seven months ago, near Swedish?"

Joy nodded.

"That's where Dylan Colson was born. Seven months ago."

58

It was all a dream.

Voices kept telling Maria about the most horrible thing that had happened to Dylan.

Nurses, a doctor, then Lee, whispered it over and over.

It all *seemed* so real.

Detectives and the bag of Dylan's clothes: his shoe, his T-shirt, his blanket, all smelling of his sweet baby scent mixed with gasoline and smoke and death.

Strange, how dreams were, but it wasn't *really* happening. It was a dream. Like with the bird hitting her window in the night—only she did not *really* wake. She did not *really* take Dylan to the store and leave him with Shannon Tabor out front.

No way.

See, that was all part of the dream. It never happened.

Dylan was never stolen by a woman who then murdered him in a fire.

It didn't *really* happen.

Did it?

Because if it did—if it did happen, then it meant—

it meant—oh God—horror gushed from the pit of her stomach, then subsided.

The sedative was working.

Barely.

Hands forced Maria to sit back down, to stay in her hospital bed. As more time passed and she stared into the chain of solemn faces, she knew.

She knew.

It *was* real. It *did* happen.

She felt the horrible truth coil around her, constrict and crush her, as it prepared to open its jaws and swallow her whole. She was not dreaming. She was living a nightmare.

Help me, please! Please, help me!

Suddenly her torment flared with anger, detonated with fury, as it had when she attacked the van to rescue Dylan. And now, as this evil worked to destroy her, she raged against it.

No.

It couldn't happen like this. She would fight. Maria demanded to get dressed and go to the chapel.

Her battle was with God.

She stood, shaking off Lee and the nurses who tried to stop her.

"Let her go, but not alone," Dr. Binder said.

Maria knew the chapel.

It was where she'd come to ask God to keep Dylan safe and healthy when she and Lee first learned that he was coming into their lives. Now, as Dr. Binder and two nurses watched, here she was again, not to implore God's help, but to demand an accounting.

The fracture-pattern of stitches lacing her head accentuated the anguish in her face. With Lee holding her, Maria looked up to the large oak cross suspended on the wall.

How can You do this? How could You give us Dylan only to take him away? Like this! How could You do this?

The water from the hanging wall fountain bubbled.

I can't accept that he's dead. I just can't. You show me. I want to see him! I want to hold him! It's not true, unless I see. Because I don't think that You would be such a cruel God, to take him away and let me live. To punish me for leaving him for a few seconds.

It was only a few seconds. I'm so sorry. Please.

Lee tightened his hold on her quaking body.

Because if You take him from me, I'll follow him and I'll find him and be with him. Because I'm his mother.

Maria fell to her knees before the cross.

Oh God. I can't live without him.

59

In the hall outside the chapel where Maria pleaded with God, Grace's cell phone rang.

"We've got a break," Boulder told her. "The dead adult in the fire is a *male* and there's no evidence of the baby in the fire."

"Nothing?"

"Not a trace. We still have a shot here, Grace. Take down this number and password. Get to a land line. We're starting a conference call with the FBI, right now."

Grace grabbed Perelli.

A nurse found them an empty office with a speaker-phone. They shut the door and joined the call. The emergency case status meeting was arranged through the FBI. It involved Seattle PD, King County Sheriff's Office, Washington Highway Patrol, and several other departments. More agencies would be updated later.

"This is McCusker at the FBI, I'll coordinate this and we'll move fast. First up, David Tanaka."

"The adult victim of the fire is not female, as presumed," Tanaka said. Grace and Perelli exchanged looks while taking notes.

"CSI got a print in the house," Tanaka said, "and we got a hit: Axel Tackett, white male age forty-one. Tackett was on parole after serving time in Coyote Ridge for drug offenses. We've got his file.

"Axel Tackett's identification as the deceased adult was confirmed through his DOC dental chart. And"— the sound of a page being turned crackled over the line—"three of his ribs were chipped, consistent with stabbing. A ten-inch serrated knife was located by CSI among the debris in the fire. That blade is consistent with the injuries inflicted on Beth Bannon."

Kay Cataldo joined the call.

"A shoe recovered from the fire debris also is consistent with the shoe in the surveillance video taken of Dylan Colson's abduction and the impressions found at the Bannon homicide."

"Tanaka here. We believe Axel Tackett was stabbed several times but alive during the fire and died from smoke inhalation."

"What about Dylan Colson?" Grace asked.

"No evidence of his remains in the aftermath."

"Nothing?" Grace said.

"Not a trace of him. We've scoured the scene. Went through it with the cadaver dog. Tackett's blood is B positive, a rare type, and it is evident everywhere. Dylan is O positive, a common type, and not a trace. We can put Dylan Colson in the house, and I would testify to that. But there is absolutely no single indication of the child's remains in the fire. Nothing."

"Then there's a chance he's alive?" Grace said.

"Absolutely."

"And if he's alive he's likely with Nadine."

"Things are already in motion to issue an alert and hold a news conference," McCusker said.

Through the small office window, Grace glimpsed Lee comforting Maria in the hall and whispered her own small prayer.

Help us find Dylan.

Before it's too late.

60

After the conference call, Grace Garner stood over the humming hospital fax machine willing it to go faster.

She was keyed up from the break in the case; adrenaline and caffeine surged through her as the machine discharged pages.

A media storm had befallen the Seattle Police. While it was still early morning, newswire reports prompted increased demand for information on the fatal fire in the Colson case. Questions were coming in from the national press, CNN, FOX, the Associated Press, *USA Today,* CBS News, and the *Washington Post.*

They'd put all this attention to use soon, Grace thought, collecting the last pages her sergeant had faxed her.

She joined Perelli, Maria, and Lee in the tranquillity of an empty meeting room permeated with the lemony scent of furniture polish.

"What's happened?" Lee asked when Grace entered. "Has there been a break?"

"Please tell us," Maria said.

"Dylan was not a victim of the fire. He was not found at the scene, according to our best and most recent information."

Maria covered her mouth with her hands.

"He's alive!" Lee said.

"That's a strong possibility because we have no evidence to confirm that he was hurt at the scene."

"Where is he?" Maria asked. "God, where is he?"

"We're working on locating him and we're going to need your help."

Grace opened her folder and placed a recent photo of Axel Tackett on the table. His square jaw was raised slightly in defiance, while his eyes burned with bitterness from his prison-hardened face.

"That's who was driving the van!" Maria said.

"Have you ever seen him before?"

"No, never."

"Tackett's been confirmed as the person killed in the fire."

"Who else?"

"No one."

"What about Nadine Getch?" Maria asked.

"No evidence of her remains was found in the fire."

Lee looked hard into Grace's face, then to Perelli, then back to Grace.

"Then where's our son?"

"We think Nadine has fled with Dylan."

"Oh!" Maria groaned. "You've got to find her!"

"In a few minutes, we'll be holding a news conference to put out a new nationwide alert. We're only hours behind her now. But we need you to help us."

"What can we do?"

Because the evidence pointed to Nadine as the person who'd murdered Beth Bannon and Axel Tackett, the Seattle Homicide Unit had completely ruled out Lee as a possible suspect.

"But it's your connection to Beth Bannon, your fin-gerprints on her car and the envelope, and Nadine's connection to her, that may help us, Lee. If we knew more about it, it could help locate Nadine. Can you tell us anything more, any details?"

Grace slid photos of Bannon and Nadine closer to Lee, along with the envelope with the Colson's home address.

"Think, Lee. We know Beth Bannon helped place babies with couples who couldn't have them. We know that Beth came in contact with you and that Nadine came in contact with Beth. In fact"—Grace flipped a page—"CSI just confirmed that a fingerprint taken from the residence where the fire was, which we believe belongs to Nadine, matched a latent found in the Toyota."

Lee stared at the photographs. He followed Grace Garner's attention to the photocopy of the envelope ad-dressed to him and studied the postmark. Buried deep in his mind, in a distant corner that had been blocked, a memory appeared, twinkling like a star, light-years away. As he focused on it, it pulled closer until more detail was revealed.

Hissing.

Rain.

A train and truck had collided in the rain.

An emergency call had come after Dylan was born.

But *when* had it come?

Think.

"The day after Dylan was born, I went back to the hospital to see him and Maria, and I stayed late. I remember it was a cold night and there was a pretty wild storm going by the time I headed to my truck. Then I got an emergency call. A truck had hit a train at a crossing."

Remembering more, Lee stopped.

"Wait. There were two women who couldn't start their car. Before I got the call. That's it. In the parking lot by the hospital. One of them was her, had to be her." Lee tapped Beth Bannon's photo. "It was dark, it was a Toyota. She had the hood up. I tried to help her, but couldn't get it to turn over. I even reached under, ready to hook her, but then I tried her battery post. And we got it going."

"But there was no invoice?" Perelli said.

"That's right. I had Bannon and the other woman in the cab to warm up and keep dry, and I told her no charge. She wanted to pay me. I said no. We kinda joked and that's when she must've taken the envelope from my dash. It's a mess. My trucker's newsletter. Look, that's what she wrote on it, 'Follow up with payment.' But I told her it was on the house because I was a proud new daddy and all, on cloud nine, you know. She said she was happy for me because that night was a sad night for her friend."

"Her friend?"

"Yeah, the other woman. She didn't speak?"

"Was it Nadine?"

"I don't know. It was night, it was raining, and I never really saw her face."

"Lee." Perelli looked hard at him. "How come you never remembered any of this before?"

"I help a lot of people. Through random roadsides. Or people flag me over. A lot of times, I don't charge, you know, if it's a loose battery cable or something. I don't remember every face. And we'd just had Dylan and that night coming out of the hospital, my radio goes off and my dispatcher is asking me to help with the truck-train thing. Nobody hurt but it kept me busy."

Lee added he never really associated anything bad with that time. He was so happy, he had a million things on his mind, being a new dad. He was ecstatic because against all the odds, he and Maria had a new baby.

Grace flipped through the pages of her case notes and told Lee and Maria that Beth Bannon went to a lot of confidential support classes and groups; one of them for women who'd lost babies, which met at a small community hall in Ballard.

"Lee, when you helped Beth Bannon, the night she had her sad friend in the car? It was likely Nadine."

A few seconds of silence passed as everyone absorbed the facts.

"She thinks Dylan is her baby," Maria said.

All eyes went to her.

"This Nadine, who stole Dylan—she thinks he belongs to her, that's what's happened."

Maria drew Nadine's picture closer, searching her eyes. Then she gently placed it on the table.

"He's not yours," she whispered, "you give him back."

Lee tried to put his arm around Maria, but she

shrugged him off. The flats of her hands slapped hard on the table as she remained locked on Nadine's face. "Where are you? You give me back my son!"

61

A fly walked along the forehead of Hollywood's hottest eligible hunk until Shirley Brewer mashed it with her flyswatter.

With an expert flick, she sent the dead insect to the trash, then resumed studying her tabloid on the counter while finishing her breakfast: a glazed apple Danish and black coffee.

Another lazy morning at the Sweet Dreams & Goodnight Motel. Located on the wooded fringe of one of those neighborhoods few people gave much thought. The motel, with its warped window frames, peeling paint, and leaky plumbing, was owned by Shirley, her good-for-nothing, shiftless husband, and the bank.

She had to laugh at her pitiful self, or else she'd cry. One day, you're a shapely eighteen-year-old from Tacoma with dreams of being a singer. Then you blink, forty years vanish, and you're three hundred pounds of regret. At least today's Danish was fresh.

She halted chewing long enough to squint through the streaked office window. A car had rolled up. A guest? Already? Couldn't be. Likely someone lost looking for directions.

The transom bells jingled.

A woman, in her late twenties, say. Good figure. Hair short and hidden under her big hat, large dark glasses that did not hide the shiner on her left cheek.

If Shirley had learned anything in all her years as an innkeeper, it was how to read people instantly and she had this girl's story down in a heartbeat.

"I'm going to need a room."

Shirley's eyes went to the car for another person.

"How many people?"

"Just me."

"How many nights, hon?"

"I don't know."

"It's forty-five per night, but"—Shirley tried not to make much of the woman's bruise—"we're running a special today. How does thirty sound?"

"Good, thank you."

"Just fill out this registration card."

The woman's fingers were scraped and her hands trembled a little. *Lord of Moses, what she must've been through,* Shirley thought, before noticing the tattoo on the back of her hand.

That's an interesting one.

The woman signed in as Jane Smith from Spokane.

Smith. Right.

"You drive all night?"

"What?"

"From Spokane?"

"Oh. Yes."

Shirley turned and plucked a key for Room 19 off a peg.

"It's got a nice comfy new mattress and bathroom. Nice and quiet. To the far end of the courtyard. You can park around back. And if you walk down the path through the woods at the edge of the property, it'll take you through the forest to the creek. It's pretty and shaded down there. A good place to think in private."

"Thank you."

"And, hon? You're doing the right thing."

"Excuse me?"

"Well, it's none of my affair, but it's obvious." Shirley indicated the bruised cheek. "He hit you, so you left. It might have been a hard decision, but, sweetheart, it's the right one, for damn sure. Am I wrong?"

Jane Smith stood in silence for a moment.

Thinking.

"Please, don't let anyone know we're here. He's got a lot of friends, *even police friends*. If he finds me I don't know what he'll do. Promise me you won't tell anyone."

"Don't worry. You're safe here." Shirley dropped her voice. "My poor excuse for a man took a swing at me long time ago when he was drunk. I brained him with a skillet and that ended that."

She winked. "Remember, park around back. No one will see your car."

After Jane Smith left, Shirley resumed eating breakfast and studying her tabloid.

There. That's one good thing done today.

She sighed, then switched on the small color TV she kept on the counter by the maps. Might as well see what was happening in the news today.

62

Room 19 reeked of cigarettes, stale beer, and despair.

The rear courtyard was compact and lined with thick shrubbery and a stand of trees, making the unit and her car invisible from the street. Nadine thought it was perfect. And it was pure luck that the nosy cow at the counter considered her an abused woman from Spokane.

After the fire, she just drove.

Aimlessly.

She was exhausted and knew she should get some sleep to clear her mind but she couldn't rest until she figured out what to do.

She was afraid.

Everything had gone wrong. Everyone had lied to her. She trusted no one. She had to find the truth. When she finished unpacking all that she needed from the car, she drew the curtains. Removed her hat and glasses, went to the bathroom and looked at her hands.

She was still shaking.

They weren't stained with paint.

That's blood.

She washed them. Gritting her teeth as she scrubbed.

Then, standing before the mirror, she stared at herself, touching the bruise on her cheek. Axel had managed one punch. *One last punch.* Who would've figured his final act after deceiving her would help her.

Why did you lie to me, Axel? I trusted you. I loved you. I shared dreams of building a new life with you. But you were just like the others. When will I learn that the only person I can trust is me?

It had happened so fast with Axel. She'd had no choice. In the days before they were to depart, after she'd discovered he'd left his computer on, she'd read his cryptic files. And last night, as they were packing the car to leave, she'd learned of his plan.

It had to be a joke, she thought.

Was he really planning to murder her? *Kill her?* Stage a suicide, then sell Dylan to a black-market group in Vancouver, British Columbia, for $25,000 and make it all look like she and Dylan had died in a fire?

She was stunned but had no time to risk letting her guard down.

That was why she'd carried the knife in her waistband, under her shirt.

When Axel called her into the garage, to show her "a surprise" at the front of the van, she was ready to surprise *him.* The instant she smelled the gasoline, walked among the dizzying fumes, saw Axel's shadow flash as he raised his hands to slide a plastic bag over her head, she was ready.

But he wasn't.

The blade flashed as she drove it hard and deep into his abdomen, pulling it out and thrusting it into him again and again. Shocked, he managed to hit her before he fell over, his voice all liquidy with blood. He pleaded in vain as she heaved him into the van and finished what he'd set out to do.

Liar!

She screamed at him as the garage ignited.

Axel was like Beth Bannon. What Beth did was also unforgivable.

It was evil.

Even when Nadine had given her the chance to redeem herself, Beth continued lying. *Why do so many people lie to me? Why do they always pretend to be my friend, then lie to me?* She couldn't understand it.

She'd arrived in Seattle alone and in trouble. She began seeking help in hospitals and clinics. That was how she met Beth, at a class for mothers who'd lost their babies.

"I'll help you, Nadine, I promise."

But Beth lied.

Nadine had discovered that Beth actually gave babies to couples; couples who God did not think were fit to have babies of their own. Nadine felt betrayed.

Enraged.

She was left with no choice but to follow Beth to where she lived in North Seattle and confront her. Beth was shocked when she appeared at her door that night. Beth tried to play it cool, all nonchalant and whatnot. Pretending like she was still going to help, refusing to acknowledge the truth even after Nadine confronted her with it. She tried, heaven knew how she tried, to give Beth every chance to help her set things right.

Still, Beth refused, leaving Nadine with no other choice.

Some people simply responded better to a threat.

Unfortunately, not Beth.

Even when Nadine held out the knife, she acted all calm and understanding, as though Nadine had failed to grasp the truth.

It was Beth who was lying.

Nadine replayed that night over again. Had she missed anything?

Beth had just made herself popcorn and was settling in to watch Sleepless in Seattle. *How sappy.*

"We need to talk now, Beth. I told you, I came to Seattle pregnant and alone."

"Yes, you told me that."

"The hospital took my baby and gave it to another couple."

"Yes, that's what you told me, but I'm not sure—"

"Liar! You know the truth. The hospital took my baby right after it was born and gave him to you."

"To me? No, that's not true."

"Then you gave my baby away."

"Nadine, that never happened, now please put the knife down and listen."

"No! You listen! You tell me who has my baby!"

"No one has your baby. Please put the knife down."

"Where's my baby, Beth?"

"I swear, I don't know."

"You are a lying bitch! A stupid, lying bitch!"

"Nadine, you need more help than I can give you."

"Where's my baby? You took him and you gave him away!"

"No."

Unable to tolerate another lie, Nadine stabbed her. Beth screamed as blood flowed.

"Oh God, please stop."

"You gave my baby to that tow truck guy that rainy night."

"Please, no. I don't know what you're talking about!"

Nadine stabbed her again.

"What's his name? Where does he live?"

"No, no."

"I overheard you that night. You talked about his new baby, how happy he was. You talked about money. I saw you write something on an envelope. Now, tell me!"

Nadine stabbed Beth again; this time it was harder. Deeper. Beth collapsed.

"Help me, please."

"Stop lying!"

Nadine stubbed her and stabbed her, so many times it was as if Beth broke. Her blood gushed and sprayed in all directions like fountain works, warm and sticky. Yet still she refused to tell the truth.

"Well, you just lie there lying and dying, Beth Bannon," Nadine told her corpse as she washed the knife and her hands, cleaning herself pretty thoroughly before carting off Beth's files.

And here they were.

Nadine turned to the three cardboard file boxes she'd

taken that day, documents that she'd now hauled into the motel room, along with Axel's laptop. After dealing with Beth, Nadine searched her papers and found the envelope that led her to the Colson home in Ballard.

See, it is true.

The Colsons had her baby and soon Nadine would rescue him, she assured herself when she found their home in Ballard and began spying on them.

Liars! All of them, liars!

But no matter how hard Nadine searched Beth's documents, she never found what she needed, the records that proved Dylan was her son.

"I'm going to look real hard right now until I find them and that will end things once and for all, won't it, sweetie."

Nadine leaned over the bed and kissed Dylan, who was asleep.

"See, they all tried to take you away from me. They all lied and they all died. We're going to be together forever and ever. Yes we are."

Nadine hummed as she searched the files.

63

Jason was rolling his Falcon along the Seattle streets from Joy Montgomery's home to Ballard. He needed to show Nadine's picture to the neighbors, maybe the supermarket cashiers and the people at Lee Colson's tow shop.

Jason was planning his next steps when his phone went off.

"It's Grace. You're the first person to get this, but we believe Dylan Colson is still alive."

"What? Hold on! Hold on!" He pulled over. "Say that again."

"We found no trace of the baby's remains at the scene."

"Who's dead, then?"

"Nadine's boyfriend. An ex-con named Axel Tackett. I gotta go."

"Wait, wait. Spell that and give me his D.O.B." After taking down the information, he said, "Where's Dylan?"

"We believe Nadine fled with him after setting the fire."

"She murdered Tackett?"

"She's the prime suspect."

"For Beth Bannon too?"

"Yes."

"Man. Where is she? You got a lead on a location?"

"Working on it. It'll all be out soon with a press conference. You've got the scoop. I'll see you there. I have to go."

"Hold on, Grace. What about Lee Colson as a suspect?"

"Cleared."

"Is all this on the record, or am I sourcing you?"

"On the record, we're squared now."

"Closer to being squared."

"Very funny."

Jason called an editorial assistant at the paper and dictated a breaking news update for immediate posting on the *Mirror*'s Internet edition. Then he called Spangler's line and left a voice-mail message, alerting him to the development and urging him to put someone good on the police scanners to listen for a possible takedown.

After hanging up his phone rang again.

"Jay," his old man said. "I've got to meet you right away."

"Not now, Dad. There's been a major break."

"I've got something you must see."

"What is it?"

"Prison, police, and psychiatric records for Nadine Lasher. That's her real name. Nadine Sienna Lasher."

Twenty minutes later, Jason met his father at a booth at Fat Ray's Diner, off the northeast campus of the University of Washington.

Jason's old man passed him the records, some fifteen pages from several agencies—Toronto Police, Royal Canadian Mounted Police, Correctional Service of Canada, something from psychiatric services from the province of Ontario.

"She's Canadian, born in Toronto." Henry Wade spooned sugar into his coffee.

"I see that. This is dynamite. How'd you get this so fast?"

"Krofton's connected. A lot of this stuff, in various forms, is public up there. But the agency got its request fast-tracked through the FBI liaison at the U.S. Embassy in Ottawa. You can bet a fuller package moved even faster and is now with Seattle PD and at the FBI field office downtown."

As Jason examined Nadine's records, a compelling story emerged.

Hours after her birth, she was found wrapped in a worn, torn ski jacket, abandoned on the steps of a downtown Toronto church.

She grew up a ward of social welfare agencies, raised in the homes of foster parents, where, at times, she was abused. At twenty-three, she was a desperately lonely gift-shop clerk who, oddly, still lived with her morally strict foster parents.

Nadine had an affair with a married stockbroker and became pregnant. He broke his promise to leave his wife and marry her. He demanded Nadine get an abortion, then broke off their relationship.

Nadine refused to get an abortion but attempted suicide.

When her foster parents learned of her affair and

pregnancy they were appalled and shamed. They sent her off to relatives in Niagara Falls, where she gave birth to a son. Her foster parents then demanded she give up her baby for adoption.

Nadine agreed, but secretly kept in contact with the adoptive parents. At this time, unknown to anyone, Nadine was undergoing psychiatric counseling for delusions and drug abuse.

Meanwhile, the happy adoptive parents had agreed to grant Nadine periodic visits. About a year after her baby boy was born, the adoptive parents were days away from finalizing the adoption.

During her last visit with her son, Nadine abducted him and fled. It triggered a massive search involving police, volunteers, tracking dogs, and helicopters. The trail led to a remote area north of Toronto, where searchers found Nadine sitting alone by the shore of an isolated small lake.

She was humming a lullaby to herself.

Searchers could not find the baby. Divers probed the lake. Police dragged it for three days. No body was ever recovered.

In custody, Nadine told detectives that it was wrong for the father of her baby to have lied. Wrong for her foster parents to have forced her to give up her son. And wrong for the adoptive parents to take him from her.

"How could the baby ever be happy without his real mother?" she was quoted in court transcripts as telling homicide investigators.

During her trial, she remained steadfast in her

account of the abduction, stating that she had no clear memory of the whereabouts of the baby. After three days of testimony, Nadine Sienna Lasher, owing to her altered mental state at the time of her acts, was sentenced to five years in prison.

A year after she was sent to a prison for the criminally insane, Nadine underwent several severe psychotic episodes. She summoned detectives. She had something more to tell them.

In a long, emotionless monologue, she blamed others. Having been lied to by everyone, she'd been certain that her baby's adoptive parents were going to move far away once the adoption was complete.

"I knew I would never see my boy again, that's why I took care of him."

"What did you do, Nadine?"

"I sent my baby to Heaven."

"Can you show us where? Where you sent him to Heaven?"

Detectives drove Nadine north of Toronto and deep into the bush country but far from the original spot where she was first found. Nadine took the police deep into a forest clearing, where she pointed to a shiny heart-shaped stone under a stand of wildflowers.

An autopsy confirmed that the baby had been buried. Alive.

64

Nadine stared live from TVs across the United States.
So did Dylan Colson.

Photos of their faces were followed by the faces of Axel Tackett and Beth Bannon.

By midmorning, Nadine Sienna Lasher, a.k.a., Nadine Getch, was the nation's most wanted fugitive, sought in the abduction of Dylan Colson and the homicides of Beth Bannon and Axel Tackett.

Police believed Nadine was still in the greater Sea-Tac area and were appealing to the public through the alert system and the press for anyone with information to call.

"She is considered armed and dangerous, and should not be approached," Agent McCusker told more than one hundred reporters gathered at the news conference held by the Seattle FBI, the Seattle Police, and the King County Sheriff's Office.

"And now, Dylan's parents, Lee and Maria Colson, will say a few words. They will take no questions."

The room's emotional intensity shot up under the lights.

Brilliant flashes from still cameras rained down on

the Colsons as they sat behind the mountain of micro-phones and recorders. Heads bowed, they held hands while struggling to begin. Maria wore a print bandana to cover her stitches. She touched the corners of her eyes. Lee was unshaven. Relatives and friends lined the wall behind them.

"Dylan is our world," Maria said amid the whir-click of cameras. "He is everything. Nadine, if you can hear my voice, please, I'm begging you, please, just let him go."

Maria covered her face with her hand, then she buried it in Lee's chest, intensifying the camera flashes. For newswires and newspapers, *that* was the shot. A portrait of pain. The mother of a stolen baby boy pleading to the fugitive murder suspect who'd abducted him.

Lee cleared his throat and swallowed. He blinked rapidly before he said, "Nadine, Dylan is our son. We know you're taking good care of him. We know you have no intention of hurting him. Please, let him go. People want to help you. Please." Lee rubbed the tension in his jaw. "Thank you."

The Colsons left and McCusker concluded things as the description of Nadine appeared on broadcasts next to her face.

"We're asking anyone who has any information as to the whereabouts of Nadine Lasher and Dylan Colson to call your local police agency immediately," McCusker said. "We are only one call away from locating Dylan and bringing him home safe to his mother and father."

65

"You're liars! All of you!" Nadine shouted at Lee and Maria Colson, who pleaded to her from the TV. Her eyes raced around her motel room; the stained walls were closing in on her. They were coming.

She gazed upon Dylan, asleep on the bed.

"You're mine. They can't take you from me."

Stinging from lack of sleep, her eyes widened as she inventoried the room. The foul-smelling carpet had disappeared under the scattered files, papers, and notes she'd searched. Beth's material.

It wasn't there.

Why wasn't it there?

Her painful memories of how she'd arrived in Seattle, alone, scared, and pregnant. She'd given birth to her son but they would not let her see him.

Why?

Well, Nadine had figured it out, it had to have happened like the last time. They took him and gave him to a childless couple. And she was not going to let that happen again. She told Beth everything, told her what had happened. Begged her to help her find her baby.

Who had her baby?

Beth had to know. She helped people find babies.

Axel was supposed to help too. That was why she wrote to him at Coyote Ridge before he got out. He believed in her. Shared her dream to build a life together with their baby. That was how it had been—until Nadine found out for herself that Lee and Maria had stolen her baby.

Papers rustled as she rummaged through the scattered files for anything that would prove it. Tears blurred her eyes. Why wasn't it here? She could not let them take her boy away.

What's this?

A note, handwritten by Beth, a fragment from another note. She slid to the floor as she read it, not believing, the words coming like blows.

I'm very concerned about Nadine. She's mentally unstable, insisting she's given birth to a baby boy here in Washington State within the past year when it's just not true. I know little about her past, but her delusions and fantasies are disturbing. She needs help.

Nadine gasped.

Mentally unstable. Delusions. Fantasies.

How could Beth say such hurtful things?

"There's my son on the bed, Beth! He's not a fantasy. He's real!"

Nadine's world was falling apart. She had to do something fast.

What was that?

A siren.

Far off.

Was it getting closer or going away?

She couldn't risk waiting to find out. She couldn't let them stop her from being with him. Nadine got to her feet, brushed the tears from her eyes, wrapped Dylan in a blanket, took him in her arms, and left.

She found the entrance to the path and stepped into the cool darkness of the woods. Soothed by the sun-dappled light, she followed the trail as it twisted along a downward slope. As she neared the water, she heard its rush beckoning. Branches grazed her as she came closer to the creek and a final decision.

It was an isolated sanctuary within Seattle.

No one else around.

Nothing but trees and the creek, the water's flow drowning out the sounds of the city.

Nadine stood at the water's edge with Dylan in her arms and tears rolling down her face.

She was so tired of lies, so tired of fighting for what was hers. Dylan's warmth against her felt so right. So perfect. Looking at his sweet face, feeling his sweet breath, she understood now.

Understood exactly what he was.

He was her angel baby from the bad time come back from Heaven.

Her answered prayer. Come back to take her with him.

Slowly, Nadine slipped off her shoes.

The moist mud of the bank was cool on her toes.

It felt like *release*. It felt right. Like a dream.

Her dream.

Their dream.

Remember the dream.

They were going to move into a beautiful little house with a big wraparound porch with hand-carved spindles in the railing. They'd have a big porch swing where they would sit on summer nights, sip lemonade, and look up at the stars.

They'd have a pretty yard with a big old shade tree in the back where he could play. She'd buy him a baseball and a glove and a football and she would play catch with him. And on weekends they'd go for drives into the country for picnics and ice cream, then pick wildflowers and wade in a stream. Birthday parties in their house would be special. Christmas and all the holidays would be perfect, like in the magazines she read at the supermarket checkout.

They were going to be the kind of family she'd always dreamed of having. Ever since she was a little girl. And they were going to live in the kind of house she'd seen a million billion times in her mind.

It would have a big fireplace where they would sit and listen to the rain on stormy days, or keep cozy on winter nights. Their house would have a big kitchen where she would make the best home-cooked meals ever, and it would have big bright rooms filled with light.

Filled with love.

They would go there now.

Nadine edged into the water, felt it rise above her

ankles, swirl and suck around her calves, knees, thighs, and climb coolly to her waist.

Dylan stirred in her arms.

His blanket, her pants and shirt glowed surreally against the dark water and green of the wood. She edged farther out, feeling the slippery, moss-slicked rocks under her toes and the current pushing against her.

Dylan was waking.

Squirming.

"Hush. We're almost home, angel, almost home."

66

The mouth. The chin. The butterfly and spiderweb tattoo.

Lord of Moses, could it be her? The girl the police were looking for?

Shirley Brewer pulled her attention from the TV news bulletin to the peg that held the key for Room 19. She looked at her telephone before she checked the guest registration card.

Jane Smith with her face bruised. Her fingers scraped.

Shirley had this one down for a runaway, an abused woman. She couldn't be this "Nadine" they were looking for, could she? There was no baby. *But there was that tattoo on the back of her hand.* Shirley tapped the card on the counter.

All right.

Before she called anybody, she'd check it out, just to be sure.

Grunting, she reached for her hickory cane and her ring of master keys, then headed to the linen storage room to collect some fresh towels and her thoughts. She'd just make a little innocent check. To be sure. No sense sounding an alarm if it wasn't her.

And she prayed that it was not her.

Lord, two murders, a missing baby.

Shirley was uneasy but not afraid. She'd dealt with all kinds of people and had learned that being in this business was not for the faint of heart.

Still, her grip on her cane tightened.

Her swollen legs bothered her more and more these days, she thought as she tottered across the deserted courtyard. When she came to the back unit by the trees, she saw Jane Smith's blue Ford Focus and took note of the license plate.

All quiet here.

The car was unlocked and the windows were down. Seemed a little odd. People always locked up. Poking her head inside, she took stock of the interior. It was empty, clean, no sign of anything wrong. She stuck out her bottom lip upon seeing the rental dealer plate.

She knocked on the motel room door.

"Hello, dear, I brought you more fresh towels."

No response.

"Dear?"

She knocked again, louder, then tried to see through the crack in the drawn curtains. Where could she be? Breezes swept through the treetops and she glanced to the woods. Maybe she went for a walk to the creek. Shirley slid her key into the handle and opened the door.

"Hello, dear. I've brought you more towels."

Lord Almighty.

Her jaw dropped.

Papers were strewn over the floor, the nightstand, the chair, the TV, the desk. They buried a laptop and much of the bed, where a suitcase had spewed its contents. This was not a mess. It was an explosion of rage, of something gone terribly wrong, Shirley thought, moving closer to the bed.

There, under the papers, she saw a baby's bottle, a small pack of fresh disposable diapers. As Shirley touched other baby items, worry twisted in her stomach and kept twisting until it took her breath away.

She did have a baby.

Then Shirley Brewer, who had battled drunks, crackhead hookers, pimps, and the frightening pieces of scum who landed here, groaned with fear. For as she shifted her weight, the light adjusted and she saw the words dripping in red letters across the mirror.

"He's My Baby!"

Shirley had to call the police now. She reached for the phone but froze.

"What are you doing in my room?"

Nadine stood in the doorway.

"Oh, dear, you startled me! Oh, I'm sorry. I just brought you these fresh towels," Shirley said, disturbed by Nadine's condition. "Goodness, you're soaked to the bone."

Nadine said nothing. Breathing hard, she was drenched, her hair, her clothes; water dripped from her, darkening the carpet at her feet. In the moment the two women looked at each other, the truth passed between them and the air tightened as if someone had just pulled back the hammer of a gun.

"Dear." Shirley swallowed. "Where's the baby?"

Nadine was lost in a trance, staring at nothing.

"Sweetheart, where's the baby?"

"He's my baby."

"I'd love to see him."

"He's safe. He'll always be safe."

"Where?" Shirley's knuckles whitened on her cane as she moved closer. "Honey, where is he?"

"Hey!" A distant voice outside. A man calling. "Hey, miss!"

In that instant, Nadine snatched her small bag from the round table near the door, ran outside, and got into her car.

"Wait!" Shirley started after her, but the Ford's door slammed and the ignition turned. "Please! Wait!"

The engine revved and the tires squealed.

"Wait! Miss!"

The man emerging from the forest was in his forties, with glasses, a blondish beard, and a ball cap. His clothes were soaked too. He arrived just as the Focus roared away.

"Hey, what the hell's going on?" Puzzled, he looked to Shirley for an answer. "I'm downstream taking bird pictures when I see this girl in my viewfinder. I thought she was drowning, so I set my gear down and rush across the creek to help, and she runs away. Ma'am?"

Shirley was chanting the license plate of the Focus. Over and over as she hurried back into the room, seized the phone, and called 911.

"Lord, hurry!" she told no one as the line clicked.

"Jee-zuss, what the hell happened in here?" The man looked around the room. "Is that woman all right?"

"Go back to the water"—Shirley pointed her cane at the birdwatcher.

"Why?"

"Go back to the creek and look for a baby!"

"What?"

"A baby—did you see a baby?" Shirley spoke into the phone, "Hello, police! Lord—!"

67

Time had run out.

Given what Jason Wade now knew about Nadine's past, and now that she'd murdered two more people, he held little hope Dylan Colson would be found alive.

If they find him at all.

The downtown boardroom had emptied fast after the press conference had ended. Most news crews had packed up and left, a few stragglers were on cell phones talking to editors. He needed a moment alone with Grace Garner but had lost sight of her and the Colsons when his phone rang.

"It's Spangler. The parents were riveting. What else you got?"

Stepping out of earshot of others, he decided it was time to tell him everything. "Some exclusive, compelling bio stuff on Nadine."

"What sort of stuff?"

"She did this before in Toronto, abducted and killed a baby. I've got her file from Canada."

"*What?* Where the hell is it? I want that file now."

"I'll get it faxed to you."

"I want you to get more from the parents. I want you to get us an exclusive with the Colsons now!"

"I don't know"—Jason looked around—"they took them away."

"Find them and do it, Wade! Don't let us down now!"

Grace would know, Jason thought after hanging up. But where was she? He needed her. He could feel time hammering against them. Nate Hodge, the *Mirror* news photographer, was in the hall, on his phone discussing his pictures with Bitner, the photo editor.

"Nate." Jason grabbed his shoulder. "Did you see which way Grace Garner and the Colsons went?"

Staying on his phone, Hodge pointed down the hall to the right. Coins jingled in Jason's pocket as he hurried, taking the corner as Perelli and Dupree shot by him in the opposite direction, concern stamped on their faces, cologne-scented breezes in their wake.

Something's going on, Jason thought. As he turned to watch them, he bumped into Grace, her face tense with urgency.

"Grace, I have to talk to you about Nadine's criminal history, about Toronto."

"Not now, Jason!" Her phone was pressed to her head as she followed Perelli and Dupree.

"Grace, please, I need two minutes alone with the Colsons."

"Dammit, Jason, not now! Something's happened!"

"What's going on?"

She couldn't answer as she rushed by for the emergency exit stairs. He was following her when he caught sight of Lee Colson, alone at the end of the hall, stepping into a washroom.

Hodge called after Jason, but he'd followed Lee into the washroom. Colson was doubled over the sink, his hands shaking as he splashed water on his face. He met Jason's reflection in the mirror. Colson looked utterly defeated.

"Excuse me, Lee, I'm so sorry. Jason Wade from the *Mirror*."

"I know who you are. You're the one who found Beth Bannon."

"Lee, I was wondering if—"

"So if you're so good, can you tell me what's happening?"

"I was going to ask you—I mean, I saw Grace and the others hurry out of here."

"They've just received a new tip but won't tell us anything. They say they don't want to raise our hopes. They want to take us home and have us wait. We can't take this. We just want to find our baby boy. Goddammit! I feel so damn helpless." He pounded the counter.

The door swung open as Hodge swept in, phone to his ear.

"Jason, Bitner says it's all over the police scanners now. They got a 911 call—someone spotted Nadine! It's a good tip, down to the tattoo."

Hope blossomed on Colson's face.

"Where?"

"Hang on!" Hodge listened to his phone. "In a Ford Focus somewhere near Aurora, direction unknown. They've put up the chopper. They'll likely try to box her in, then take her down. Come on, Jason, we'll take my Blazer, let's go!"

"Hold on," Lee said, "take us with you!"

Hodge and Jason stared at Lee.

"We need to be there. Maria and I will go with you."

Jason seized the opportunity.

"Okay, do this: get Maria away from the uniforms now."

"I can do that."

"Just say the relative who is going to take you home has the car in the back downstairs, say the FBI arranged it."

Lee nodded.

"Then meet us in the stairwell on the ground floor like now! Immediately."

"Wait," Lee said to Hodge, "did the 911 tip say anything about Dylan, did they see him?"

Hodge put the question to Bitner back at the paper, who shouted to the *Mirror*'s intern listening to the scanners.

"There were indications of a baby," Hodge said. "Something about sending fire department divers to a river, but no baby was seen. We'd better move, now!"

68

Nadine's world was crumbling.

As tears stained her face she drove through the traffic along Aurora Avenue. She had wanted to end it all at the creek. It was such a beautiful place—spiritual, really—but the stranger had interrupted her.

So it was not meant to happen there.

Nadine swallowed air.

She couldn't bear to look at herself in the mirror, with her drying skin tightening, her hair frizzed, her clothes damp and chafing. She knew she looked a mess.

She brushed at her tears.

Her life was a mess, nothing more than a series of lies until it dawned on her that everywhere she'd turned, everyone she'd ever trusted, had tried to convince her that she was wrong. To make her believe that somehow her entire life was a lie.

Well, they were wrong.

Every goddamn one of them.

Liars.

That's what they were.

A horn beeped, jerking her attention back to her

driving. Nadine didn't know exactly where she was going but she knew exactly what was true.

Dylan was hers.

He was the one person who did not lie.

The one person who loved her back.

"You're so quiet, angel." Stopped at a red light, Nadine looked to the rear floor where Dylan was lying. "In a little while, Mommy's going to fix it so they won't lie to us anymore. We're going someplace where they won't ever find us. Oh, green light."

Nadine threaded the car through traffic, which, for some reason, seemed to be increasing.

"We're going where I can love you and hold you forever. Where nobody lies."

Nadine started humming a lullaby as her small blue Ford moved along Aurora, passing a sign indicating they were coming to the Aurora Avenue Bridge, which spanned Lake Union.

"Soon we'll be in Heaven."

69

God, please let me find my baby.

Buckled in the backseat of Nate Hodge's speeding SUV, Maria Colson clamped her hands together and prayed. The cross-talk over the police radio in the Blazer intensified as dispatchers began betraying emotion over the air.

"Suspect's vehicle sighted on the approach to the bridge. All units stand by—"

Hodge took every shortcut he knew but time was racing against them. They could hear distant sirens howling, see the police and news helicopters far off.

"All units, that sighting is confirmed. We do have the car approaching the bridge—"

"Hang on."

The Chevy's big eight cylinders hammered as Hodge stomped on the accelerator.

At first Nadine could not fathom why traffic had slowed to a crawl near the bridge.

As her Ford crept forward, she realized road construction had created lane reductions and delays.

Nadine squinted through her windshield in a futile effort to see ahead.

Suddenly, her Focus shuddered and the motor died. Her fuel indicator showed that her car was out of gas. Nadine slapped her hands on the whcel. Drivers behind her, already angry because of the gridlock, began honking. Some attempted to squeeze around her, creating more traffic problems and more honking.

Nadine had a plan. She got out, opened the rear door, took Dylan into her arms, and began walking toward the bridge.

He was such a good baby.

So quiet.

In the woods behind the Sweet Dreams & Goodnight Motel, Grace, Perelli, and Dupree had joined an army of police, firefighters, and paramedics.

Their radios crackled across the water, echoing through the forest.

Shirley Brewer and the bird man were also there, watching officials from the FBI, Seattle PD, King County Sheriff's Office, Washington Highway Patrol, and neighboring jurisdictions look for a tiny body.

Fire crews had hauled rubber boats down the slopes and slapped them into the water. Other investigators waded in while K-9 units scoured the banks.

Based on what had happened here, Grace feared that Nadine had drowned Dylan and fled.

Would this be her third homicide in the case? Grace bit her lip as her cell phone rang with an update.

"It's Boulder. They're closing in on the Ford,

Nadine's been spotted near the bridge on Aurora and she's definitely got a baby with her."

"Alive, Stan? She could be carrying a corpse. Is the baby alive?"

From the newest transmissions, Jason, who'd been sketching a rough map of sightings, had it and pointed.

"She's southbound coming to the bridge."

Hodge's Blazer was northbound, frozen in traffic but within sight of the bridge. The nearest marked police units, sirens wailing, weren't getting much closer.

"All units, new call from a motorist on Aurora reports woman exiting the vehicle with baby, on foot on west side southbound—"

"Ten-four, we're still too far back, stuck in this traffic—Larry, how's it looking for you?"

"Not good."

At this point the Blazer filled with the vibrating transmission from Guardian One, the King County police helicopter.

"We've got a visual—she has a child in her arms and is walking toward the bridge. Dispatch, can we get a call through to the road crew down there to wake them up to what's going on? Somebody's got to grab her now!"

The rear of the Blazer thudded as Lee hammered the side door in frustration. "Goddammit!"

Maria pleaded, "Somebody do something!"

Jason felt gooseflesh rise. Were the Colsons about to hear the murder of their baby over the air? He turned to Hodge, who had gritted his teeth and shifted gears.

"Hold tight, everyone!"

The Blazer's motor growled as Hodge veered into oncoming traffic sounding his horn, flashing his four-way lights. *I swear, Your Honor, it was a matter of life and death.* The Chevy pinballed through traffic, around construction pylons.

"Faster!" Maria screamed.

Rising high over Lake Union, the Aurora Avenue Bridge offered sweeping views of Seattle, and of ships navigating the Ballard Locks and the Lake Washington– Lake Union Ship Canal on their way to the ocean.

Nadine had walked to the middle of its span when someone tried to stop her.

"Hold it right there!"

Two men wearing white T-shirts, jeans, hard hats, and orange vests were running toward her. She saw walkie-talkies clipped to their belts.

"We want to talk to you for a moment, please!"

Her face clenched, Nadine raised Dylan just over her head. He began to cry.

"You get away from me!"

The men flashed their empty palms. Then, amid sirens, horns, and the thumping helicopters, Nate Hodge's Blazer screeched to a halt and Marie and Lee rushed toward Nadine, who backed hard against the bridge's railing.

"Nadine, please. I'm Maria, Dylan's mother! Please put him down!"

Nadine's memory raced back to when Maria had jumped onto Axel's van to stop her from taking Dylan, remembering how her eyes reflected the desperation she now carried in her heart.

Nadine was confused.

Don't be tricked.

She looked at the people circled round her: the two construction workers, Maria, her husband, Jason Wade, and Nate Hodge, who was photographing it all as police vehicles approached.

"Stay back! All of you!"

"Yes, Nadine."

"He's mine, Maria! You stole him from me!"

Nadine lifted Dylan to the railing, holding him on it.

"No, please, Nadine!" Tears filled Maria's eyes as she edged closer, ever so closer, fighting her instinct to reach for Dylan, to lunge for him.

She was still too far.

"You stole my baby, Maria, and you lied!"

Maria nodded.

"Yes, he's yours and I know you love him so much, no one understands that, but I do!"

Nadine nodded as she listened.

"So I'll tell everyone here for you, Nadine, he's your baby because you love him the most. I understand." She pointed to Jason. "This man is a reporter. He's writing down the truth."

Nadine nodded slowly.

"But I love Dylan too. So please, could I hold him one last time, to say good-bye, please?"

Nadine repositioned her fingers on Dylan's waist, keeping him on the railing edge while she thought, as Maria, and the police behind her, moved closer.

Far back, a sharpshooter with a scope was lining up a head shot.

"Please, Nadine, may I hold him, one last time?"

"No!"

Maria leapt forward, her hands covering Nadine's; now both women had hold of Dylan. Maria screamed, feeling Nadine growling and driving her feet hard into the ground, trying to propel herself, Dylan, all of them, over the side.

Maria fought back. Dylan wailed as the women struggled for him. The others had rushed forward to pull them away from the side. Maria had Dylan now, but in the surge, Nadine had succeeded in getting herself over the side. Hands reached for her but she fought them as she slid from their grip. A police officer had seized one wrist as her body dangled high above Lake Union.

Nadine never screamed.

She never uttered a word. Instead she fought with her free hand and kicked fiercely to loosen the officer's grip even as another officer reached for her.

But he missed.

Nadine worked herself free.

As she fell she stared into the sun and smiled, for in her final moment, before she died, she understood that God had let her hold Heaven in her arms.

And all would be forgiven.

Far above her, Maria Colson had collapsed to the road holding Dylan as Lee Colson held them both in his arms. They stayed that way for a long time amid the sirens, helicopters, traffic, and news cameras that soon crowded the bridge.

DAY SIX

70

The next morning a massive crisp photo of Maria rescuing Dylan from Nadine's death grip commanded the *Mirror*'s front page.

It ran under the headline

BABY RESCUED
AS ABDUCTOR FALLS TO DEATH
FROM BRIDGE

The paper had cleared eight inside pages for its exhaustive coverage, which included large, stunning news pictures. There was one taken by the birdwatcher showing Nadine waist-high in the river with Dylan in her arms. There were maps, graphics, a time line, and some 12,000 words of coverage. Spangler assigned fourteen reporters to the story and designated Jason as the lead writer.

He got a photo byline.

Key to the *Mirror*'s reporting was the fact that, other than Nadine's chance meeting with Lee because of Beth Bannon's car trouble that rainy night, she had no link to the Colsons.

Canadian authorities confirmed that Nadine Sienna

Lasher had been convicted for killing the baby she'd had as a result of her relationship with a married man in Toronto; the court found she was in a disassociated state when it gave her a five-year prison sentence.

"Obviously, her mental instability had reemerged after her release and upon her arrival in Seattle. We are satisfied she is responsible for the murders of Beth Bannon and Axel Tackett and the abduction of Dylan Colson," Grace Garner was quoted as saying in a release issued by the Seattle police.

It went on to state that Nadine had moved to Washington after starting a relationship with Axel Tackett, a convict she'd met through a website for inmates seeking pen pals. However, investigations by the FBI, Seattle Police, and King County medical officials failed to confirm that she had ever delivered a child in Washington State.

In the wake of Dylan Colson's dramatic rescue, balloons, flowers, cards, and stuffed toys began arriving at the Colson home in Ballard.

Relatives, friends, neighbors, and a string of politicians visited to share the Colsons' joy at being reunited with their son.

Elated in their relief, Maria and Lee received them all, accepting the good-natured observations of how Maria refused to let Dylan out of her sight, even in their home.

At every turn, Maria and Lee thanked every police agency, every person who searched, called, and prayed for Dylan's safety. Maria also offered sympathy for the families of the homicide victims and for Nadine.

"No, I don't hate her for what she did," Maria told CNN. "She had a troubled mind and I hope she has found peace. If anything, what she did has made me love my son even more, if that's possible."

In answering follow-up questions from Grace, Perelli, and Dupree, Lee had accepted that given the evidence that police had at the time, they had reason to suspect he may have been involved.

"I understand. No hard feelings." Lee shook hands with all of them.

Subsequent investigations through e-mails and phone records generated by Axel Tackett led the FBI and Royal Canadian Mounted Police to make several arrests on both sides of the border of people suspected in black market baby-buying and adoptions. Joy Montgomery's confidential cooperation also helped. Officials saw no need to challenge the Montgomerys' adoption of Emily.

As they stepped from the Colson house, Grace spotted a familiar red 1969 Falcon parked across the street.

Leaning against it with his arms folded, Jason Wade smiled as she approached him alone.

"You're looking mighty pleased with yourself, Jason."

"Could say the same about you."

"What're you doing here, haven't you milked this story enough?"

"Actually, I was looking for you."

"Why? The case is closed."

"Not where we're concerned, Grace."

Her smile grew a bit as she eyed him, brushing away the silky strands of hair a breeze pushed across her face.

"I don't date," she said.

"Do you eat?"

"Sometimes."

"How about one of those times, we just eat together?"

She searched his eyes and liked what was there, but she wasn't sure.

"Grace, don't you sometimes get a bit tired of eating alone in your apartment?"

She looked away and smiled. Jason followed her gaze down the street to her partner, Perelli, sitting behind the wheel of their unmarked Malibu, nodding big nods.

"But not a date, because I don't date."

"Hell no."

"Sure, I'll eat with you, Jason."

He nodded.

"I'll call you."

"Maybe I'll call you first." Grace Garner gave him a bigger smile as she walked away.

That night, Jason drove to his old man's place south of the airport. They drank Cokes while a couple of steaks sizzled on the barbecue and they watched the jets lifting off and landing.

They didn't speak much, sitting there listening to the planes, enjoying the sun setting over the Pacific.

"Thanks for everything, Dad."

His old man shrugged.

Jason stared at the ice in his glass, waiting for the right moment, then decided it might never come. After watching a 767 climb out over the ocean, he said, "So what happened all those years ago when you were a Seattle cop?"

His old man squinted toward the horizon from under his ball cap.

"I mean, Boulder was getting into it with you. I know you were on the job for a few years, then quit. Dad, what the hell happened?"

His old man removed his hat, looked into it as if the answer were there, replaced it, and continued staring at the jet that was disappearing in the horizon. Probably headed to Tokyo, Hong Kong, or Hawaii—someplace far away.

"I'm going to tell you about it."

That surprised Jason.

"Over the past years, a day hasn't gone by that I haven't thought about telling you."

"Shoot."

"Just not today. I'm just not ready, son."

He turned to face him and the unease Jason saw in his old man's eyes was enough to convince him that he had to let his father tell him when he was ready.

"Sure. Steaks look about done."

One of Beth Bannon's church groups claimed Nadine's body in what one Seattle columnist called an irony worthy of Shakespeare.

The columnist had learned that the group maintained

a small cemetery in a remote reach of Washington State where it saw to the burials of miscarriages, orphaned runaways, street people, and paupers.

It had arranged for a small headstone that would read:

NADINE SIENNA LASHER

"Heaven's door opened
and
washed away every fear"

AUTHOR'S NOTE
& ACKNOWLEDGEMENTS

Getting this story to you was not a solitary effort. My thanks to my editor, Audrey LaFehr, and everyone at Kensington who played a role in the production, promotion and distribution of the book. Again, my thanks to Wendy Dudley, Mildred Marmur, Jeff Aghassi, John and Jeannine Rosenberg, Shannon Whyte, Donna Riddell, Beth Tindall, Therese Greenwood, Prime Crime in Ottawa and the Florida gang, who always save me a seat at Bouchercon. A special thanks to Barbara, Laura and Michael.

I would also like to thank my British publisher, MIRA UK, for their fantastic work. And I tip my hat to the crew at www.shotsmag.co.uk. As well, my thanks to my Toronto agent, Amy Moore-Benson, and my London agent, Lorella Belli.

Thanks to friends in the news business for their over-whelming support and thanks to the staff of some of crime fiction's leading publications, *Crime Spree, Mystery Scene, Deadly Pleasures* and *Mystery Readers Journal*. And my special thanks to sales representatives, bookstore managers and booksellers I've come to know for putting my work in your hands. Which brings me to you, the reader. Thank you for your time, for without you, a book remains an untold tale. I hope you enjoyed the ride and that you'll be back for the next one.

Don't miss the next Jason Wade novel,

PERFECT GRAVE.

Read on for an exclusive look at the first chapter

1

For Sister Anne, death was always near.

But tonight, it *felt closer* and she didn't know why.

Tonight was like any other in the Compassionate Heart of Mercy Shelter at the fringe of Seattle's Pioneer Square District, where she was offering tomato soup to those who had lost hope. Their pasts haunted their faces. The pain of their lives stained their bodies with lesions, needle tracks, and prison tattoos.

Moving along the rows of plastic-covered bingo tables, Sister Anne saw how her "guests" occasionally looked up from their meals to the finger paintings on the basement walls, pictures taped there by the children of the shelter's day care program. Portraits of happy families holding hands under sunny skies and rainbows.

No dark clouds. No frowns. No tears.

Glimpses of heaven.

She was moved by the juxtaposition of the dreamy images and the cold realities of these unfortunate souls, handcuffed to mistakes, tragedies, and addictions, searching the artwork of inner-city children for answers.

Silent cries for help.

Offering help was Sister Anne's job. Her mission was to rescue broken people. To give them hot food, hope, and the courage to mend themselves.

"Would you like more soup, Willie?"

A gravelly whisper emerged from the crumb-specked beard of the former aircraft mechanic, who'd lost his job, his house, and finally, his family, to gambling.

"I don't want to trouble nobody, Sister."

"It's no trouble, dear. Sister Violet tells me you're doing well in recovery."

"Haven't missed a session in two months."

"Keep the faith, dear heart. You're my hero."

Sister Anne gripped his shoulder and pulled him close, indifferent to the smells of alcohol, cigarettes, body odor, and despair that were common here. The nuns of the order met the challenge of their mission, but Sister Anne embraced it.

For whether she was handing out wrapped sandwiches to homeless men, or comforting runaway teens and abused women, or whether she was entering prisons to counsel inmates, Sister Anne was a tireless warrior for charity.

She never lectured or preached; she served with humility, for she, too, had made mistakes. Yet none of the other sisters knew her story, or how she came to have her "God moment," which had inspired her devotion.

Sister Anne was private about her previous life.

In fact, upon first meeting her, few people figured Anne Braxton to be a nun. An easy thing to do since the Vatican's push in the 1960s to modernize the church. For the sisters of this small order, it meant they did not live a cloistered life behind the stone walls of a convent or maintain the tradition of wearing habits, wimples, and veils.

Tonight, Sister Anne wore faded jeans and a Seattle Seahawks sweatshirt, dotted with gravy and smelling of tuna casserole. With her scrubbed face and cropped hair feathered with gray, it was easy to peg her as a forty-something volunteer from a middle-class suburb. The small silver cross hanging from the black cord around her neck and her simple silver ring betrayed none of the inner fire that had fused her to her community.

For she had shouldered the anguish of those she'd worked so hard to help. Next to Willie was Beatrice, who'd been a schoolteacher in Ravenna when she accidentally backed her minivan over a six-year-old girl on a school trip. The girl died. Beatrice fell into a depression and was slipping away until the night police were called to the Aurora Avenue Bridge and talked her out of jumping into Lake Union. Since then, Sister Anne had been helping Beatrice forgive herself.

Sister Anne did the same with Cooper, a haunted soldier, whose tank took a direct hit in the rear. Everyone in the crew died. "Cooked alive."

Only Cooper got out.

Sister Anne prayed every day for Cooper, Beatrice, and Willie, refusing to let them believe they were worthless, unloved, and at fault for what had happened. No one is to blame, she would tell them, and the new people who arrived with similar tragedies every day at the shelter. Each one of them mattered and she wanted them to know that, especially at the end of the evening before they vanished into the night.

"Thank you for coming. God bless you and good luck." She hugged each of them as they departed.

Later, while collecting plates, her thoughts turned inward as she reexamined her past, her guilt clawing at her until she pushed it away.

But it kept returning.

Tonight, Sister Anne was the last to leave, staying behind to study the next day's menu. Again, the odd feeling drew her back through the years to the time when everything changed. It had been happening more and more over the past weeks, as if something was closing in on her.

Was God telling her something?

As she locked up, she stopped at the door and considered the line of prayer from St. Francis posted there: "It is in dying that we are born into eternal life."

She thought about it for a moment, then headed for the street. On the bus, she looked at the banner ads for unwanted pregnancies, condoms, distress centers, police tip lines urging people to report suspicious behavior. We live in a world of pain and we all have our crosses to bear.

She closed her eyes.

Her bus ascended the hills between First Hill and Yesler Terrace, toward a small enclave of clean, modest buildings straddling the eastern edges of the two neighborhoods. Mercifully, it was a short ride.

Echoes of distant sirens and a far-off car alarm greeted her at her stop, reminding her of a recent rash of car prowlings and a few break-ins at the fringes of her neighborhood.

Walking along the rain-slicked sidewalk, she saw the high-rise luxury condos of First Hill towering over the public housing properties of Yesler Terrace. Beyond them, across I-5, Seattle's glittering skyline rose into the night. To the north she saw the Space Needle, to the south, the stadiums where the Mariners and her beloved Seahawks played.

Sister Anne's home was a few short blocks away in the cluster of well-kept town houses. A generous parishioner had donated one to the archdiocese. Hers was the middle building. She reached for the door and stopped cold.

It was slightly ajar.

Goodness.

Her concern melted to annoyance. It had a temperamental mechanism. Upon entering, she'd detected the aroma of baked onions, pepperoni, peppers, and cheese and sighed. Her new neighbors, the young nuns from Canada, were partial to pizza every now and then but had yet to master the trick of completely locking the front door. Well, the silver lining here was that it spared her from fiddling with her front-door keys. Inside, the building was quiet as Sister Anne climbed the stairs to her second-floor apartment, where she lived alone.

Evening prayer, a cup of tea, and a bit of rest for her weary bones. She flicked on the lights of her small apartment and felt a ping of unease. Something wasn't right. She couldn't put her finger on it but something felt *wrong*.

Oh, it's nothing.

She was being silly because she was exhausted. But hanging up her jacket, she still couldn't shake a niggling feeling of *a presence*. Something in the air. The smell of cigarettes? But no one in this building smoked.

She stepped into the hallway leading to her bedroom and froze.

Her clothes cascaded from her dresser drawers. Her closet had been ransacked.

Someone's been here.

She looked toward her phone. A floorboard creaked and before she could react, a strong, gloved hand reached from behind and covered her mouth. A large, rock-hard arm hooked her neck in a viselike grip, crushing her windpipe, lifting her body. Her toes brushed against her hardwood floor as she was carried to the bathroom and her face thrust before the mirror.

The eyes of her attacker stared into hers.

He held her there long enough for her to recognize him and exhume long-buried pain. Then a knife blade glinted at her throat.

"Scream and you'll die," he said. "Understand?"

She nodded and he loosened his hold over her mouth.

"You know why I'm here."

She knew.

"It's gone," she swallowed. "I told you, it's gone."

"You're lying! Where is it?"

His grip tightened until she whimpered. The blade scraped over her skin, breaking it. Blood webbed down her neck, tears filled her eyes, and she said, "We can never erase the sins of our past."

His anger burned.

"No," he said, "but we can pay for them."

Her eyes widened suddenly as the blade sliced deep across her throat. Her hands tried to stem the blood.

"I forgive you," she whispered.

He let her collapse gently to the floor as if she were his dance partner. He watched her struggle for something in her pocket. A rosary. Her blood-stained fingers squeezed it. He watched for several moments until Sister Anne's face emptied of life. Then he returned to her bedroom and resumed shuffling through her personal papers and photographs.

Stopping at a recent snapshot of a boy. Searching the kid's eyes and face, the man studied it long and hard until he almost smiled. He now had the link to the thing that belonged to him.

All he had to do was claim it before time ran out.

© Rick Mofina 2007

PERFECT GRAVE
by Rick Mofina
Available September 2010